SATURD[illegible] NIGHT IN THE CITY OF THE DEAD

Who will survive? In a kill-or-be-killed world, are you the hunter or the prey? **Who can you trust?** In the final pandemic, will your friends become your enemies? **Who is the monster?** The raging child? The creature in the cellar? The man with the gun? Or is it *you*?

In this collection of stories, we explore the outer reaches of *The Exodus Plague*. A man wakes in an unfamiliar room. A luxury cruise liner becomes a plague ship. Three children invite a stranger into their home – with horrific consequences. The enemy is everywhere. Trust no one.

For some background on these stories, read "Notes From The Apocalypse" at the end of the book.

HUW COLLINGBOURNE

dark neon

ISBN: 978-1-913132-15-6
Published by: **dark neon**

http://www.darkneon.com/

Download Free Stories

To download **free stories** now and to be the first to hear about new books, join Huw's mailing list at:

http://www.darkneon.com/newsletter

or scan this QR code:

Also by Huw Collingbourne

The Exodus Plague

Book 1: The Snow
Book 2: Imprisoned
Book 3: Escape

The 1980s Murder Mysteries

Book 1: Killers In Mascara
Book 2: The Glam Assassin
Book 3: Death Wears Sequins

You can find the Exodus Plague series on Amazon by scanning the above bar code or via this URL:
https://tinyurl.com/7d2rukta

Table of Contents

PREFACE

The snow fell and overnight the world changed. This book tells stories from the world of the near future, when the worst that *can* happen *does* happen. Welcome to *The Exodus Plague*.

I've also written a series of novels set in the same world. You can read the stories in *this* collection before, after or even while you are reading those novels. These stories are independent of the novels – though there are a few characters in some of these stories that also show up in the novels, as explained in '*Notes From The Apocalypse*' at the end of this book.

So settle down in a cosy armchair and let me take you into a world where only the strong, the lucky or the ruthless will survive.

Room 23a

The room was unfamiliar to me. I looked at its high, white-plastered ceiling, I looked at the two ugly, wooden-framed armchairs, I looked at the faded curtains with their hideous *fleur-de-lys* pattern, I looked at the big, sagging bed in which I was lying. I was certain that I'd never been in this room before in my life. I had no idea whose room it was or where it was. For all I knew it might have been in London or it might have been in Timbuktu, apart from the fact that I had the feeling that Timbuktu was a hot place and the room I was in was decidedly cold.

I pulled back the bedsheets. I was naked. I didn't recall going to bed, naked or otherwise, so who had put me there? Had I been in an accident? I stood and wandered over to take a closer look at the hideous curtains. They were hanging from big wooden hoops on a big wooden pole. When I pulled back the curtains, the big wooden hoops rattled noisily which made me grit my teeth. I realised that I had a colossal headache.

"I must have got plastered," I thought, "last night. And ended up in someone else's bedroom."

The light through the window was blindingly white. That didn't help my headache. Everywhere outside was white. Brilliant white. Apart from the sky, which was luminously blue. "As blue as a kingfisher's wings," I thought to myself.

I turned back to examine the room. In addition to the bed and the two armchairs, there was also a small, pine coffee-table, a chest-of-drawers painted canary yellow, a ceramic washbasin attached to one wall and a huge, disused fire-grate surrounded by elaborately moulded pillars – the sort of nauseating things of which the Victorians were inexplicably fond.

The chimney behind the grate had been blocked off and it now contained a three-bar electric fire which I wasted no time in turning on. Elsewhere in the room, there were several untidy piles of books and a stuffed teddy-bear wearing a bobble-hat. A heap of clothes lay on the floor in front of the teddy-bear. I assumed they must be mine so I put them on. They fitted me perfectly but looked dreadful. The trousers were dark green, the shirt was bright pink, the shoes were two-toned brown brogues and the jacket was a rather moth-eaten herringbone tweed with leather patches sewn on the elbows. I couldn't believe that I'd ever bought any of that stuff. But in the absence of anything else to wear, they would just have to do. I decided against wearing the underpants and socks, which gave evidence of prior use. Fortunately, I had been able to find clean underpants and socks in the chest of drawers. As it was still perishingly cold in the room, I also borrowed the teddy-bear's bobble-hat.

There was a mirror on the wall over the mantel-piece. I took a look at myself. I almost reeled back in shock. It was not my clothes that shocked me, though in other circumstances they would have been shocking enough. It was my face.

Or rather, it was not *my* face. The face looking back at me from the mirror was one that I did not recognise. On the whole, I hoped it wasn't mine. Given a free choice of faces, this wasn't one that would have been close to the top of my list of preferences.

Not that it was, in essence, a bad-looking face. The bone structure was good, the jaw jutted just the right amount, the slightly wavy hair was of an attractive dark blond colour. But the whole effect was spoiled by the eyes. The eyes were red. Not just mildly bloodshot but glowingly crimson red.

My first reaction was to look away. I walked over to the window again. I looked down upon a broad expanse of pure, unsullied snow covering the ground outside. The snow ended at the wall of another building, some hundred yards or so away. That building looked like something vaguely classical. It was a long, two-storey affair with Roman-style columns propping up the roof at intervals.

I walked back to the mirror and forced myself to take a closer look at my eyes. The 'whites' of my eyes were entirely red due to a network of inflamed capillaries. I wondered if I might be suffering from episcleritis or possibly subconjunctival haemorrhage. Then I wondered how I'd even heard of episcleritis and subconjunctival haemorrhage? Was this the sort of thing that most people knew about? Maybe I was an optician? But even if I were, that didn't explain the mystery of why I was in a room I didn't recognise in a place I'd never visited with a face I'd never seen.

There were two courses of action open to me. Either I could sit on the floor, warm my hands by the glowing bars of the electric fire and start panicking; or else I could go outside and start investigating. I chose the latter option. I grabbed an overcoat and scarf which were hanging from a hook on the door of the room. Then I exchanged my two-tone brogues for a pair of Wellington boots which were lying on the floor to the left of the window. I opened the door and – ran straight into another door. For some reason, there were two doors where you would typically expect only one. The inner door opened inwards. The outer door opened outwards. I opened the outer door and stepped into a cold, stone-floored hallway with a wooden balustrade. There was a flight of stairs to my left, leading down to the ground floor, one level below.

The outer room door swung shut behind me. I look at it. It was a solid oak door bearing the number, in brass characters: "23a". Below the number there was a little brass frame containing a handwritten card which stated: "T. E. Farquhar". The name meant nothing to me. I didn't even know how to pronounce it.

I ran down the echoing stone staircase, then along a short but wide hallway towards another oak door, this one much bigger than the door of my room. I pulled open the door and I practically gasped at the beauty of the scene before me. The perfect expanse of snow which I'd seen through the window was enclosed on four sides by long, low buildings in the neo-classical style. These buildings formed the boundaries of a vast courtyard dotted with trees whose bare branches were decoratively weighed down by snow. Apart from me, the courtyard was deserted.

I turned right and walked alongside the wall of the building containing room 23a, keeping the snowy courtyard on my left. After a while, I came to the end of the building. At first, I had assumed that the building on my right formed a seamless corner with the similar long, low building directly in front of me. But this was not the case. The two buildings did not adjoin. There was a substantial gap between them which opened onto a short road that led towards some tall iron gates. The gates were closed and, as I soon saw, padlocked. The snow along the short road was well-trodden. A large number of footprints converged upon a small, one-storey building immediately to the right of the padlocked gate. Through the windows of that building I could see an electric light. There was also somebody inside. I pushed open the door and walked in.

"Ah, Mr Farker, sir!" said a small, plump man who was sitting behind a sort of reception desk, "I 'as it for you!"

I didn't know who the man was and I didn't know what he had for me. I also wasn't at all sure that I was who he thought I was. In the hope that all might soon be revealed, I decided to play along.

"Oh, have you?" I said.

"That I have!" said he, proudly.

The man was, I noticed, wearing a dark jacket and a bowler hat. The bowler is not a hat that is much in fashion these days. I tried to think what sort of people wore them. I had a feeling that a bowler hat was the sort of headgear favoured by disreputable bookies at race-courses. But this wasn't a race course and I very much doubted whether the man standing behind the desk was a bookie.

He turned towards an old-fashioned set of pigeonholes fixed to the wall behind him. In case you have never seen an old-fashioned set of pigeonholes, I can best describe them as an ancient-looking wooden construction of criss-crossing planks forming a matrix of little cubbyholes. From one cubbyhole the man in the bowler hat took a small padded envelope and handed it to me.

"Came not half an hour ago, sir," he said, "Delivered by hand, it was."

I wondered how else a letter might be delivered? By foot? By nasal orifice? But the plump man had an officious air about him which gave me the feeling that he might not appreciate my asking the question. So I took the letter from him and said, "Thank you, Mr. …um?"

He frowned as though he wasn't sure if I was pulling his leg by pretending to have forgotten his name. "No need for any 'mister' to you, sir," he said, "Pipply will suffice. Always has, always will."

"Yes," I smiled, "Thank you, Pipply."

As I was turning to leave, I glanced back and said, "The gates are locked, I suppose?"

"Now don't you worry about that, sir," he responded brightly, "You're safe here. There's nothing can get through them gates in a hurry. And even if they did, they'd have me to deal with."

I was startled to see that he was holding a revolver in his hand.

*

It turned out that the letter which Mr Pipply had given me wasn't a letter after all. What I mean to say is that the padded envelope which Pipply had taken from my pigeonhole didn't contain any correspondence. It did, however, contain a small, brown plastic screw-top bottle. On the bottle was a label. On the label was written "T. E. Farquhar. 2 to be taken 3 times a day." Inside the bottle were some green and yellow capsules. I sat in my room and stared at them. There was no indication of what sort of ailment the capsules were intended to treat. I put them onto the floor next to the teddy-bear. I was trying to think what to do next when there was a knock at the door.

The door wasn't locked. "Come in!" I shouted.

I heard the outer door being opened. Then the inner door was opened. A young woman stood there. "You were sporting your oak," she said.

"Was I?" I had no idea what she meant.

"Your outer door," she added, "was closed. Which means you don't want to be disturbed."

"Ah?" I tried to sound as though this was not news to me, "It must have blown shut. In the wind."

She laughed. She had rather a nice, tinkling sort of laugh. "There isn't any wind and a damned hurricane wouldn't blow that bloody door shut! Are you coming to lunch?"

It occurred to me that I was staring, open-mouthed at her. This was not due to her exquisite beauty, which might indeed have justified such a reaction, but to her eyes. Her eyes were hazel. I suspected they might, on other occasions, have been quite attractive eyes. On this occasion, however, they were quite exceptionally bloodshot.

*

Lunch was served in a hall on the other side of the courtyard (or 'quad' as the woman insisted on calling it). Rather than taking the direct route by striding through the snow straight towards the hall, we partially circumnavigated the quad by turning left, then right, then right again. I didn't comment on this bizarre behaviour. I just followed where she led. I seemed to have a vague memory, however, that there was a strange tradition in Cambridge colleges which permitted dons to walk on the lawns while lesser mortals were obliged to remain on well-designated paths.

Cambridge colleges? Why had that idea sprung into my head? I looked again at the long, low buildings enclosing the quad. Of course. It was a college. And while I didn't know for certain that it was in Cambridge, it seemed exactly the sort of college that might be.

"So Pipply must be the college porter!"

"What?" The woman turned to look at me. I hadn't realised I'd spoken my thought aloud.

"Pipply," I said, "The man in the bowler hat."

"What about him?"

"He's the college porter?"

She gave me a strange look – part way between a smile and a smirk. "Are you sure you're feeling all right, Terrence?"

Terrence. Was that really my name? Terrence Farquhar? I didn't feel like a Terrence Farquhar. I felt more like a David or a Michael. David Brown, maybe? Or Michael Smith?

"Yes," I said, "I'm feeling fine."

"You have been taking the capsules, haven't you?"

"I, um…"

"Terrence," she said sternly, "For the trial to mean anything we all have to follow the correct procedures."

Trial? What sort of trial was she talking about? Had I volunteered for something? Some sort of drug trial, maybe? Well that might explain why I was so disoriented, why I'd forgotten so many things. Maybe it was a side-effect of the drugs? Maybe I was hallucinating?

"What colour capsules are you taking?" I asked.

"What an odd question. Blue, of course. Everybody takes blue capsules."

*

Lunch was self-service. A miserable-looking man with an insanitary walrus moustache dolloped portions of something involving meat and mashed potatoes onto plates with remnants of previous meals adhering to the edges. We carried our plates to one of numerous long wooden tables in the hall and sat on an uncomfortable bench. No sooner had we sat down than we were joined by a tall, willowy young man with short black hair.

"Hi Fiona. Terrence," he said.

"Good afternoon, Angus," replied Fiona, "and how are the black holes progressing?"

Well, that sorted out the problem of names, at least. The woman was called Fiona, the man was called Angus. They both knew my name which struck me as curious since I had no recollection of seeing either of them before.

Angus sat next to Fiona and tucked in with gusto to the unappealing meat and potato stuff piled up on his plate, "Fiona thinks that's all physicists do," Angus explained between mouthfuls, "Try to find black holes."

"Well, isn't it?"

"I've explained that already, I'm not an astrophysicist. Astrophysicists study big things. I do a different sort of physics altogether. I, um, study small things."

"Quantum mechanics?" I suggested.

Angus looked confused. "Mmm," he said, "That kind of thing."

"You are all equally insane," Fiona said airily.

"What's the matter?" Angus said abruptly, looking at me.

"The matter? Nothing. Why?"

"You were staring."

"Was I? I'm sorry I… I must have been thinking of something."

I realised he was right. I'd been staring at his eyes. He had the same deep red, bloodshot eyes that Fiona and I had. But the man with the walrus moustache who'd served out the food didn't have bloodshot eyes. Nor did Pipply the porter. Just we three.

I had to tell them. It was silly to keep avoiding it. These two appeared to be friends of mine so if I was going to mention it to anyone, it made sense to mention it to them.

"The thing is," I said, "I'm feeling a bit odd."

"Odd?" said Angus, "In what way?"

"Well, there's things…" How could I explain this? Tell them that I had no idea who they were? That I wasn't even very sure who *I* was? No, that would sound mad. I'd have to broach the subject more obliquely – "I had a headache when I woke up this morning," I said, "and ever since then, well, I seem to keep forgetting things."

"What sort of things?" said Fiona.

"Well, like Pipply. I forgot his name."

"Really?" said Angus.

"Really."

Angus and Fiona exchanged glances. They looked genuinely concerned.

"Have you been taking the medication?" Angus asked.

"The capsules?"

"Yes."

"Of course," I lied.

"I wonder…" said Fiona.

"What?" I said.

"Well, you know, there've been rumours. I mean, we don't know for sure, do we?"

"What rumours?"

"Placebos," Angus said, "To do the tests properly, some of us won't be getting the real medication. That's what I've heard anyway. I don't know if it's true or not. You should know."

"Me. Why me?"

"Well," said Angus, "you are the medical student. It's in your line of work, isn't it. Randomised trials, controls and protocols and all that sort of thing."

I thought about that. "Yes," I agreed, "The correct RCT protocol would require some participants to be given placebos."

"There you are, then," said Angus, "That's it. You should let them know it's having side-effects, then get them to give you the proper thing."

"RCT?" said Fiona.

"Randomised Control Trial," I explained, "It's a standard scientific methodology aimed at reducing the bias of…"

What am I talking about? I thought. RCT, protocols and methodologies. What the Hell was I rambling on about? How could I possibly know anything about all that? Angus had said I was a medical student. I didn't think I could be. I didn't seem to know anything about medicine. And I was pretty sure I didn't like the sight of blood. Didn't medical students have to dissect corpses? Well, surely, I would never be able to do that!

"What colour capsules are you taking?" Angus said.

"Aren't they all the same?" I asked.

"Blue, you mean?"

"Absolutely. I mean, it stands to reason. All the capsules would have to be the same colour, whether they contain the real drug or just a placebo. Not much point having different colours, is there! Then everyone would be able to tell the real ones from the fakes."

"Yes," Angus smiled but he didn't seem convinced, "I suppose so."

We carried on eating our meal. We were the only people in that cavernous hall. I wondered where the other students were.

*

Back in my room, I opened the brown plastic bottle and poured some of the capsules into the palm of my hand. One end of the capsule was green. The other end of the capsule was yellow. According to the label, I should take two capsules three times a day.

I hadn't taken any all day. I didn't know if I'd taken any on the previous day because I had no memories of any previous days at all. For all I could remember, my life may as well have begun that morning.

I tried to think what might have happened to me. All I knew was that I was in a Cambridge college and I had two friends called Angus and Fiona. All three of us had unnaturally bloodshot eyes. Which probably meant that all three of us were suffering from the same medical condition. It seemed that we were taking part in some sort of drug test. The drugs were inside the capsules. But the capsules that Angus and Fiona were taking were blue whereas mine were yellow and green.

Angus thought my amnesia might be due to the fact that my capsules were placebos – not the real drug at all, just some harmless and ineffective alternative. Another possibility was that I had simply decided not to take the capsules and was now suffering the consequences. Yet another possibility – and the one that frightened me most – was that it was the drugs inside the capsules that had robbed me of my memory. I carefully tipped the capsules from the palm of my hand back into the little bottle.

"They think *they* are testing *us*," I said to teddy, "Well, I can do my own tests too. I'll pretend to take their bloody capsules but really I won't. Let's see what effect that has!"

I stared at myself in the mirror again, fascinated by the deep red colour suffusing the sclera – the so-called 'whites' – of my eyes.

"I'm talking to a teddy-bear," I muttered.

"Yes, you are," I agreed. And I laughed. I was feeling better already.

*

That afternoon I lay on my bed and watched the ceiling. There was a moulded pattern (a cornice?) running all around the edges. At first it looked fairly simple – just a series of parallel lines with some decorative vine leaves in the corners. But the more I looked at it, the more complicated it became. I saw that what had at first seemed to be simple lines were in fact quite complex fractal shapes that interlocked like intricate cogwheels. Each cog on the wheel was itself a smaller cogwheel. And each cog on the smaller cogwheel was a yet smaller cogwheel. And all the little wheels were turning.

Suddenly I sat up in bed. I realised that I couldn't possibly see so much detail even if it had been there. Which it certainly wasn't. I went to the washbasin, splashed cold water over my face, towelled myself dry and took another look at the ceiling. There was nothing unusual about the cornice. It was a plain plaster moulding made of parallel lines with decorative vine leaves in the corners.

I picked up the small plastic bottle, opened it, shook out two capsules into the palm of my hand. I had no idea what they contained. I had no idea even who'd left them for me. Maybe Pipply would know?

*

"The package that arrived this morning, sir?" Pipply said, "It was the usual chap who delivered it. William, I think his name is."

"Not a regular postman?"

Pipply smiled, "We don't seem to be getting regular post just now. I expect when everything gets back to normal we will."

"So who's William?" I asked, "I mean, where does he come from?"

"He's just the delivery man, that's all, from the LMB."

I wanted to ask Pipply what the LMB was but he was giving me such a peculiar look that I thought better of it. I didn't want to arouse his suspicions.

I decided to change the subject. "Not many students around, are there?"

"In college, sir? Well, no, not at this time of year. Term doesn't start for another week."

*

"The LMB?" Angus said. We were sitting in the library. He was reading a book called 'Quantum Physics For Dummies'. It was either a more advanced book than the title suggested or else Angus had seriously slipped behind in his studies. I'd found an old copy of 'Biggles Flies West' which I was browsing without paying much attention.

"The porter told me that's where the capsules come from."

"Oh, really? I didn't know that. For some reason, I thought the Cavendish Labs were behind them."

"So what is it, then? The LMB?"

"I'd have thought that was more your line than mine, what with you being a medic."

"You were obviously wrong then."

"It's the Laboratory of Molecular Biology. They do lots of clever stuff, I believe."

"What kind of clever stuff?"

"Oh, you know. Diseases. Flu, SARS, Covid, neurodegenerative diseases, Alzheimer's… you name it, they do it."

"Alzheimer's?" For some reason, that word sent me into a mild panic. People with Alzheimer's forget things. They forget where they are, who other people are. But it's mostly old people who get Alzheimer's, isn't it? Whereas how old was I? Early twenties? Surely that was too young.

"Why have we got red eyes?" I said suddenly.

Angus stared at me. "Serious question?"

"Dead serious."

"Have you been taking the capsules?" Angus said.

I nodded.

"Maybe they really are the placebo then. How much have you forgotten?"

"Quite a lot," I said.

Then Angus told me about the catastrophe – "It all started with the snow…"

*

Ever since I'd woken up that morning, I'd been aching to find some explanation. An explanation of why I was in a room I didn't recognise in a Cambridge college I'd never heard of, why I didn't know my own name and why the person staring back at me from the mirror had eyes filled with blood. I thought an explanation would put my mind at rest. I was wrong. I would have been happier not to know.

The snow began in earnest during the second week of January. Once the snow began falling it was disinclined to stop. Overnight the entire country was brought to a standstill. Trains were unable to run, roads were blocked, whole towns were entirely cut off. But that wasn't the worst of it. The worst was yet to come.

People started becoming sick. At first, it seemed to a affect older people the worst. Many old people had the full range of flu-like symptoms – coughs, sneezes, fever and delirium. And then came the blood. Haemorrhaging. Vomiting blood. Like some sort of haemorrhagic fever. Whatever the disease was, it acted quickly. Within a week or so, almost an entire generation of people had died.

Mostly the younger and fitter people survived. Up to a point, anyway. Their bodies fought off the pathogen. But their minds did not fare so well. The disease affected their brains. They became violent, aggressive, it was as though they'd lost their inhibitions, they no longer had any sense of self-restraint.

"Like Pick's Disease?" I said.

Angus had closed his book by this time and had been strolling around the library as he'd told me about the catastrophe.

He stopped pacing. "And what, may I ask, is Pick's Disease?"

"It's caused by a build-up of tau proteins in the neurons…"

"In English?" Angus suggested.

"Ah, yes, sorry. Well, put simply, Pick's Disease attacks the brain. It causes frontotemporal lobe degeneration…"

Angus raised his eyebrows at me.

"It causes part of the brain to malfunction," I said, "which often results in profound behavioural changes. Sufferers may become hostile, aggressive, they seem to misperceive their environment, misunderstand what people do and say."

"As if they are on acid?" Angus asked, "LSD? Hallucinogens."

I hesitated. "Possibly." The fact of the matter is that I had no idea what effects LSD might have on a person. As far as I knew, I'd never taken any. But since I knew so little about myself, I might have been wrong in that assumption.

"So what causes this Pick's Disease?" Angus asked.

"I don't know."

"Does anybody know?"

"I don't know that either."

"Maybe you should find out."

"And maybe you should mind your bloody business!"

"Don't shout," Angus said in a whisper, "This is a library!"

"Ha! Bloody Ha!" I yelled, "There's nobody here but us."

"And you are behaving like an idiot," Angus added.

I suddenly stepped towards him and grabbed him by the throat. In that split second, I wanted to throttle him. Angus reached up, took my hands, and gently loosened my grasp. I stood for a second blankly staring at my hands as though they belonged to somebody else.

"I'm sorry," I said, "I… I really don't know…"

"You don't know what came over you?"

"Right."

"Take your medication," Angus said, "It's the only way."

*

Back in my room, I stared at the little bottle of capsules again. I unscrewed the cap and tipped a capsule into the palm of my hand.

"How do I know about Pick's Disease?" I asked the stuffed teddy-bear who was sitting on the floor glaring at me.

The teddy-bear said nothing.

"It's because I'm a medical student," I said. But I didn't know if that was true. I couldn't recall being a student.

I prised open the capsule and tipped its contents into the palm of my hand. It was a plain white powder. It could have been anything. Chalk? Sodium bicarbonate?

"Cocaine?"

"What?"

"It could be cocaine."

It was the teddy-bear. He was talking to me at last.

"Oh, shut up!" I said.

I licked a fingertip and dipped it into the powder. Then I licked the powder off my finger. It tasted bitter.

"Crushed aspirin," I said, "Must be the placebo."

I dipped my finger into the powder again and once again licked it off.

"Oh well, at least aspirin will help my headache."

I tipped another capsule into my palm and swallowed it in one gulp. Then I went to explore Cambridge.

*

I didn't leave by the front gate. The last time I'd seen it, the gate had been padlocked and the porter didn't seem keen on unlocking it. However, there is another way out via a loose bar in the cast-iron fence that runs along the eastern end of the college. This provided the time-honoured way for students who had been illicitly sleeping over at other colleges to regain entry after the gates had been shut for the night.

Once out, I wandered into the middle of town. The first thing that struck me as odd was how deserted the town was. Even though it was only the middle of the afternoon, most of the shops were shut and there were very few pedestrians. The second thing that struck me as odd was the tank parked on King's Parade, right in front of King's College Chapel. There were a couple of soldiers leaning against the tank, chatting and smoking cigarettes. They each had guns in their hands. I'm not an expert on guns so I can't tell you what kind they were. They were big buggers, that much I do know. They looked like the sort of guns that could mow down a battalion or two of enemy combatants without pausing for breath.

But what enemy combatants were they likely to encounter in Cambridge? The few people I saw, trudging doggedly through the snow, looked harmless enough. There was an elderly, white-haired gent who was holding an animated conversation with himself – clearly a don and, in my opinion, very probably a physicist. There was a middle-aged woman with a tight bun who cheerily called out "Bloody fascists!" as sailed past the tank with her tweed cape flapping in the breeze behind her. I put her down as a Classicist. Then there were younger people. Students, I supposed. Most of those wandered about dazedly smiling to themselves. They all had red eyes.

A young woman approached me. She was about eighteen or nineteen, I guessed. She was clutching a bunch of paper flowers in her hand. She smiled at me. "Peace," she said and handed me a flower.

Then she walked over to the soldiers. I saw her holding out a flower. The next instant, one of the soldiers had struck her in the face with the butt of his gun, knocking her to the ground. She lay in the slushy snow with her flowers scattered all around her. My immediate reaction was to go to her, to help her to get up again. But I saw the soldier watching me. He had his right hand close to the trigger of his gun. I slouched onwards. I put the paper flower into a pocket.

Then I went back to my room and took two more capsules. By dinner time, I was feeling much better.

*

That night I went to the college bar. Angus and Fiona were already there. There were two other people sitting at a table in the corner. Serving behind the bar there was a big chap with muscles that seemed to be fighting against his tee-shirt. The barman recognised me. He said, "You up for the game on Saturday, Terry?" I replied, "Yeah, sure." I didn't use his name because I didn't know what it was. I also didn't know what game he was talking about. Judging by his physique, I thought it was more likely to be rugby than bridge. Then I looked at my physique. I realised that I was just as muscular as the barman. I was also taller than anyone else in the bar. "Good grief!" I thought to myself, "I'm a rugby player!"

"How are you feeling?" Angus said.

"Fine," I replied.

"I heard you had a bit of setback this afternoon," Fiona said.

She was being polite. Angus had clearly told her about the incident in the library when I'd tried to strangle him.

"A bit of a panic attack," I said vaguely.

"Have you taken your…?"

"Medication? Yes, I have. I'm feeling much better now."

"That's good," Fiona smiled, "We are really lucky, you know."

I didn't feel lucky. "How do you mean?"

"The medication keeps everything under control."

"Are you sure that's a good thing?"

Fiona glanced at the two students sitting at the other end of the bar. She leant towards me and said in a whisper, "We're still alive, aren't we?"

I didn't understand. "Angus told me that the disease only kills old people."

"It does," Angus said, "As far as anyone can tell. But it has other effects on people our age. You know, removes inhibition and all that. The medication keeps that under control."

I turned to Fiona again – "You said we should be glad because at least we're alive. Lack of inhibition isn't exactly fatal, is it? You don't die of it."

"You do if a soldier sees you," she said.

It was in that moment that I decided that I had to get away.

*

When I went to bed, I expected to pass a sleepless night. A great deal had happened to me that day and my thoughts were racing. In fact, I slept soundly. I took two capsules before going to bed and I woke up when the alarm clock went off at half-past eight.

"How long have we all been here?" I asked Angus and Fiona over breakfast.

The huge hall was empty again apart from us. I wondered what had become of the two people we'd seen at the bar the previous night. Not to mention the rugby-playing barman. Either they weren't breakfast eaters or they'd had advance warning of the tasteless pulp that purported to be scrambled eggs and bacon and had concluded that starvation was the preferable option.

"I can't remember being here last term," Fiona said, "To be honest, I thought I was a student in Manchester. But I'm not sure."

"I think I stayed here over Christmas," Angus said, "I'm doing a doctorate. I think this is my second year."

"What's the subject of your doctorate?" I asked.

"Physics," he replied, "I'm not sure what exactly. It will all become clear, no doubt, when term begins."

"What's the date now?" I asked.

This was a question that had not occurred to them and they didn't know the answer to it. The best they could come up with was that they thought it was January. "But it might be February," Angus added.

"How old is Pipply?" I asked.

"Pipply?" Fiona said, "Pipply the porter, you mean?"

"Is there any other?"

"He's quite old. In his sixties, I'd say."

"I saw some even older people in town," I said, and I told them about the grey-haired don and the woman who'd shouted at the soldiers. "If this disease kills old people, they should be dead. Shouldn't they?"

"Probably have a natural immunity," Angus said.

"Or they might have been immunised against the disease," I added.

We poked dispiritedly at the scrambled mush on our plates for a while. Then Fiona said, "But if they'd been immunised, someone would have had to know about the disease before it even arrived."

"That's what I was thinking," I said.

*

After breakfast, I took two capsules and washed them down with a glass of water. The snow in the quad, I noticed, was starting to melt. Some icicles outside my window were dripping. The thaw was on its way. Maybe things would start getting back to normal now.

I went to see if Pipply had opened the front gates yet and, to my astonishment, he had. I was just about to stroll through the gates and wander down into town when Pipply came running out of his lodge. "Mr Farker! Mr Farker!" he cried, "There's a package for you."

He gave me the package and I opened it. It contained a small brown plastic bottle. Stuck to the bottle was a label on which was written "T. E. Farquhar. 1 to be taken 3 times a day (in addition to any other medication)." I flipped open the cap of the bottle and shook a single capsule into the palm of my hand. It was blue. I popped it into my mouth and swallowed.

When I walked through the gates I turned right instead of left, which took me in the direction leading out of town rather than into it. I had only progressed a few hundred yards when an armoured car happened to drive past. There were two big loudspeaker horns fixed to the roof of the car. Inside I could see two soldiers – one driving, the other holding one of those very big guns that they seemed to like so much. Both soldiers were staring at me. The loudspeakers suddenly blared out: "Pedestrian, return to town. I repeat. Return to town. Now!"

I didn't feel incline to argue. I turned around and walked back to college.

*

"They do it for our safety," Fiona said later that evening. We were in hall again, eating one of those meals whose ingredients are impossible to guess without a few clues. This one was called Grilled Rump Chipsteak with Vegetable Mêlée.

I'd been telling Angus and Fiona about my close encounter with the armoured car.

"Cambridge is a safe haven," she said, "You have no idea what it's like when you go outside its boundaries."

"And have you?" I said, "Any idea, I mean?"

"One hears rumours," she replied.

"Everyone's infected," Angus said, "Everyone who's still alive, that is."

"Then we must be infected too," I said, "But the capsules suppress the symptoms."

"You think so?" said Fiona.

"Don't you?"

"I've never really thought about it."

"I discovered this really amazing thing today," Angus interrupted, "If you put two snooker balls on a table and you roll one towards the other, when they hit, the first one stops dead and the second one goes zooming off under its own power."

"Conservation of momentum," I said.

"What?"

"Newton's Laws of motion. The second one, I think."

Angus looked crestfallen. Then he brightened up. A gleam came into his eyes. "Do you think it's correct?"

"Well, I suppose it must be, mustn't it?"

"I'm not so sure about that. I've been considering it deeply and I think I've found a flaw. Not just in the second law but in all three. They are contradictory, you see. Accept one and you must reject the others."

"An interesting idea," I said, "You might want to talk it over with your director of studies."

"My director of studies… have I got one?"

"I'm sure you will have by the time term starts."

"Yes, you are probably right."

"The thing is," I said, returning to the topic that we'd been discussing before, "I'd like to see what's outside Cambridge. I mean, for all we know, there's absolutely nothing wrong with the rest of the country. All this stuff about old people dying and young people going on the rampage, it might be complete nonsense. For all we know, everyday life in Bath, Bristol and Birmingham continues just as it always has done."

"If that were the case," Fiona said, "why would the Army have been deployed to protect Cambridge?"

"That's what I mean to find out," I said.

I had been hoping to convince Angus and Fiona to come with me. But I didn't think they had the necessary spirit. They seemed remarkably uninquisitive. Almost bovine in their indolence. So I would just have to go it alone.

*

After dinner I took two of the green and yellow capsules and one of the blue capsules. They definitely had a calming effect. The panic attacks and feelings of aggression no longer plagued me.

At half-past seven there was a knock on my door. It was Fiona. She'd come to ask me if I wanted to go to King's. I said, "At this time of night? Why would I want to do that?" She told me there was a performance of Bach's B Minor Mass. I had nothing else to do so I went.

King's College Chapel is a glorious absurdity. By any normal standards, it is far too big and immensely too magnificent for a mere college chapel. It seems to labour under the delusion that it is a cathedral. The air was perfumed with incense and the organ was rumbling through some baroque piece as we entered and took our pews.

The chapel was far from full. There were a few elderly men and women; and maybe a dozen or so people of student age all of whom, as far as I could tell in the ecclesiastical gloom of the candle-light, had the customary bloodshot eyes.

I had been anticipating a performance on a grand scale with a full orchestra, soloists and the world-famous King's College Choir. Alas, that was not to be. There were six elderly singers, a cellist, a violinist and the organ player. It was the B Minor Mass on a tight budget. The singers' voices were drowned out by the organ. Given the quality of their voices, this was probably all for the best.

Room 23a

Living in Cambridge was like being confined to Bedlam. I was starting to think I was the only completely sane person there. I went back to my room and took two green-and-yellow tablets and one blue one. Then I went down to the bar and had a few drinks with Angus and Fiona. Angus had brought a snooker ball and a large frying pan. By rolling the ball around in the frying pan he was able to explain how it was only the friction between the surfaces of the ball and the pan that eventually caused the ball to stop moving. Therefore, in a frictionless environment the ball would continue moving for ever.

"And that," he said triumphantly, "is the basis of the machine I'm making."

"What machine is that?" I asked.

"Isn't it obvious?" he said, "It's a perpetual motion machine."

I was about to make a joke but from the look on Angus's face I could tell that he was serious.

"Oh," I said, "That's interesting."

*

I decided to keep a diary. I went back to my room and took a small ring-bound binder from the heap of assorted junk on the floor. I felt that I was at a momentous point in my life, perhaps at a momentous point in all of human history, and that this deserved to be documented. I didn't know what the date was so I wrote "Day 1" on top of the first page in the book. Beneath that, I wrote the following:

> *I don't believe what they are saying about the catastrophe. I don't believe the story that something arrived with the snow. I don't believe that anything has happened to Britain as a whole. It's my belief that something has happened in Cambridge. That's why there are soldiers everywhere. Cambridge has been put into quarantine. They are not trying to protect us from the outside world. They are trying to protect the outside world from us.*

Saturday Night in the City of the Dead

Underneath that I wrote (in capital letters):

I HAVE TO GET OUT OF CAMBRIDGE. I HAVE TO ESCAPE!

I took some capsules and went to bed.

*

When I looked in the mirror the following morning, I was surprised to see that my eyes were less bloodshot. A good night's sleep had also made me feel less pessimistic. Of course, so much had happened to me and to the world that it was hardly surprising that I had been starting to feel a bit paranoid.

Even so, I'd been allowing my imagination to run away with me. Thinking rationally, it was obvious that the Army was acting in a defensive role, trying to keep Cambridge safe from harm. When you are not accustomed to seeing soldiers on the street it is all too easy to jump to the conclusion that they are acting against your interests rather than for them.

I'd been suffering from the same sense of paranoia about my medication. When the porter had given me my first bottle of pills, I had been very suspicious. I had even wondered if my problems – everything from my bloodshot eyes to the amnesia – had been created or exacerbated by the medication itself. Which is, of course, a classic symptom of a paranoid delusion. There was nothing to suggest that there was anything remotely sinister about the capsules. I had been ill. They were helping me to recover. That's all there was to it.

Over breakfast, Angus explained some of the theory behind his perpetual motion machine. I didn't understand the technical details. It involved a snooker ball falling inside a revolving tube and the secret was the conservation of rotational momentum. I had to admit that he really seemed to have stumbled upon something important there. I had a feeling that he might be on the brink of a breakthrough that would revolutionise our understanding of the world we live in and, as a useful bonus, would also permit the creation of a totally clean and inexhaustible form of energy.

Then I went back to my room and took my medication. I only had two of the green-and-yellow capsules left which worried me but when I popped into the porter's lodge, Pipply handed me another package. When I opened it, I found it contained a small brown plastic bottle. On the bottle was a label. On the label was written "T. E. Farquhar. 3 to be taken 4 times a day." I went back to my room, opened the bottle and tipped a couple of capsules into the palm of my hand. They were silver with red stripes. I popped three into my mouth and swallowed them. I decided that I wouldn't even mention the silver-and-red capsules to Angus and Fiona. They were still only getting the blue capsules. Everyone got the blue capsules. I had obviously been moved up a level. I must therefore be a special case. I popped another capsule into my mouth, just for luck.

*

The day after that I wasn't feeling too good. Looking at my diary, I find this entry:

> *Not feeling too chipper today. Charlie Rubenstein called to see me. He says I'm just the sort of person they are looking for.*

It must have meant something to me when I wrote it. Looking at it now, though, I can't make any sense of it. Who's Charlie Rubenstein? I've been racking my brains but I can't recall anyone of that name. I wonder what I meant when I wrote "He says I'm just the sort of person they are looking for"? Just the sort of person that *who* is looking for? Weird. I can't even recall writing that. But it's my handwriting and it's there in my private diary so I guess I must have.

*

By the time I'd started taking the red capsules, I was feeling on top of the world. Lent Term was in full flow by that time. The snow had all melted and we were having a cold and blustery spring.

Fiona had acquired a transistor radio from somewhere so we were able to receive the BBC news. The television channels weren't broadcasting by that time. I think that was due to all the power cuts that people were having. According to the BBC, there had been rioting in some of the bigger cities but the Army had now taken control, law and order was being re-established and the national infrastructure was gradually being restored.

We'd had no real problems in Cambridge. We hadn't even had power cuts. I realised how lucky I was to be a student there. The rest of Britain had been through some tough times but the Government had implemented various emergency plans and soon everything would be as it should be.

*

I burnt my diary today. I asked Pipply what month it was. He says it's April. How time flies. Anyway, who cares what month it is? It's pointless trying to keep track.

I put my diary into a saucepan, poured some lighter fluid onto it and set fire to it. I nearly ended up setting fire to my room too. I didn't realise lighter fluid was quite that vigorous. I had to open the window and poke the saucepan outside. I almost set fire to my curtains in the process.

Sir Eric Martingdale, who's Master of this college, happened to be passing beneath my window at the time. Great flakes of black ash rained down upon him from on high. He looked up at my window, saw me sitting there holding a flaming saucepan, waved to me, and said, "Farquhar, is that you? How are you settling in this term?"

"Very well, sir," I replied.

"Good, good," he said, and off he went, completely unflustered, as though he was entirely used to seeing students waving flame-engulfed saucepans out of their windows.

I wonder how long I've been at college now? We are well into the Lent Term, that much I know. I don't seem to have done much in the way of actual study yet, however.

A woman in a white coat arrived today. She erected a desk in the Fellows' Combination Room. All the graduate and undergraduate students (there are more than a dozen of us now) had to line up. She gave us some sort of inoculation. I don't know what it was for but I'm sure it's good for us.

This afternoon I was walking along the street into town when I saw an undergrad from another college running in the opposite direction – by which I mean, away from town. I was shocked. Naturally. Why would anyone want to run away from Cambridge? There's everything anyone could ever want here. Whereas, outside its borders, well, who knows what could happen? It's a dangerous place out there.

I think he must have been one of those anarchist types. They call themselves The Resistance. What are they resisting, though, that's what I can't figure out? Naturally, a soldier shot the undergrad. He was running full pelt one second and the next second – *bam!* – half his chest was blown out in a mighty spray of blood. Once upon a time I would have felt sorry for him. Not any longer though. People like that are dangerous. Subversive. They make things bad for the rest of us.

*

A funny thing happened this evening. Angus, Fiona and I were in the bar when Sam, the junior porter came in. They were having problems with that religious nutter again. There are a few of them about. They are the plague of Cambridge. This one goes by the name of Perkins The Pardoner and he is a particularly egregious example of the species.

He keeps cursing people. Biblically. I had no idea quite how many curses The Bible contained until I heard old Perkins trotting them out. So anyway, old Perkins was standing outside the gates making a bloody nuisance of himself. The Master had told Pipply to get rid of him. Pipply had told Sam to get rid of him. Sam came into the bar and told me to get rid of him. Actually, he told everyone who was in the bar to get rid of him but since I am bigger than all the others, quite naturally they pushed me to the front of the queue.

I wasted no time at all in dispatching the unsavoury eremite. Though I have to admit that Fiona's threat to bop him on the head with a snooker ball might have helped to convince him of the seriousness of our intent.

There are some new people in college. Not sure when they arrived. The thing is, I don't think they are students. There are two youngish chaps and a very tall woman. Plus a dog, about which the less said the better. There's something very strange about the two chaps. They have funny eyes. The woman's eyes are OK. But the chap's eyes are not. They are not bloodshot. Not a trace of red to be seen. That makes me suspicious.

I'll keep an eye on them. They might be members of the bloody Resistance. I'm a peaceful person as a rule. But I have no sympathy to waste on anarchists. I'll keep a close eye on the buggers. Make sure they are taking their capsules. People who don't take their capsules are dangerous. I know exactly how to deal with them and I have no hesitation in doing so.

The catastrophe was a great blessing. It got rid of the bad and the corrupted, it disinfected the world so that we could start anew. Whatever we do now, we must not let the corruption return. Oh yes, I'll be keeping a very close eye on the two young chaps and the tall woman. Not to mention the bloody dog.

A DIRTY WEEKEND IN BLACKPOOL

Agnes Butterford knew what his game was from the moment he suggested it. "Oh yes!" she thought, "I know what you're game is, my lad." Because when a married man asks an unattached woman of mature years to accompany him on a weekend in Blackpool, there is only one reason. Not that she really minded. I mean, Eric wasn't unattractive. For his age. And besides, she had nothing else to do. So Eric picked Agnes up on the corner of Market Street on the Friday afternoon in his Volvo C70 soft-top convertible with luxury fitted mohair hood and they drove down to Blackpool. Eric had booked a room in advance. It would be a long weekend. They were to stay there Friday, Saturday and Sunday nights, driving back to Bradford on the Monday morning.

Agnes worked in a hairdressers' shop. As receptionist. On the front desk. She took appointments, dealt with payments, all that kind of thing. The job was not without its points of interest but, even so, Agnes did not feel overwhelmed by unbridled excitement. What's more, the girls who worked there – Sandra and Claire and Tammy – all seemed to think that Agnes led a very dull and predictable life. Oh no, Agnes thought, those girls don't know the half of it. Well, she'd have a few stories to tell them when she got back!

Mind you, a sophisticated weekend with Tom Cruise in Saint-Tropez would have been Agnes's first choice. But since that wasn't on the cards, a dirty weekend in Blackpool with Eric would have to do. At least, Eric was generous with his money. When he took you out, you didn't have to pay for a thing!

However, if she'd known how it would all end, Agnes would have had second thoughts. It was the blood that upset her the most. She'd always been a bit squeamish. The sight of an underdone steak made her come over quite faint. If she'd had the slightest suspicion that the weekend would end with so much blood – splashed over the walls, running down the curtains, dripping off the Tiffany-style lampshade – well, she would certainly never have agreed to go.

Agnes assumed that they would have a nice, quiet, uneventful little weekend by the seaside. Maybe Eric would take her for a meal somewhere fancy. Maybe they'd go dancing. Blackpool isn't at its best in January but even so, there are plenty of things to do if you know where to go.

Eric owned his own car dealership so it had been no problem at all for him to get away early on Friday and come back late on Monday. It had been a bit trickier for Agnes. The 'Swanky Snipz Hair Salon' relied upon Agnes. Albert, the boss, was always telling her that – "We rely upon you, Agnes," he would say. Agnes was the only person who really understood their computerised booking system. And she also helped out by sweeping up the hair which, by rights, is not a receptionist's job. But Agnes was owed some days off so they'd just have to do without her.

Eric had to smooth things over with his wife. He'd told her that he was off to a conference. Agnes didn't need to tell her husband anything because she had left the lazy, good-for-nothing swine the previous year and she never wanted to see his rotten face ever again.

It was bitterly cold when they arrived in Blackpool. The weather forecast said that snow was on its way. They didn't pay much attention to that. If you paid attention to weather forecasts, you'd never do anything – that's what Eric said.

It was a nice enough little hotel. Cosy and just five minutes' walk from the seafront. But really it was more of a guesthouse than a hotel. It had four *en suite* bedrooms, a dining room and a bar. Being as it was out of season, all the bedrooms were vacant except for the one that Eric had booked which was called the 'Orchid Room'. Eric had assured Agnes that it was by far the best room there. Agnes thought of asking Eric how he knew that. But the answer to that question was so obvious that she didn't bother.

The woman who ran the hotel was a bit la-di-da. "All airs and graces and no knickers," was how Agnes described her. Eric and Agnes arrived at half-past five and the la-di-da woman told them that dinner was served at seven "on the dot" and they would need to order in advance "to allow the chef to prepare the food to your requirements."

Chef! Agnes had to laugh. They didn't have a chef. The la-di-da woman cooked it all herself but she was too stuck-up to admit it. If they'd had a proper chef Agnes might not have ended up getting the food poisoning. And if she hadn't got the food poisoning, Eric might be alive to this day. However, you can't know these things in advance, can you? If you could, you'd do everything differently. For instance, Agnes wouldn't have chosen the Prawn Surprise for a starter. And then she wouldn't have ended up killing Eric with a meat cleaver.

At seven o'clock on the dot, Agnes and Eric were sitting at the little table with its rose-patterned, frilly table-cloth, and a lovely view onto the small front garden and the road beyond. Eric had chosen a Grapefruit Exquise for starter and Agnes had opted for the prawns. The Grapefruit Exquise turned out to be half a grapefruit with a glacé cherry in the centre. The Prawn Surprise was mainly surprising for its lack of prawns. It took the form of a pinkish glop which appeared to be made of salad cream with a few fishy lumps nestling in the bottom. Whether those fishy lumps had any connection to prawns was anyone's guess. Agnes couldn't help thinking that it tasted a bit "off" but she didn't mention it. Best not to make a fuss. Any anyway, maybe the main course would be better.

It wasn't. Agnes had trout for her main course and Eric had steak and kidney pie. He claimed it was the best steak and kidney pie he'd ever eaten, which Agnes found hard to believe. Her trout was only half thawed and was almost raw in the middle. Still, the wine was all right. It was a Beaujolais. Agnes would have preferred Mosel but the establishment's wine list didn't extend that far. They were given a choice of Beaujolais, Hungarian Riesling or beer, so they went for the Beaujolais.

By the time they'd got around to the dessert (they both had ice cream which, surprisingly, was quite good), it was starting to snow outside. Agnes thought the snow made the evening all the more romantic. It reminded her of the film with Bing Crosby. "Which film's that?" Eric asked. "You know," Agnes said, "The one with the snow." Eric smile – "Oh yeah, that one." Eric didn't really much care for snow. He had to get back on Monday morning, after all, and the last thing he wanted was to have to drive through snow. Still, as long as it made Agnes feel romantic, that was a good thing. When she felt romantic, she tended to get a bit more physical with him and that, after all, was the whole point of their dirty weekend. Besides which, it was only a flurry of snow. It probably wouldn't even settle.

But the snow did settle. At first, the big flakes fell and just melted away. But after a while, some of them stuck. By nine o'clock, there was already an inch or so of snow on the pavements outside.

By that time it was too late to go to a show so Eric suggested going to a wine bar. He knew a very nice wine bar no more than ten minutes' walk from the hotel. But Agnes said she didn't feel like going.

"Why's that, love? Is it the wine you don't fancy?" Eric said, "We could go dancing, maybe? Is the Blackpool Tower Ballroom open this time of year? I can phone up and find out, if you like…"

"No, no, it's not that," Agnes said, "It's just that I… I don't know, I'm feeling a bit under the weather for some reason."

"A few glasses of wine will soon get you on your feet," Eric suggested.

"No, really, love. I think I'd rather stay in. I'll have a nice, long bath. You go out. I'll probably feel a lot better when you get back."

"I can't go out without you, love," Eric said, though he tried not to sound too certain about that, just in case Agnes agreed.

But Agnes didn't agree. "There's nothing for you to do here," she insisted, "Once I'm in that bath I'll be there for hours. You know what I'm like. You might as well go out to a wine bar or a pub or something. Then when you get back I'll be as fresh as a daisy, just you see if I won't!"

"All right, love, if you insist. Eric kissed Agnes on the cheek. She liked to be kissed like that. She thought it was more well-mannered than kissing on the lips. Eric didn't mind. Once he'd been to the pub and Agnes had got herself all titivated up, he knew he'd be able to kiss her wherever he wanted to.

So Agnes started running her bath and Eric went out into the cold, snowy night. Without Agnes, he had no intention of going to a wine bar. There was a pub nearby that served good bitter and had a barmaid who was very soothing on the eyes. So that's where he headed.

By the time Agnes had finished running her bath, she barely felt like getting into it. Her stomach was feeling none too good and her head was starting to throb. She couldn't seem to get the taste of her Prawn Surprise out of her mouth. If only she'd chosen the grapefruit, she'd probably be feeling fine. There had definitely been something fishy about the prawns.

She wasn't in the bath more than five minutes before she had to leap out again with considerable speed. She had a sudden urge to vomit. She rushed towards the toilet and only just got there in time.

Agnes always kept a small range of essential medicines in her handbag so she took a couple of paracetamols for her headache and sucked on a couple of stomach-settling pills for her tummy ache. Then she got into bed, turned off the bedside lamp, pulled the blankets over her head and settled down for five minutes' doze.

She was woken by the sound of screaming.

She pulled back the blankets and listened.

Silence.

Then there was the sound of something being smashed. It sounded like crockery.

She sat up in bed. She was about to reach out to turn on the lamp but, to her confusion, it wasn't necessary because there was enough light filtering through the curtained windows to enable her to see the room fairly clearly. She got out of bed and went to the curtains and opened them. There was snow everywhere. The roof-tops of the houses opposite were covered in snow. The road was deep in snow. The small front garden down below was buried in snow. And the snow was still falling heavily.

She glanced at the green glowing numbers of the digital clock on her bedside table: 09:27. She must have slept soundly throughout the night. Well, at least she felt all the better for it. Her stomach still wasn't quite right. And her head still ached a bit. But, on the whole, she felt pretty good. Maybe she and Eric would be able to go for a decent meal somewhere that evening. Somewhere that didn't serve Prawn Surprise. Maybe they'd even be able to take in a show?

There was a loud bang from downstairs. Like furniture falling over. Then a smashing sound. Like glass.

Oh my God! Agnes started to panic. Maybe the house was being burgled. And there was she, all alone in her room, wearing a negligée that was far more revealing than she would want anyone other than Eric to see her wearing, let alone a burglar!

Eric. Where was Eric? He'd said that he was just going to pop out for a few drinks. So why wasn't he here? She didn't remember him returning. But then again, she didn't remember anything because she'd slept so soundly. He must have come back, mustn't he?

"He's probably downstairs having breakfast," she told herself.

There was another sound of something being smashed from down below. Eric was a noisy eater but even he wasn't that noisy. What on earth was going on down there? Agnes would have to get dressed and go and take a look.

Then she heard the sound of heavy footsteps coming up the stairs. Towards her room. She realised she hadn't locked the bedroom door. Well, she and Eric had been the only people staying in the guest house. There hadn't seemed any need. Seconds later, the door was flung open. Agnes breathed a sigh of relief. It was only Eric!

She went towards him, "Eric love, what the hell was going on downstairs?" She laughed, "You wouldn't believe what was going through my mind. I thought there might be a burglar and…" She stopped in mid-sentence. There was something wrong with Eric. He was dishevelled. His clothes were wet, his hair was unkempt. His eyes were staring wildly.

His eyes. There was something very peculiar about his eyes. They were bloodshot. He must have been drinking. His eyes did have a tendency to get bloodshot when he'd had a skinful. He also tended to get aggressive. Agnes had known a few men like that in her time. When they are sober they are soft-spoken, mild-mannered and polite. But once they get boozed up, their nasty side comes to the fore. Eric was like that. Up to three pints he was OK. Four to five and he'd start getting belligerent. Any more than five pints and he was like the Incredible Hulk.

Agnes stared at him. She reckoned he must be well on the wrong side of five pints.

"Eric?" she said hesitantly, "Is everything all right, love?"

Eric's reply took the form of a guttural grunt. Almost a growl, in fact. Agnes assumed the worst. He must have been on an absolute blinder. Ten pints. Maybe more.

"Come and sit down, Eric love."

He said nothing. Just stared at her. For a moment, Agnes thought he was crying. But those weren't tears. They were drops of blood. Big, sticky drops of blood were oozing from his eyelids and slowly rolling down his cheeks. The blood wasn't just coming from his eyes either. There was blood coming from his nostrils too.

"Oh, my God, Eric! What's wrong?"

The panic was coming back again. Agnes had never liked the sight of blood. Even what she called her "little monthly problem" made her feel queasy. Seeing blood oozing from places where blood should never ooze from made her feel distinctly faint.

"I love you…" Eric said.

What? He'd never said that to her before. Never. He'd said he liked her. He told her she was really fun to be with. But love? That wasn't a word he'd even mentioned before.

Eric moved towards her. He held out his arms as though he was about to embrace her. Agnes didn't know what to do. She took a small step towards him then had second thoughts and backed away again.

"You need a doctor," she said, "I'll get my phone."

Eric shook his head. The blood was flowing faster now. From his eyes, from his nose. It was dripping down the side of his neck too. In horror, Agnes saw that blood was bubbling out of Eric's ears.

"Don't go," he said.

"My phone," she said, "It's in my handbag."

He gripped her wrist, pulled her towards him. "I told you don't go," he snarled.

"Eric," she squealed, "You're hurting me."

Immediately he released his grip. "This isn't me," he said softly, "Agnes, my love. I'm slipping away. I don't know what's happening. I…"

Agnes didn't stay to listen. She slipped past him, through the open door onto the landing. She ran down the stairs, into the dining room.

The dining room had been wrecked. Tables and chairs lay on the floor. A china cabinet had been toppled. Fragments of smashed crystal glasses and blue willow-pattern plates lay scattered across the carpet. But Agnes barely noticed any of that. Because her attention was completely focussed on the body. The la-di-da lady hotel owner was lying on her back. It looked like a very uncomfortable position to be in. Her body was sprawled across a mound of broken crockery and smashed glass. But she was obviously past caring. Because while her body was lying on the floor, her head was sitting in the centre of the table next to the window. It seemed to be staring out at the steadily falling snow.

Agnes felt sick. She put her hand over her mouth. There was a noise behind her. A foot scrunching on broken glass. She turned. It was Eric. He looked angry and he looked mad. He shouted at Agnes and called her another word that she'd never heard him use before but this time it wasn't "love". Eric was blocking the doorway to the passage. There was only one other door in the dining room. Agnes went towards it. It was a swing door. She pushed; it swung. She was in the kitchen. There were knives there. Lots of knives. She picked one up at random and carefully ran her thumb along the blade. It was blunt. She picked up another knife and did the same thing. It was blunt too. Agnes wasn't surprised. The la-di-da woman had been an awful cook. If she'd employed a proper chef, the knives would have been as sharp as razors. Just her luck! If she ever went on another dirty weekend in Blackpool, she'd insist into staying at a proper hotel with a proper chef. You never knew when that might come in handy.

Then she saw the meat cleaver. It was lying next to a wooden chopping board. It didn't look as though it had ever been used. She tested the blade with her thumb. It drew blood. That was exactly what she needed.

He was there. In the doorway to the kitchen. Agnes smiled at him. "Eric, my love," she cooed, "you've been overdoing it. You need to relax. Come and have a nice cup of tea."

He looked confused. The poor thing. For a second, Agnes felt sorry for him. But she didn't feel so sorry that she was prepared to loosen her grip on the meat cleaver that she was holding behind her back.

She couldn't think what had come over Eric. Even a ten-pint blinder wouldn't account for the destruction and slaughter that had taken place in the dining room.

"I don't know what's happening," Eric said.

Agnes thought, "Well, that makes two of us then," but what she said was, "I'll put the kettle on, shall I? And then I can phone for a doctor."

His reaction was instant. "No doctor!" – and he lunged towards Agnes.

Almost before she knew what she was doing, Agnes whipped her hand from behind her back. Swinging the meat-cleaver high over her head, she brought it down with all her might, straight into the middle of Eric's skull. The sound it made on contact reminded Agnes of the sound her butcher made when he was chopping up a rack of lamb: steel crunching down hard on flesh and bone.

Eric staggered back. He landed against the stove and put out a hand to break his fall. He stood there, propped against the stove, staring wide-eyed at Agnes, as though he couldn't work out what had just happened. Eric was drenched in blood by now. The blood that had been trickling from his nose and from his eyes and from his ears was joined by a tidal wave of blood cascading down his forehead. The meat cleaver stayed where it had struck – right in the very top of Eric's head.

"Agnes?" Eric said.

"Yes, Eric?"

"I meant what I said."

"What was that, Eric?"

"I love you."

Those were Eric's last words. Then he closed his eyes and his body slumped forward, away from the stove and landed with a soft *whump!* upon the linoleum kitchen tiles.

Agnes put her hand over her heart. Those had been Eric's dying words – "I love you". Agnes sighed. It was like a scene from a romantic novel. Well, apart from the meat-cleaver and the decapitated body in the other room.

It was a shame, though, that Eric had made such a mess of everything. Agnes walked back through the dining room. She wiped the blood off the Tiffany-style lamp standing on the mantelpiece.

Then she glanced down at the negligée she was wearing. It was covered in blood.

Oh well, there was nothing for it. She'd just have to go and have another bath – a nice, long soak this time – freshen herself up and get dressed in some nice clean clothes. That would make her feel so much better.

Well, she thought, at least she'd have something to tell the girls back in the hairdresser's. They all thought that Agnes led such a dull, predictable life. Oh no, Agnes thought, they don't know the half of it!

She glanced out of the window. The snow was falling more heavily than ever. She wouldn't be able to get back this weekend after all. A pity. She couldn't wait to tell everyone about her dirty weekend.

THE ACCORDION PLAYER AND THE MONKEY

It was Brian's idea to go to the party. He'd met this girl called Sandra who was a friend of a girl called Jenny who worked in the accounts department of the magazine where Brian was a subeditor. Sandra had said she was throwing a party on Saturday and everybody was welcome.

So that's how Brian had ended up in the posh house in Westbourne Park on the night of the Great Snow. He'd been in two minds at first but then he'd gone to a pub in Bayswater and he'd bumped into a guy called Justin who sometimes wrote bits and bobs for Brian's magazine.

It was one of those parties where everyone either gets rat-arsed on the free booze, out of their head on someone else's drugs or else just has lots of sex. Brian had been hoping for the latter option but luck wasn't with him so he settled for the booze.

It was funny that Brian didn't manage to get off with any of the women at the party. Because birds always fell for Brian. That was what he called young women – "birds". Brian had watched all the old films from the '60s with Michael Caine and Terrence Stamp and all that lot and he'd picked up the lingo, which he thought sounded cooler, *groovier*, than modern slang.

"I reckon the birds here are lezzies, that's my theory," said Brian.

"What?" said his mate, Carl.

"You know, dykes. Birds who fancy other birds."

"That guy over there seems to be doing all right for himself," Carl replied.

The guy to whom Carl was referring was called Alistair. He was tall, had a lithe, muscular physique like a swimmer and had the sort of perfect, wavy blond hair that fashion models sometimes have but men in real life never do. Except for Alistair.

"He's a poof," sneered Brian.

"Maybe that's what women like?" said Carl.

At some point Alistair started wandering around holding a silver tray upon which were lots of little bright yellow marzipan pigs. Everyone took a pig. Brian took two. The main attraction of the pigs was not the marzipan outer layer but the inner nugget of pure Afghan cannabis resin which they contained.

Ten minutes after eating the first pig, Brian was feeling mellow. Then he ate the second pig. Ten minutes after eating the second pig, Brian felt as if his legs were made of rubber but that didn't matter because when he walked he floated two or three inches above the ground.

That was when he struck lucky. A plump, red-haired girl wearing a transparent cheesecloth shirt sidled up to Brian and whispered in his ear – "Shall we have sex?"

Brian couldn't believe his ears. Maybe the cannabis had been stronger than he'd realised. Maybe he was suffering from auditory hallucinations. He smiled sloppily at the girl and said – "Where?"

"Out there," she said.

"Out where?" he asked.

"In the garden."

"In the garden?"

He walked to the back window and glanced outside.

"It's like the Antarctic out there," he said, "Polar bears might walk across the ice cap at any moment."

The girl giggled. "That's the Arctic you are thinking of."

She caught hold of his hand and pulled him in the direction of the back door. He assumed she was teasing him. There was no way they were going to have sex out in that blizzard! But the girl kept tugging his hand, so Brian followed.

It was bitterly cold out there. The red-haired girl started to unbutton Brian's shirt. Brian didn't fancy her any more. She was too desperate somehow. She was fumbling with Brian's belt now, then trying to undo his zip. He pulled her hands away, started to do up the belt again.

"What's the matter, man?" the girl said.

"I'm gay," Brian lied.

"That's cool," said the girl, "I'm undecided. But I can be gay if you want."

He pushed her away. She wasn't the sort of bird he fancied anyway. Brian liked them tall and willowy. Like Sandra. Where was Sandra anyway? Brian pushed his way back into the living room. Oh, there she was. She was rolling about on the rug in front of the fire with Justin – the guy who freelanced for Brian's magazine sometimes.

That was the last straw. Brian had had enough of the party. It was still early. He glanced at his watch. It took a while to bring it into focus. He wasn't sure whether it was 11 o' clock or 12 o'clock. Or maybe it was 1 o'clock. Anyway, whatever the time, it was a Saturday night. And on Saturday nights, you are supposed to enjoy yourself.

Brian staggered upstairs to get his overcoat which he'd left in a heap on a bed in somebody's bedroom. At that moment, two naked people were rolling about on top of his overcoat. Brian didn't much care for that. So he elbowed the top person in the ribs, causing them to roll onto somebody else's overcoat.

"Bloody party" he grumbled, as he buttoned up his coat, "It's like the last bloody days of bloody Pompeii. Or Constantinople. Or whatever."

Then he stumped miserably down the staircase, opened the front door and went out into a mad swirl of falling snow. He didn't know where to go to next so he wandered through the streets for a while on the lookout for whatever he could find. A nightclub maybe? Or some other party he could crash where the birds wouldn't be so hoity-toity.

What he actually found was an old man with an accordion and a monkey. The monkey was wearing a knitted woollen cardigan and hat and was sitting on the man's shoulder. The man was playing the accordion and singing sad songs about love and loss.

Brian stopped to listen. They were under a bridge down a side street. It was one of those narrow, old streets that pop up unexpectedly in London, looking little changed since the days of Dickens and Jack The Ripper. The snow hadn't settled under the bridge so Brian was able to see the cobblestones.

When the man finished playing, the monkey began chittering at Brian and put its tiny hand out towards him. This was all part of the act, Brian supposed. To get money out of the spectators. Oh, what the heck, why not? It was a good enough act, after all. Brian put his hand into a pocket and took out a pound coin. He held it out to the money who immediately snatched the coin and then dropped it into the top pocket of the accordion player's overcoat.

"You want to be careful," the accordion player said.

"Who?" Brian said, "Me?"

"I don't see anyone else here, do you? I'm just saying, look at my eyes."

"Your eyes?"

"Do you see anything strange about my eyes?"

The accordion player stepped out from the shadow of the bridge so that his face was illuminated by a nearby streetlight.

"No," said Brian, "I can't see anything strange about your eyes."

"That's what I mean," the accordion player said, "You want to be careful."

Brian smiled. The man was an idiot. Probably a meths drinker. Still, he played the accordion well and the songs he sang almost made Brian want to cry. Which was odd. Because Brian was not the sentimental sort. But it was late and he'd had too much to drink and he was still high off the cannabis in the marzipan pigs, so it probably wasn't surprising that he was in a weird sort of mood.

Later on, when he'd wandered off to another part of town, Brian wasn't sure if he'd really met the accordion player and his monkey at all. I mean, why would anyone be out in a blizzard in the early hours of the morning with an accordion and a monkey? It didn't make any sense. All the same, he remembered what the man had said about his eyes.

Brian carried on walking. He saw some people making snowmen. He walked over to them. The snow was deep here. It sifted down into Brian's shoes as he walked through it.

"Nice snowman!" Brian called out.

One of the people turned around. A man. A big man with a bushy black beard. "What's it to you?" the man said. He sounded oddly aggressive.

"Nothing," Brian said, "I was just saying. It's a nice snowman."

There was something funny about the man's eyes. Brian thought it would be a good idea not to get too close to him, so he backed away in the other direction. He realised that he was walking down the middle of a main road. There should be cars coming along it. But the road was too choked with snow for that. The snow ploughs would be along soon, no doubt. He stared up at the snow. He'd never seen such big flakes. They seemed to shimmer like a pigeon's throat or a soap bubble. There was a word for that, Brian thought. He was a subeditor, he should know it. Luminous? No, that wasn't it. Incandescent? No, that wasn't it either.

Opalescent. That was the word. The snowflakes looked opalescent. Like opals that seemed to glow with an inner light.

There were two people on the other side of the road. A young man and a woman. They were having an argument. Calling one another names. The man said it was the woman's fault. The woman said it was the man's fault. Brian couldn't figure out what the argument was about. Just the usual Saturday night/Sunday morning bust-up. The woman hit the man. The man hit her back. This was more serious than the average bust-up. They were really going for one another now. The woman bit the man's hand. Then the man hit the woman with such force that he knocked her off her feet. She slammed hard into the ground. She didn't get up again.

"Shit!" Brian thought, "He's killed her."

Then the man spotted Brian.

"What are you looking at?" the man said.

Brian looked at the woman lying motionless in the snow.

"Nothing," Brian said, "Nothing."

Brian wasn't the hero type. If people wanted to fight in the streets, that was their business. It was nothing to do with him. He walked on.

In another street he saw some people gathered around a fire. The fire had been made from planks of wood and bits of furniture. They were roasting a great side of meat in the flames. It smelled disgusting. From the way they looked at him, Brian got the impression that he wouldn't be welcome to join them. In fact, he got the impression that if he didn't leave pretty damn' quickly they'd be perfectly happy to roast Brian on that fire. Brian left pretty damn' quickly.

Then, later, he was in a shopping street. On the left there was an electric goods shop. On the right there was an off licence. The windows of both the shops had been smashed. So had the windows of a greengrocer's, a cheese shop and a chemist's. People were carrying away all they could get – bottles of wine, chunks of Stilton cheese, TV sets, bags of potatoes…

Where were the police?

The snow was still falling. The looters were struggling to get through the drifts of snow, carrying their burdens. Two women and a man were trying to take away a washing machine. The load was too much for them. They dropped it in the middle of the street and went off to look for something easier to carry.

The roads were all blocked with snow. That's why there were no police. As soon as the snow ploughs got going, they'd be here. Wouldn't they?

He turned down another street. Two muscular young men, stripped to the waist, were having a bare-knuckle fight. One man slammed his fist into the other man's nose; his head jerked back and a spray of blood flew over the cheering crowd that had gathered around the fighting men.

He turned down yet another street. A man lunged out of a doorway with a carving knife in his hand. He slashed out at Brian. The man was babbling and cursing but his words made no sense. Brian turned away and slipped in the snow. The man made a guttural growling noise. Brian tried to get up. There was a hand on his shoulder, then another hand on his other shoulder, pulling him to his feet.

"Come on!"

Brian looked up. It was a young woman. Well, more of a girl, really. She can't have been more than eighteen. Good-looking. Fair hair.

"Follow me."

Brian looked at the man with the knife. He was just standing there, cursing to himself and swishing the knife through the air. He gave no indication of even noticing Brian and the girl.

"I've been watching you," the fair-haired girl said.

"Really?" Brian smiled. Automatically, he came out with a cheesy chat-up line, "And do you like what you see?"

The girl frowned. "I thought you might be worth saving. Suddenly I'm not so sure."

Brian had often fantasized about being picked up in the street by a good-looking bird like this one. But he had never imagined it would happen like this.

"You look all right," she said.

"Just all right?" The cheesy chat-up lines came so naturally to him that he couldn't seem to stop himself.

"I'm taking you back to my place," the girl said, "and don't you dare say another word or I'll leave you to the mob and they'll probably tear you limb from limb. And I'm already starting to wonder if that might not be such a bad idea."

Brian had opened his mouth to say something. He shut it again. He had a vast collection of chat-up lines but none of them seemed quite appropriate in the present circumstances. He decided silence would be his best bet until he could figure out what exactly was going on. The girl walked away and Brian followed. She wended her way through a network of small streets and alleyways, always watching, especially when turning corners, to make sure that nothing unexpected was waiting there. Finally she arrived at a house in a small, dead-end street. Brian noticed that it was no longer completely dark. Dawn was breaking, such as it was – a thin, grey light struggling through the densely-falling snow. The girl unlocked the front door and they went into a dismal hallway with cracked linoleum on the floor and paint flaking off the walls.

"Nice pad you have here," Brian said.

"Ha-bloody-ha," the girl replied.

They walked through to the back of the house. She pushed open a door. They went into the kitchen. There were two people sitting at the kitchen table – a young man with a neatly-trimmed beard and a young woman with short, dark hair. They were holding mugs of tea in their hands. When the door opened, they turned to look. The young man immediately jumped to his feet. The young woman sat there with eyes wide, looking scared.

"It's all right," said the girl accompanying Brian, "He's normal."

"How can you tell?" said the young woman with short, dark hair.

"Because he's an idiot. The others are maniacs. This one is just a twat."

Brain opened his mouth to say something but the fair-haired girl glared at him. She didn't seem to be a big fan of Brian's witty repartee. So he closed his mouth again and smiled inanely.

The young man held out his hand, "I'm Ron," he said, "and this" (he nodded towards the dark-haired woman) "is Marian."

Brian shook Ron's hand. "Brian," he said.

Brian looked at the blond girl who'd brought him there.

"What?" she said.

"You haven't said your name."

"Does it matter?"

"It does to me."

"I swear," she said, "if you come out with one more stupid line like that, I'll swing for you. For what it's worth, I'm Cyndi."

"Thanks, Cyndi. For rescuing me, I mean."

"You rescued him?" Marian said, "Wow! What happened?"

Cyndi related the story about finding Brian being threatened by the man with the knife. She also told them about the other things she'd seen – the looting, the fighting, the random acts of violence.

"What's happening to people?" Marian asked.

"Beats me," said Cyndi, "Everyone's gone nuts."

Brian told them about his experiences: the party, the people making a snowman, the people roasting something over a fire, the man with the accordion and a monkey.

"A monkey!" Marian said, "In this weather!"

Then Ron told Brian their story. The three of them were students. This place was their accommodation. Term hadn't started yet and the two others who lived in rooms upstairs hadn't returned. The three of them had watched a film on TV the previous evening and had a few beers. Then they'd gone to bed. They were woken up an hour ago by someone banging on the front door. It was the old lady who lived next door, Mrs Wheeler. She was in quite a state. Her husband was acting strangely, she said. Could someone come and help her? Ron had gone next door to have a look. The old man was sitting in an armchair wearing only his pyjama bottoms. Blood was seeping from his nose and mouth. Ron tried ringing for an ambulance. It took him ten minutes to get through. A harried sounding woman told him that she'd log his call but not to expect an ambulance soon "because of the roads. And everything else."

So Ron had helped Mrs Wheeler to cover her husband with blankets to keep him warm and then he came back to the house and turned on the radio to find out what was going on – what was the "everything else" that the woman on the phone had mentioned?

The BBC was playing endless music interspersed with news headlines: "Rioting has been reported in London, Manchester and Birmingham. Due to the weather conditions, the emergency services are warning the public that there may be considerable delays from the police, ambulance and fire services. We are expecting the Prime Minister to make a statement to the nation at nine o'clock. And now, we return you to the music."

"And that's all we know," said Ron.

"Which is why I went out to see for myself," added Cyndi.

"Why are people rioting?" Brian asked.

"Opportunism," Ron said.

"Don't be so cynical," said Marian.

"Well, have you got any better ideas?" said Ron.

"What did you mean," asked Brian, "when you said that I was normal?"

Cyndi shrugged. "Apart from the fact that you're an idiot, you mean?"

"Yeah. Apart from that."

"Look at your eyes."

"I can't. Not unless you've got a mirror. Why? What's wrong with my eyes?"

"Nothing."

Brian didn't understand what she meant. But he thought about what the accordion player had said. He'd said something about some people's eyes being strange.

They turned on the radio at nine o'clock. The Prime Minister's statement had been postponed. There was a story about a retirement home in Bristol that had reported an inexplicable outbreak of some sort of haemorrhagic fever. "Like Mr Wheeler next door," Ron commented, "Maybe something's going around."

"Just a coincidence," Marian said.

Marian made some beans on toast for breakfast. After that, Brian slumped in a settee in another downstairs room and dozed off. It was almost one o'clock in the afternoon by the time he woke. Marian and Cyndi were sitting in the kitchen drinking coffee. The radio was playing music.

"There's hot water in the kettle," Cyndi said, "and coffee in the jar."

"Only instant?" Brian said.

"Do you have to work at being so unlikable," Cyndi asked, "or does it come naturally?"

There was the sound of the front door opening and shutting. Moments later, Ron came into the kitchen. He was wearing a parka with a fur-trimmed hood. He brushed snow off the parka before taking it off.

"Things are getting worse," he said.

"How much worse?" said Marian.

"A lot worse."

He made himself a mug of coffee and sat at the table. "There's dead people."

"Where?" said Marian.

"Everywhere." He hesitated, "I called on Mrs Wheeler next door."

There was a long silence. Nobody wanted to ask.

"Mr Wheeler died during the night."

Cyndi gasped – "No!"

"And Mrs Wheeler's looking none too good."

"Have you called an ambulance?" Marian asked.

Ron shook his head – "Can't get through."

"God damned snow!" Cyndi said.

"I think something is killing old people," Ron said, "Like they were saying on the radio. About haemorrhagic fever. I think that's maybe what's happening."

"Fever!" Marian looked alarmed. If Mrs and Mrs Wheeler had it, does that mean we'll get it too?"

Ron shrugged, "I don't know. There are other problems though. The gangs Cyndi and Brian saw last night. They are all over the place. Young people. Teens, twenties. Maybe some in their thirties."

"Looters," Marian spat the word out, "They think that because the police can't get through the snow they can get away with nicking whatever they want to."

"Yeah," said Ron, "Maybe that's all it is. Only…"

"Only what?" said Cyndi.

"Well, have you seen their eyes?"

"What about their eyes?"

"Red. Bloodshot."

"Who?" Marian asked.

"Just about everyone. As far as I can see. All the gangs. The looters. Most of them have really red eyes. It's weird."

"You mean they have the fever too? Like they've been talking about on the radio? Like Mr Wheeler had?"

"Don't know," said Ron, "Maybe it affects young people differently. Some diseases do. Flu does sometimes."

"Covid does," Marian added.

"I don't know," Ron said, "All I know for sure is that it isn't safe out there. We need to barricade the doors or something. Stop them getting in."

Brian didn't want to be barricaded. Brian wanted to get home.

"You don't want to be out on the streets now," Ron warned him, "It's madness out there."

But Brian was determined. "It's only a twenty minute walk."

"Not in this snow, it isn't," Cyndi warned him.

But Brian was insistent. Ron advised him to wait until darkness fell. It would give him a better chance to get back without being seen. So Brian stayed with the three students for the rest of the afternoon. They drank tea and they ate biscuits and they listened to the radio. The news reports became bleaker and bleaker. There were more reports of old people dying from the mystery haemorrhagic fever and more reports of looting and rioting in towns all over Britain. The Prime Minister's statement to the nation had been postponed until 1 o'clock and then it had been postponed again until six o'clock. Brian didn't know if the statement was ever made though. At half past five, he left the house.

Ron had given him an old pair of Wellington boots. Brian was grateful. His shoes were no protection against the snow. He put his shoes in a carrier bag and took them with him. It wasn't too long before he saw the bodies. They had been left where they'd fallen. The snow was already starting to cover them.

There the sound of breaking glass, followed by the shrill *bleee-bleee-bleee!* of a burglar alarm. Two youths had just smashed the window of a jeweller's shop with sledge-hammers. They scrambled through the broken window and scooped up handfuls of watches. They were taking their time. There was no need to worry that anyone would come and stop them. As the lads casually walked past Brian, one of them turned towards him and smiled. By the light of the streetlamp, Brian noticed that the youth's eyes looked odd. Where they should have been white, they were dark. Brian couldn't be sure what colour they were. He thought they might have been red.

The youth with the strange eyes threw something at Brian. It fell in the snow at his feet. Brian stooped to pick it up. It was a Rolex watch. For a brief second Brian thought of going over to the jeweller's shop and putting the watch back inside. Then he realised what a meaningless gesture that would be. Someone else would come along and steal the watch again. That's how the world was, all of a sudden. He threw away his cheap old watch and put the Rolex onto his wrist. It fitted perfectly. Maybe the New World Order wasn't so bad after all.

Even so, he thought it might be better to avoid any main streets – streets with lots of shops in. They attracted looters. And some of the looters might turn violent. So he kept to side streets. He thought he knew this part of town reasonably well. But everything looked different in the snow. After a while, he realised he must have been going around in circles.

He started worrying. He was lost. Maybe he'd never find his way home. Not that night, at any rate. And if one of the gangs found him, what then? There were no police around to help. No emergency services of any description.

"Typical of this bloody country," he moaned to himself, "A little snowstorm and everything goes to wrack and ruin. Where's the bloody Army, for God's sake?"

Just then he walked into a wide open street and – "My God!" he said, "A miracle!"

The Army was there!

He tried to figure out where he was. On the other side of the road stood the wrought iron gates to a park. It must be Kensington Gardens then; either that or Hyde Park – he was never sure what the difference was. At any rate, he reckoned he must be somewhere near Lancaster Gate and the road he was on must be the Bayswater Road.

The snow was now deep and smooth and it was falling so thickly that he could barely see more than a few yards in any direction. Even so, he was pretty sure that this was the Bayswater Road. And, being such an important road, one of the main routes into and out of central London, naturally the snow ploughs had been out to keep it open. Well, up to a point anyway. There wasn't any actual traffic moving along the road. But there were some armoured cars and a military ambulance. At least, Brian *thought* it was an ambulance. At first sight it looked more like a tank – a huge, lumbering thing with caterpillar tracks – but it didn't have a gun at the front, though it did have red crosses inside white squares painted on the sides. Armed soldiers were milling around all over the place. There were some civilians with them, talking to the soldiers. It was a strangely comforting scene, Brian thought. Not exactly normality but, anyway, it showed that the Government was getting things back under control.

Brian smiled to himself. For a while, he'd started to think that there might be more going on than met the eye. Ron, Marian and Cyndi's paranoia had been getting to him. Haemorrhagic fever! What the hell was that all about? It was just some old people who'd got sick and died. Old people always died in winter. Flu, hyperthermia, heart attacks, old age… all perfectly normal. And as for the looting and rioting – well, with kids these days, any excuse would do.

A soldier glanced at Brian. Brian smiled at him, gave him the thumbs up sign, "Well done, mate!" he said, just to be friendly.

"Sir!" the soldier shouted back, "Put your arm down, sir."

"What?"

"Your arm, sir, put it by your side. Both arms by your side. Away from your body."

Brian did as he was told. The soldier was walking towards Brian. There was an older man with him. He looked like a civilian. He was too old to be a soldier and he wasn't wearing a uniform. He was wearing a long overcoat and a broad-brimmed hat. He had a small torch in one hand.

When they reached Brian, the soldier snapped, "What's in that carrier bag?"

"Shoes," Brian replied.

The soldier told him to open the bag. Brian did so. Having ascertained to his satisfaction that the shoes in the bag did not constitute an offensive weapon, the soldier went to stand to one side while the elderly man approached him. "Good evening, sir," the elderly man said, smiling, "Are you a local resident, by any chance?"

Brian nodded. "Down towards Bayswater. What's this about?"

"Just answer the doctor's questions," the soldier said.

The old man was still smiling. "It's just a formality, sir. Would you mind if I take a look at your eyes."

Brian was about to make a joke but he noticed the soldier staring at him. That was a very big gun he was holding. Brian replied, "Please, go ahead."

The old man lifted the top eyelid of Brian's right eye and shone a small torch into it. Then he went through the same procedure with Brian's left eye.

"What's the matter?" Brian said, "Anything wrong?"

"No, no, quite the contrary," said the old man, "Did you happen to go out last night, sir?"

"Yes," I said, "Why?"

"You've been out in the snow, then?"

"Yes. Yes, I have."

"Fascinating. Fascinating." The old man turned to the soldier and nodded briefly. Then he wandered off towards another soldier who was talking to a young woman.

The soldier next to Brian, said, "Over there. In that queue." He indicated a line of four people standing next to an armoured car. There were two people wearing hazmat suits – fully sealed body coverings including gloves and helmets – who seemed to be dealing with the people in the queue.

"You did hear me, son?" the soldier said, "I said, go and get in that queue."

"What for?" Brian protested, "I'm on my way home."

"Not any more, you're not, sunshine."

Brian went where the soldier was pointing. One of the men in the hazmat suits placed him at the end of the queue. Brian couldn't figure out why the two men were wearing hazmat suits but nobody else was. People only wore that stuff when there was serious danger of infection, didn't they? Or poisoning? But if the men in the suits were in danger, then so were the soldiers. And so was the old doctor. In fact, so was everyone – including Brian. So that didn't make sense. Unless, of course, the people who weren't wearing hazmat suits had been inoculated? But inoculated against what?

Brian took a look at the other people in the queue. They were all quite young. The youngest was probably about sixteen. The others were in their twenties. Brian looked at their eyes. They were normal. None of them were bloodshot.

*

He was in a bed in a hospital ward. They'd driven for hours to get there. In the armoured car. Which was very uncomfortable. Brian had chatted a bit to the others who'd been rounded up along with him but they didn't have much of interest to tell him. None of them understood what was happening any better than Brian did.

When they arrived at the hospital they found a large number of other people sitting or standing around waiting to be told what to do next. None of them were very old. They were mostly people in their twenties. A few in their thirties. One or two in their forties. A few teenagers too. None of them had red eyes.

Presently some doctors and nurses came along and separated them into groups. Brian was taken to a small private room. The nurse who took him to his room was a plump, rosy-cheeked woman with a lilting Irish accent. Brian asked what was going on. "Oh, nothing to worry about, you'll just be having a few tests. You'll be right as rain again soon, don't you worry now."

He was taken to have a shower and when he came out again, he was given some horrible hospital garment to wear instead of his own clothes. After a while, a doctor came along – a tall, eagle-nosed individual with swept-back silver hair and a stethoscope dangling ostentatiously over his long white coat.

Brian was in the doctor's consulting room now, lying on the bed. The doctor asked him how he felt.

"Tired," Brian replied.

"Apart from that, any symptoms?"

"Like what?"

"Oh, hot flushes, shortness of breath, soreness, palpitations?"

"What kind of palpitations?"

"That's for you to tell me," said the doctor.

Brian looked confused.

"I think we can take it there are no palpitations, then. No redness of the eyes either."

Brian noticed that the doctor had brought a small white kidney-shaped tray with him. Lying in the tray was a syringe. The doctor picked up the syringe, then he took a little bottle from a cardboard box standing on a metal trolley next to the tray. He stuck the needle into the top of the bottle and pulled the plunger to suck the fluid into the syringe. Then he went through that business they always do of tapping the syringe and squirting it. Brian wasn't sure if that was to get rid of air bubbles or if it was just for dramatic effect. Either way, he didn't like the look of it.

"Wait a minute," he said, "are you going to inject me?"

"Afraid of injections, are you? Don't worry, old man, just look the other way. It'll all be over in a jiffy."

"What's in it?" Brian said, "That injection. What is it?"

The doctor was already dabbing some moist cotton wool over Brian's arm. "Oh, nothing to worry about. It's just some tests we're carrying out."

"Tests? Why? There's nothing wrong with me."

The doctor smiled. "Yes, that's what's so fascinating."

"But I don't want any tests. I don't want any injections."

"Not optional, I'm afraid, old man."

He put the cotton wool back into the kidney-shaped tray and approached with the syringe needle glinting beneath the stark fluorescent lighting.

"Not optional?" But sure I have to know what it is. Surely I have to give my consent."

"No, as a matter of fact, you don't, old man. Not in a time of national emergency. Now stay quite still. This won't hurt a bit."

Brian felt a sharp pricking pain as the needle slid into his arm. And then his arm felt as though it was on fire, as though it had been pumped full of acid. That was when Brian blacked out. The last thing he remembered before sinking into oblivion was the label on the cardboard box from which the doctor had taken the small bottle of fluid. It had one of those weird biohazard symbols on it – three joined, broken rings, overlapping a circle. Beneath the symbol some words were printed. Brian hadn't been able to make any sense of them. He thought they said: The Exodus Project. Whatever that meant…

AN UNEXPECTED GUEST

Miss Ceridwen Hughes lived alone in the old stone cottage on Bryn Hud hill, above the little village of Cwmdistaw. She had been born there and she had lived there for all of her eighty-seven years. The cottage was cold and it was draughty; it had no central heating or television. In fact, it had changed very little since the days when her mother and father had lived there with Ceridwen and her two elder sisters, Mair and Angharad. There was still the old, high-backed wooden settle. There was still the Lord's Prayer, "Gweddi'r Arglwydd", embroidered and framed on the wall.

The only major changes had been the electricity and the wood-burning stove. As long as her mother had been alive, the house had been heated by an open coal fire and lit by gas flames flickering and hissing in the glass-shaded mantles on the wall. Ceridwen had a cast-iron wood-burning stove put in after the coal deliveries stopped. She had the electricity fitted when someone from the council said the gas was unsafe and would have to go.

Well, there was no electricity now. Five days earlier, the lights had gone off and they hadn't come back on again. Now, in the evenings, Cerdiwen did her sewing and her crocheting and her knitting by the light of candles. There were two candles in brass candleholders on the mantelpiece and another one in a saucer on her little worktable.

It was on one such evening that the stranger called. Ceridwen had been crocheting some cushion-covers at the time. When she heard the knocking, she thought it must be the wind blowing because nobody ever came calling on her at night. Her little cottage was two miles away from the village and she no longer had any very close friends. She had outlived them all.

Then the knocking came again. When she listened, it didn't sound as if it was very windy. So, strange as it seemed, she had to conclude that there was someone at her door. She laid down her crocheting and her crochet hooks on her worktable and pushed herself out of her chair with difficulty. Her old joints were getting stiff these days and the cold only made them worse.

She took a brass candlestick from the mantelpiece and hobbled down the passageway towards the front door. There was that knocking again. Not very hard. Not very loud. More like a child tapping at the door than a grown man. Still, you could never tell these days. You heard such stories about people breaking into houses, hurting people, stealing things. She wouldn't open the door until she was sure who was there.

"Pwy sy yna?" she called out.

There was no answer. She tried again in English, "Who's there?"

"It's me," said a thin, uncertain voice, "Owen."

She was trying to think if she knew an Owen. There was Owen Jones the boot shop owner but he'd died years ago. There had been an Owen Thomas once who was a good-for-nothing layabout. She had a feeling he was in prison. Or maybe he'd got out again? What would Owen Thomas be doing up there though?

"Beth wyt ti'n…" – she paused mid-question. She'd lived so long on her own that she'd got used to thinking in Welsh. All her old friends had spoken Welsh. They still taught Welsh at the schools but most of the younger people didn't bother learning it any more – "What do you want, Owen?"

"Help, Mrs Hughes. Please." No, that wasn't the voice of Owen Thomas. Owen Thomas had a thin, wheedling, croaking sort of a voice. She opened the door an inch or two and looked out. She couldn't see anyone there. All she could see was snow. Falling thick like goose feathers. And lying thick on the ground too. She couldn't see a person though. The night was pitch black and the candle barely cast a glimmer. She began to shut the door.

Suddenly, he was there! He held the door open. She tried to pull it shut but he was too strong. He stepped inside. "Myn uffern i!" she said, "What the bloody hell…?" Then she recognised him, "Oh, Owen Evans is it? Dan and Margedd's little boy?"

"That's me," said the young man, "Only not so little now."

That was true. Six foot tall he was, or more.

"Well, how old are you now then? You were a little dwt last time I saw you."

"Sixteen now, I am."

"Iesu Mawr! Sixteen is it? You must have been about, what, nine or ten last time I seen you."

"Yeah, probably."

"There's tall you've got now!"

"Yeah."

"Nothing the matter, is there?"

Why would Owen Evans come calling on her of all people, and after all those years? If there was anything amiss, there were plenty of people in the village. Why would he come all the way up the mountain to her, especially with the weather being so bad?

"No, nothing the matter. Well," he hesitated, "Nothing apart from, you know…"

"The damn' snow, you mean? Well, get that duffel coat off and come and warm up by my fire. I can make some tea if you like."

It wasn't a duffel coat that Owen was wearing. It was a parka – a big anorak with a fur-lined hood which Owen had pulled up around his face.

"If you don't mind, I'd prefer to keep it on."

"You'll get chilblains," she warned sternly, "And if you don't take it off you won't see the benefit when you go out again."

"Well, that's the thing, see. I wasn't planning on going out again."

"Not going out? What do you mean?"

He sighed wearily as though he could hardly be bothered to explain – "Well, see, the thing is, I haven't got anywhere to go."

"Haven't got anywhere to…?" Ceridwen sat down in her chair and had a bit of a think about that. What did the boy mean, he had nowhere to go? "Oh, I see. Had an argument, have you? With your mam. Margedd always did have a bit of a temper on her."

"No. No. My mam, she's… I tell you what though, I wouldn't mind a cup of tea after all."

So Ceridwen filled the ancient cast-iron kettle with water and put it onto the top of the cast-iron stove.

"There isn't any milk," she said, "Well, only the dried, anyway. That does for me but some don't like it."

"I don't mind," Owen said.

"Well then," she sat back in her chair while Owen sat on the settle, "what is it brings you up here, then?"

He sighed again. "You know."

"Know? How could I know? I only just seen you, haven't I?"

"Yeah, but…"

"Well then, answer my question. What is it that brings you up here on a night like this?"

"I, well, I got nowhere else to…"

"For God's sake, boy, take that duffel coat off. Put the damn' hood down anyway."

He hesitated. His fingers went to the hood but then he took his hands away again. "I prefer to wear it, if you don't mind."

"Well, that's it, you see. I do mind. It's like talking to a bloody monk with that hood up like that. I don't believe you're so cold by this fire that you need it. And I don't believe you're so shy that you can't bear me to see your face neither."

"There's something funny. About my face."

"There's something funny about my face too. It's old and it's wrinkled and it's not going to be winning any beauty contests, I don't suppose. But I don't hide it away, do I? I don't know what you're so shy about but whatever it is, I promise you I've seen worse. Nothing will shock me."

His fingers reached for the hood again. He was trembling slightly as he slowly pulled it down, showing his face by the meagre light of the candles and the fire.

"There now, that's much better," said Ceridwen, "You're a good looking young man. I don't know what you're so shy about."

"My eyes," he said.

"Your eyes?" His eyes were in shadow. She didn't understand what he meant. "What's wrong with your eyes?"

Owen stood. He took a candlestick from the mantelpiece, gave it to Ceridwen and then brought his face close to the candle flame. She stared into his eyes. In the darkness, they looked black. There was no white; there was no iris; no pupil; every part of his eye between the eyelids was a featureless black. Ceridwen gasped in spite of her promise that she would not be shocked. But when Owen came closer to the candlelight, she realised that her first impression was wrong. The eyes weren't black. The pupil was black. The iris was dark green. But what should have been the white of the eye was a deep, dark crimson.

"Diawl!" she exclaimed, "What happened to your eyes, boy?"

"It happened to everyone," Owen said, "Well, no, not everyone. But to a lot of people."

"You been to the doctor's, have you?"

Owen shook his head. "The doctor's dead."

"Dead? Doctor Jenkins? I never heard that. Are you sure."

He nodded.

"Well, there must be other doctors. Locums or whatever."

The boy shook his head. "Not in the village. There was only Doctor Jenkins."

"Well, then, get your father or your mother to drive you to the hospital."

He shook his head again. "Can't. They're not there any more."

"Want do you mean. Not *where?*"

"Not anywhere. They're dead too."

"No! Don't say such a thing. Not even as a joke."

"It's not a joke. They're dead. Mam's lying on the black-and-white linoleum in the back kitchen. Dad's on the settee in the front room. They're where I left them."

"You left them? What do you mean by that, Owen?"

"You know."

"There you go again. I can't know if you don't tell me, now, can I?"

He smiled for the first time since he'd arrived, "I killed them. I killed them both. And then I came to you."

Ceridwen took a few moments to think about what he had just said. Then the kettle came to the boil. "How do you like your tea, Owen?" she said, "Milk and sugar, is it, love?"

"No sugar, thanks."

So they huddled around the log fire with their mugs of tea and Owen told Ceridwen all that had happened. Once he started, it all spilled out, the whole story. It had started after the great snowfall, he said. The snow was all over the place, not just the village. All over the country. Other countries too. Ceridwen must have seen it on the telly?

But Cerdiwen didn't have a television and she hardly ever bothered listening to the wireless. She wasn't interested in the goings on of the world.

After the snowfall, most of the older people got sick. A lot of them died. The younger ones, though, generally recovered. Up to a point. Only some of them were left with a sickness in the brain.

"Like me," Owen explained, "I have the sickness deep inside my head. It comes and it goes, see. One minute I feel OK. Like now, for instance. I feel calm now. But then all of a sudden, I get this urge, like. To hurt people. To kill people. Just for the fun of it. And when I get the urge on me there's nothing I can do to stop it."

"Have a biscuit," Ceridwen said, "They're in the tin on the table. There's some chocolate ones."

"Why aren't you scared?"

"Scared? What of? You? Why would I be scared of you?"

"I killed my mother and my father. I killed some others too, I think. Only I'm not sure because I forget things a lot."

Ceridwen laughed – "You and me both!"

"And now I'm up here with you. And there's nobody about for miles and miles."

"You think I'm scared that you'll kill me, is it? How old do you think I am, Owen, bach?"

"I don't know."

"Eighty-seven. I'll be eighty-eight in May. I long ago gave up being frightened of dying. Being frightened of dying gets in the way of living. No, Owen, I'm not frightened of you."

Then she told him a story. It was a story of her youth. She had been eighteen. Her mother and father had lived in the cottage on the mountain in those days. Ceridwen had been a pretty girl: slim, a good figure, curly auburn hair. Lots of boys had taken a fancy to her but she hadn't taken a fancy to them. And then one warm summer day in the June of that year she had met a young man named Gwilym. He was a sailor, home on leave. He'd seen Ceridwen walking down the street and he'd fallen in love with her.

"Love at first sight, he said it was. He was a good-looking man. Dark hair, blue eyes. He had a little dimple right in the middle of his chin. And he had a way of talking that made me feel like the most important girl in all the world. But there was nowhere for us to meet. Not in them days. There was nowhere to go in the village and we couldn't take days out without our families knowing. So we met in secret. Up on the mountain. In the ferns. Up by the old quarry. It was the best summer of my life."

Ceridwen had loved Gwilym throughout the month of June. And then, in July, he had left. He said he would be back as soon as his ship returned that winter. But winter came and went and there was no sign of him. And in March the next year, Hywel was born.

"And then, finally, in June, my sailor, my one great love came back. Gwilym came back to the village. And he saw me. And he saw my baby. And he turned away like as if we were dirt. And not a word did he speak to me ever again."

It had been hard for a young woman bringing up a baby on her own in those days. People did not think Ceridwen was a fit mother. Because, after all, what fit mother would have given herself to a man up in the ferns on the mountain the way she had done?

But Ceridwen coped somehow. She took work whenever she could – cleaning houses for people, working part time in a shop. Some people took pity on her even though they talked about her behind her back.

But she loved that baby, Hywel, with all her heart. She loved his fat little cheeks and the way he blew a bubble when he said "Mam". She loved his smile and she loved the mischief he got up to once he learned to walk enough to go around the house breaking things.

But Hywel had always been a sickly child. He had a terrible hacking cough. He wheezed in his sleep. He struggled through four years of life and then one day in the month of May he gave up the struggle and faded away and died. The new young doctor, Doctor Pritchard it was in those days, told her that these things happen but he had no name for the illness that had taken her son's life. Some live, some die and that's all there is to be said on the matter.

"Will you be wanting more tea, Owen?" Ceridwen said.

"No, no, thanks. That'll be enough for me."

"There's a spare room I've got. Upstairs. You'll be wanting to take that, I expect."

"What"

"If you are to stay here you'll have to have your own room, won't you?"

"You want me to stay?"

"I thought that was what you wanted."

"Yes, but, I told you… I get violent. I can't stop myself, see. What if I was to get violent, like?"

"Then you will go out."

"What?"

"To the village. You will go to the village."

"I could… I could kill somebody. You don't mind?"

Ceridwen smiled. "I will call you Hywel," she said, "And in the evening you will sit on the settle there and I will sit on my chair here and you will talk to me. It will be nice, just you wait and see."

Owen stared at the old woman. She's mad, he thought, completely and utterly mad. And, as he stared at her, he felt his pulse start to race. And the brightness started to shine in his eyes and the headache started to pound away in his head. And he knew the urge was coming on him again. The woman sat there so frail and helpless and alone and he knew it would be so easy, so very, very easy…

She looked at him sternly. Her eyes blazed at him.

"I will go out," he said.

She smiled. "And when you return, what will you do?"

"I will wash myself," he said, "And then I will go to my room."

"That's right," she said, happily, "Just as you did last night. And the night before."

And when Owen had gone out, Ceridwen picked up her crocheting and started picking away at it with her crochet hooks. The wool was stained with something dark and sticky. She put her hand to her nose. When she looked, there was blood on her fingertips. She was getting more and more nosebleeds lately. She took a candlestick and went to the scullery to find a paper towel to use as a handkerchief. When she sat down again, she picked up her crocheting and tried to think what she was doing. She'd been talking about Hywel with someone. She couldn't recall who. She carried on working away with her crochet hooks and bit by bit she nodded off to sleep.

When she woke up, only one of the candles was still alight and the logs that had been in the fire had burnt down to nothing more than glowing ash. She thought a noise had woken her but she couldn't recall what. Oh, there it was again. Someone was knocking at her door. She took a brass candlestick off the mantelpiece and hobbled down the passageway from her kitchen.

"Pwy sy yna?" she called out.

There was no answer. She tried again in English, "Who's there?"

"It's me," said a thin, uncertain voice, "Owen."

She was trying to think if she knew an Owen. She couldn't think of anyone. There was a Hywel though.

"Is that you, Hywel?" she called.

There was a pause. Then the voice replied, "That's right, Mam. It's me, Hywel."

SATURDAY NIGHT IN THE CITY OF THE DEAD – REQUIEM

And in those days shall men seek death, and shall not find it; and shall desire to die, and death shall flee from them.

(Revelation 9:6)

FAME

Jackson lived for Saturday night.

All week long he stacked shelves in a supermarket. The boxes came into the storage room at the back; he put them onto a trolley and he wheeled them out to the shelves. He opened the boxes with a Stanley knife and he stacked the packets and jars and tins in the correct places: tins of baked beans, jars of instant coffee, packets of cornflakes, all kinds of junk that Jackson would never think of eating or drinking. Jackson liked to keep fit. He ate healthy food. Meat, vegetables, fruit. He wouldn't touch the commercially-produced pulp that he spent his days stacking on the shelves.

"You going tonight?" That was Eddie. The closest Jackson had to a friend in the supermarket.

Jackson laughed. "What? You think I ain't?"

"I thought maybe you'd have chickened out."

"No chance, mate. I'll be there."

Eddie gave Jackson a thumbs-up. "You can do it."

Jackson was a good-looking kid. Eighteen. Dark, wavy hair, electric blue eyes. And he had attitude. When he walked down the street, he caused heads to turn. He swaggered in a way that commanded attention. Some of the swagger came naturally. A lot of it came with practice. He studied himself the way an artist studies a picture. He was his own greatest achievement.

"What time're you going?" That was Shirley. She was one of the checkout girls.

"Don't know. Eleven maybe. Maybe midnight."

"You nervous?"

Jackson smiled, "Do I look it?"

Jackson knew exactly when he'd be going. Everything was planned in advance. He'd leave his house at nine o'clock. He'd get the bus into town. He'd hang around in Swizzy's wine bar, just to see who else was hanging around – Swizzy's was the place they usually congregated – and then at five to eleven, he'd leave. It was a five minute walk to the Blocks Club. He'd be there at the stroke of eleven.

Big Billy the bouncer would be on the door. When Jackson arrived, he'd say something like "How old are you, kid?" and Jackson would reply, "Twenty-six. Twenty-seven in April," and Big Billy would say, "You look about fourteen. Not even old enough to grow a moustache," and Jackson would say, "Yeah, well, when you get to your age, old man, I guess everyone looks young." And Big Billy would laugh and he'd pat Jackson so hard on the shoulder with one of his big, meaty hands that Jackson's teeth would rattle. It was all a routine. A double-act. Jackson went to that club every Saturday night and Big Billy always went through the same routine.

Jackson quit work at the supermarket at five o'clock. That gave him plenty of time to grab a takeaway pizza on the way home. His dad worked nights, on security down at one of the hotels in town, and his mother couldn't be bothered cooking. The pizza went against all of Jackson's rules about healthy eating but Saturdays were special so he didn't care.

After he ate, he'd take a long bath. Then he'd shave and splash on some Givenchy Gentleman. He only ever used Givenchy. He'd take his time brushing and combing his hair using just a touch of beeswax to add some sheen and hold it in place. He'd tried hair-clay and pomade and spray and gel but as far as he was concerned there was nothing to touch beeswax.

Then he'd get his clothes on. A crisply-ironed white shirt, with the two top buttons open (he'd open more later), black cotton trousers, smart casual black jacket, black shoes. Always white and black. Never any colours.

By ten to nine, he was ready to go. He checked himself in the floor-standing mirror in his bedroom. His hair was good, there were no wrinkles in his trousers, no dandruff on his jacket. He dabbed on a drop or two more of the Givenchy aftershave, checked that he'd got his wallet and his phone. Then he said goodbye to his mother, who was slouched in front of the telly watching some mindless shite. And he opened the front door.

It was snowing!

"Oh, Jesus!"

"What's that you said?" his mother called out.

"Nothing! I mean, I said it's snowing."

"Snowing? You better wear a pullover then."

Pullover! What world did his mother live in? Did she really think he was going out on a Saturday night wearing a pullover? He'd have to wear an overcoat, though, to stop the snow making a mess of his clothes. He had a long, black cashmere overcoat, a bit like a Crombie only about a tenth of the price. His wages from the supermarket didn't run to the real thing. Maybe one day money wouldn't be a problem. All he had to do was make the right connections. "One day when I'm famous," he thought.

Unlike just about everyone he knew, Jackson was ambitious. It was the only thing that got him through the week. He burned with ambition so much that it ached. As he stacked the shelves, putting the cheap breakfast tea on one shelf and the expensive Broken Orange Pekoe on another, the malt whiskies here and the blended whiskies there, he dreamt of how he'd get out of this hellhole, how one day soon he'd "become someone". That's how he thought of it. He was on his way to *being* someone. He wasn't there yet but he would be real soon.

When he left the house the snow was falling in light flurries. He sat on the top deck of the bus and watched people on the streets turning their collars up and scurrying about like ants looking for a stone to crawl under. By the time he got off the bus, the snowfall was starting to get heavier. He went into Swizzy's wine bar and palm-slapped a couple of mates who were sitting by a table near the window. Bear and Basher were mates he'd got to know down at the gym. They were both big guys, fit and muscular. Bear was by far the bigger. He was over six feet tall and must have weighed about sixteen stone, most of it solid muscle. Jackson had no idea what their real names were. Everyone called them Bear and Basher.

"You going down the club tonight?" Bear asked.

"I may do," said Jackson. He didn't want to sound eager; that would have been un-cool, "How about you?"

Bear shrugged, "See how I feel. I heard you was doing that grudge thing tonight. You and The Italian."

"You heard about that, did you?"

"I did. So my guess is you'll be going down the club."

"I guess your guess is right then."

Jackson smiled. People had been talking about him, obviously. Talking about the grudge thing. Like he was a celebrity. Like he was already famous. "What are you drinking, guys?" he said, "I'll get another bottle in, shall I?"

"Chardonnay," said Basher, "The Australian one."

The wine in that place was expensive. Jackson was hoping not to spend too much money. But Bear was someone it was worth keeping in with. He was one of the 'right connections' that Jackson was trying to cultivate.

Jackson bought the wine, plus a glass of Volvic mineral water for himself, then he went back to Bear and Basher's table and sat in a vacant chair. He sat slowly. He sat elegantly. He perched on the edge of the chair and crossed the calf of one leg over the calf of the other. It was something he had practised in front of the mirror. It was informal but not sloppy. Nonchalant was the word for it.

"How you doin', man?" Bear said.

"I'm doing great, man. How 'bout you?"

Even the way he spoke was well-practised. He used the right words and the right rhythm. In Swizzy's wine bar and, later on, in the club, this was the right lingo. Of course, he'd never talk like that to people at work. That would be the wrong place and the wrong time. But on a Saturday night the rules were different.

"What's that shit you're drinking, man?" Bear said.

"Water," Jackson replied.

Bear laughed. "You kidding me?"

"No. I'm not boozing tonight. I need my wits about me."

"Did he say water?" Basher said.

"That's what he said," Bear confirmed.

"Did you say water?" Basher said to Jackson.

"That's what I said."

"Oh. Weird."

Bear leant close to Basher and whispered something in his ear. They both turned to look at the bar. There was a girl there, nineteen or twenty maybe, mid-height, blonde, wearing a tight white tee-shirt and tight white slacks that left very little to the imagination. They both sniggered at something that Bear had whispered. Jackson smiled too as though he was sharing in the joke in spite of the fact that he hadn't heard a word of what Bear had said.

"You know her?" Jackson asked.

"Not really," said Bear, "One of Donnie's tarts, that's all I know. Eleanor. You ever hear that name before?"

"Lady Eleanor," Jackson said.

"What?"

"It was a song. An old song. By…" But Bear wasn't listening.

After a while, Bear leant across to Jackson. He spoke quietly, his eyes glancing from side to side to check that no one was listening. "About that stuff. The stuff we was talking about…"

"Yeah?"

"I put in a word and Donnie says you're in."

"Great."

"As long as you got the funds."

Jackson sipped his mineral water, trying to keep the nonchalant look he'd cultivated. Donnie was some kind of dealer. Jackson didn't know exactly how it worked. But Donnie supplied Bear, and Bear supplied a few other people. Jackson had never met Donnie. He didn't even know if he was local. But Bear kept going on about him. According to Bear, it was up to Donnie to decide who Bear could sell the goods on to. Donnie was very selective.

"The funds?" Jackson said, "What kind of funds d'you need, man?"

"Five hundred to start with."

Shit! Five hundred quid! Where was he going to get that kind of money?

"Look on it as an investment," said Bear, "'Cos that's what it is. You invest in something. Then you earn the dividends."

Jackson had no idea what Bear was talking about. All he knew was that he didn't have five hundred quid going spare. He could save it given enough time. But there was no way he could come up with it right away.

"When would you need it?"

"Soon. The sooner the better. If you want to get in on it, that is. Otherwise, well, I'd have to find someone else. Which would be a shame. For you, I mean. Opportunities like this don't come along very often, if you know what I mean."

Jackson didn't do drugs. Not ever. In his opinion, anyone who did drugs was an idiot. So he had no problem at all about supplying their needs, at a price.

"Hi, Jackson!" – someone called his name. He turned to look. It was the guy he'd met last week at the club. He'd just entered the wine bar bringing a blast of cold air with him. Jackson tried to remember what his name was? Peter? Phillip? Paul? It was something like that. He couldn't recall.

"Hi," Jackson said, "How're you doing, man?"

"Me? I'm doing terrific. You going to the club later on?"

"Might do. You?"

"Well, maybe. See you there. If I decide to go, I mean."

"Sure."

"You know that guy?" Bear said when the man had wandered off to get a drink.

"A bit. Why?"

"Don't have anything to do with him, that's why. Piers can't be trusted, if you know what I mean. He's definitely a bit on the dodgy side."

Piers, that was his name. Jackson wondered what was so dodgy about him. If a guy like Bear thought he was dodgy, then he must be *really* dodgy. Weird, he'd seemed a nice enough guy.

Jackson sat there talking to Bear and Basher for a while. Well, anyway, he talked to Bear and Bear talked to him. Basher didn't say much. He just grunted every so often. And then, later on, the three of them went to the Blocks Club. The snow was really settling by then. Every time Jackson took a step, the snow made a sort of squeaky noise as his shoe compressed it. The town looked nice in the snow, Jackson thought. It looked like a different place: clean and fresh.

"I hate the snow, man," Bear said.

"What snowman?" Jackson replied.

"What?"

"I said 'What snowman?'"

Bear stared at him from beneath Neanderthal brows.

Jackson tried explaining. "You said you hate the snow, man. So I said… Never mind, it doesn't matter."

"You on amphetamines?" Bear said.

Jackson shook his head – "No. Volvic."

There were times when Jackson hated people. He hated the people he worked with. He hated the people he socialised with. All they could think about was money, sex, drugs and booze, in roughly that order. One day, Jackson would go away. Far away. Jackson was made for better things.

He glanced up at a streetlight. It made the falling snow glitter. Like tinsel. Jackson stood still for a few moments with his face turned up to the light. Big flakes of snow fell upon his forehead and his cheeks. As soon as the snowflakes landed, they melted.

"What you doing, man?" called Bear.

"Watching the snow," Jackson said.

"What's he doing?" Basher asked Bear.

"Says he watching the snow."

Basher took a few seconds to think about that. "Must have dropped acid," he said.

The route to the club took them through an underpass. There were still some cars on the road up ahead, travelling slowly, carefully, through the densely-falling snow. A pedestrian walkway led downwards, taking them into the underpass that ran beneath the road. The underpass was unlit. It was a dark, forbidding place. Jackson hated it. It had an air of menace. Especially at night. Sometimes there would be down-and-outs, slumped on the ground or propped against a wall, shouting obscenities at anyone who went by.

At other times there would be clusters of youths down there, doing drug deals or shooting up, safe from prying eyes in the squalid piss-stinking darkness. There were stories that a woman had been raped down there. Jackson had heard that some guy had been mugged, his head smashed against the pavement, his arms broken. At least there was no snow in the underpass. What's more, Bear and Basher were with Jackson and no mugger would be stupid enough to take on those two.

BOOGIE NIGHTS

As they left the underpass, the paving sloped upward again and then they turned left down an old cobbled street. The cobbles were hidden tonight, beneath the snow. They saw Blocks, its neon light flickering in the darkness: *Blcks*-flicker-*Blocks*- flicker-*Blcks*-flicker-*Blocks*, with the "o" blinking on and off randomly – that light had been faulty for as long as Jackson could remember.

Big Billy was standing at the entrance to the club, sheltering under the little archway over the door. He was shivering and he looked even more miserable than usual. "Evening, gents. You members, are you?"

"You ask us that every week," Bear said, "Same question every week. And the answer stays the same."

"It's in me contract. If I don't ask you, there'd be no point in me bein' here. And if there's no point in me bein' here, I'm out of a job. 'Ere, who's the kid?"

"That's my mate, Jackson," Bear said.

"How old is he?"

"Ask him."

"How old are you, kid?"

"Thirty-two," Jackson said, "But I look young for my age."

It was the old routine again. Jackson and Billy went through the same old gags week-in, week-out.

Big Billy laughed. "Any more of your lip, sonny, and you'll be out on your arse, snow or no snow."

Big Billy opened the door and let them into the club. Once in the foyer they had to sign in. Jackson checked in his overcoat with Annie, the cloakroom attendant.

"Careful with that," he said, "It's a genuine Crombie."

"Oh yeah?" Annie said, "And I'm Ariana Grande."

"Who?" said Jackson. Although he was teasing her, he was half serious. Most of Jackson's favourite music came from the 1970s and he didn't rate any music after about the mid '80s. He took pride in not knowing which singers were in fashion these days and which were last year's thing. His tastes in music were old school – mainly funk and classic disco: Chic, Tavares, Trammps, Earth, Wind and Fire, Donna Summer.

Inside the club, a few small groups of people had congregated in the bar area but the dancefloor was almost empty. It was still early and it would fill up later. Even so, for a Saturday night, it was quiet.

"Damn' bloody snow." It was Shirley, the checkout girl from the supermarket. Jackson looked at Shirley. Then he looked at the dancefloor. Then he looked at Shirley again. He'd never realised what a looker she was before. He was used to seeing her in the pale blue Nylon uniform she wore at work, with practically no makeup on. Tonight she was wearing some kind of tight black pantsuit. It showed her figure off to its best advantage. Jackson approved of the colour. Black. Black was slick. Shirley looked fantastic. He wondered what she was like as a dancer. Not that Jackson ever danced with a partner. He was strictly solo.

"Eddie, here?" Jackson asked.

Shirley squinted her eyes – "What did you say?"

The music was so loud, she hadn't heard the question. That was one thing Jackson liked about the club. It played the music loud with plenty of bass so that you *felt* the beat as much as you heard it.

"Eddie," he repeated, shouting this time and exaggerating his lip movements so that even if she couldn't hear him she might be able to read his lips, "Is Eddie here?"

Shirley shook her head. "Ain't seen him."

Eddie was a good bloke. The only one of Jackson's workmates who felt the same way that Jackson did. About the club, about the music, about the style. For Jackson, the style was everything. How to look good, how to carry yourself in a certain way, how to have a certain attitude that set you apart from the crowd.

"Who's the girl?"

Shirley had gone off somewhere. Jackson was leaning up against the wall, just behind the columns. The Blocks Club was inside an old building that used to be a theatre or a cinema or something. There was a balcony running along three walls on the floor above. The balcony was supported by columns. The quietest, darkest place in the club was right at the back of the downstairs floor, past the columns that held up the balcony.

"Which girl?" Jackson said.

"The one with the figure."

The person asking the questions was the guy Jackson had met at the club the previous week: tall chap, slicked-back hair. He was wearing a white shirt and dark jacket, which could have looked good only he spoilt everything by wearing jeans. He was the guy Bear had warned him about. Piers. Bear had said he was dodgy, couldn't be trusted.

"Shirley," Jackson replied, "Her name's Shirley."

"You and her…?"

"What?"

"You know."

"What? Me and her? Nah! You gotta be kidding, man. Me and Shirley!" he laughed, "We're workmates, that's all. Shirley ain't my type. She's too… you know…"

"What?"

Jackson didn't know what he meant, exactly. All he knew for sure was that a girl who worked in a supermarket wasn't his type of girl. The fact that Jackson also worked in a supermarket was beside the point. That was a temporary inconvenience. Jackson would soon be moving on to bigger and better things. Shirley wouldn't.

That's when he saw Eddie. He was wearing a white satin shirt with the three top buttons open, tight black trousers (slightly flared) and Cuban heels.

Piers whispered to Jackson, "Look at that bozo!" He was talking about Eddie, "What a dick! Probably thinks he's John Travolta!"

Bear had been right, Jackson thought – Piers wasn't someone he should get friendly with. The man was an idiot. In Jackson's opinion, Eddie looked terrific. Most of the other guys there had no style. They were wearing all kinds of off-the-peg designer tat with no sense of colour coordination – no panache, no attitude. Eddie, though, he was different. He was cock of the walk. Look at the way he was strutting through the crowd, as though he owned the place.

"Hi Jackson," Eddie had spotted Jackson straight away and come across to him, "Hi, um…?"

"Piers."

Piers held out his hand, expecting Eddie to shake it. He might as well have held out his hand to the Pope. Eddie pretended he hadn't noticed the hand. It was the right thing to do, in Jackson's opinion. It showed that Eddie had attitude.

"I thought I wasn't going to make it," Eddie said to Jackson. He was ignoring Piers.

"Why's that?"

"The snow. Never seen so much snow before."

"Still snowing, then?"

"You better believe it, man. Had to wear Wellies and a long overcoat over my gear. To stop the snow getting on it. This shirt's Armani. You know how much it cost me?"

"I can guess."

"Whatever you can guess, it cost me more. When I checked-in my boots and overcoat, Annie the cloakroom girl says to me, 'You look like Captain Bleedin' Birdseye.'"

Eddie didn't look like Captain Birdseye now though. Eddie looked slick. Piers had been right. There was a touch of Travolta about him. Piers had spat out the name "Travolta" like he thought it was an insult. Which just showed what a twat Piers was! Travolta was the ultimate style-icon as far as Jackson was concerned. Him and Pacino. In their younger days, that is. Back in the '70s. Long before Jackson had been born. Jackson had been born at the wrong time, he sometimes thought. The '70s was the coolest decade. It was no good trying to explain that to a guy like Piers. He wouldn't understand.

Jackson never drank much in the club. The wine they served there was worse than horse piss. On a regular night, he might have a cocktail or two. They served one called a Blue Moon which was OK. But tonight he planned to stay strictly tee-total. Even one cocktail might make him lose focus. If he lost focus he might make a mistake. And if he made a mistake he would lose points. It was too much of a risk.

"He in yet?" Eddie asked.

"Who?"

"The Italian."

Jackson looked around as though he wasn't bothered one way or the other. He tried to give the impression that he hadn't even thought about The Italian until Eddie had mentioned him. That was how unconcerned Jackson was.

"Can't see him."

"Maybe he's chickened out," said Eddie.

Jackson shrugged as though The Italian wasn't worth the effort even to think about. In fact, Jackson had been thinking about The Italian all week. He hadn't been able to get the guy out of his mind. But he tried not to show it. Nonchalance, that was the name of the game. Stay nonchalant, stay cool, he told himself. But it was hard. Because now that the big night had arrived, Jackson was starting to doubt himself. He was starting to panic.

We are Family

"Money goes through your fingers like water, boy."

Saturday morning. There was Jackson, trying to get through his Cornflakes in peace and the old man was already moaning at him. His poor, pathetic father with his beer belly, his greasy hair and his bad teeth, "When I was your age, I had to work for everything I had."

"I have to work!" Jackson and his dad were always arguing. It drove Jackson nuts.

"Work! Down that bloody shop? You call that work? I've supported you all your life and I'm still supporting you, that's the bloody truth of the matter."

"I buy my own stuff. When did you buy me anything?"

"You get free lodgings. Who pays the mortgage, who pays for the electric?"

"I pay my fair share."

His dad was eating bacon, eggs and beans with a mug of tea. Two spoons of sugar in the tea. He was only in his forties but he could pass for sixty. He was a heart attack waiting to happen, in Jackson's opinion.

His dad took a slurp of tea and sniffed the air like a bloodhound – "And you smell like a bloody tart."

"It's aftershave. You should try some."

"Smells poofy."

"Yeah, well, better than smelling like a bleedin' compost heap."

"Oh yeah, Mr Smart Alec," his dad said, "Think you're so bloody clever, don't you. If you were so bloody clever, you'd be at a bleedin' university, not stacking shelves in a bleedin' supermarket."

That was it. Jackson couldn't stand the old man any more. He was an idiot. Jackson got up from the table, looked in the mirror, combed his hair, looked at his watch. Half-past eight. He had to be in work at nine.

"Yeah, well, dad, as always it's been lovely talking to you but I got a life to get on with, you know how it is."

"I suppose you'll be bloody prancing about down that club again tonight, will you?"

Jackson didn't bother answering.

As he made his way down the hallway towards the front door, he heard his dad mutter, "…carries on like a bleedin' fairy."

His dad didn't have a clue. As far as his dad was concerned, a cooked breakfast, a cooked dinner, a few hours in front of the telly, a few pints down the pub with the lads and bonking the missus on a Friday night were all that life had to offer. That would never be enough for Jackson. He had one life and he was damn' well sure he was going to live it to the full. He'd been getting panic attacks recently. That damn' house made him feel claustrophobic. Living in that miserable house in that miserable town was like a punishment for a crime he hadn't committed. He had to get away. Dancing was his escape route. He'd always been good at dancing, for as long as he could remember. When he danced, he was in another world. If he could win this competition, he'd get an audition for a West End show. That was the big prize. It was within his grasp. He knew it was. As long as The Italian didn't get in his way.

The Italian wasn't really Italian even though he had an Italian name. Salvatore Grandini had been born in Market Street. His granddad, or maybe his great grandad, had been Italian, hence the name. He looked kind of Italian though – tall and dark and brooding. So everyone, apart from his close friends, called him The Italian. His close friends called him Sal. The Italian was 21. He had studied dancing at a dance school. He had competed in gymnastics competitions and won most of them. He was good, there was no doubt about that. But he was also flashy. It was the flashiness which, in Jackson's opinion, was his greatest weakness.

Jackson's style was totally different from The Italian's. He hadn't been taught anything. He had taught himself by watching and by studying. Mostly he studied films. Only the classics: Fame, Flashdance, Footloose, Dirty Dancing and (the best, by far!) Saturday Night Fever. Back when Travolta was at his peak. When Travolta was a god.

It was Eddie who'd first told Jackson about the club. That had been about a year ago, shortly after Jackson's seventeenth birthday, which, according to club policy meant that he was a year too young to be admitted. But Jackson had always looked older than he really was and he had a confident swagger about him so Big Billy the doorman let him in anyway, even though he kept teasing him about his age.

They called it the Great Dance-Off and it was a big deal in the Blocks Club. There was no telling what music you'd have to dance to. It might be some brand new dance remix with all that artificial echo and vocoder shit. Other times it might be what the DJ called a "retro classic" like Alicia Bridges or Sylvester. Jackson preferred the classics but, at the end of the day, dancing was dancing and Jackson could dance to anything.

"You'll never amount to anything, Jackson," – that's what Mr Ford, the maths teacher had always said, "You've got no ambition."

Jackson would show that bastard. There was more to life than equilateral triangles and quadratic equations. And after all, what had Mr Ford made of his life, when it came down to it? Slaving his guts out over dusty old books in a third-rate school in a second-rate town, trying to teach kids to do algebra and geometry that they'd never use and had never wanted to learn in the first place! That was no life. That was a living death.

"What's the matter?" Eddie said.

Jackson was watching the dancefloor. The regular dancers, the ones who just came to sweat and grind and get pissed, moved like uncoordinated marionettes.

"Nothing's the matter," Jackson said, "Why?"

"You seem tense is all."

"You ever think about getting old?" Jackson said.

"No. Do you?"

Jackson shrugged. "To get old and never to have done anything. Can you imagine what that would be like?"

Eddie smiled, "You're in a funny mood tonight," and he ruffled Jackson's hair. He immediately regretted that because his hand got covered with the wax stuff that Jackson used on his hair. Eddie went to the gents to wash it off. Jackson came with him to comb his hair in the mirror.

"Too beautiful to live, too young to die," Jackson said.

"What?"

"That's what Marc Bolan used to say."

"Oh. I didn't know that. That's sad."

At least Eddie knew who Bolan was. If Jackson had mentioned Bolan to most people his age, they'd have said, "Who?" And Jackson would have had to explain that Bolan had been the greatest British pop star in history. The biggest teen heart-throb of the '70s. Fourteen Top 20 hits. Four Number Ones. Killed in a car crash on the 16th of September, 1977. Age 29.

"Too beautiful to live…" Jackson muttered. He stared at his reflection, "Eddie, you know what – I'd do anything to be famous."

"You wouldn't kill someone," said Eddie, "You wouldn't sell your soul or blow up a school."

Jackson flicked back a loose strand of hair. "I'd do anything."

NIGHT FEVER

Most Saturdays, the contest started around midnight. There would be a panel of four judges and, after each contestant had strutted their stuff, the judges would hold up scores on cards. Most of the dancers were rubbish. Really amateurish. For the first few weeks after he'd started going to Blocks, Jackson hadn't had any competition. Every week he entered, every week he won. Then, in June, The Italian arrived.

From the outset Jackson had been totally outclassed. That first night, he had done his usual routine – slinky, smooth, hip-swinging stuff with just a few showy moves to keep the crowd interested. Then The Italian took the floor and he did moves nobody had ever seen before. Back-flips, handstands, break-falls. His routine had been completely insane. Breath-taking. Exhilarating. That night, Jackson had considered giving up. But he didn't. He knew that now he had a serious rival and he needed to up his game. And that's exactly what he did. He found a martial arts teacher to show him how to do break-falls. He joined a ballet class to learn how to do pirouettes and jetés. His martial arts teacher told him he was too arty-farty. His ballet teacher told him he was too aggressive. Jackson wasn't bothered. He didn't want to be a martial artist or a ballet dancer anyhow.

For the next two months, he didn't go to the club at all. Everyone thought he'd given up. And then, one hot night at the tail end of August, Jackson entered the dance-off. The Italian was there and everyone assumed he was a dead cert to win. Because they assumed that Jackson would just do one of his tired, predictable old routines again. But he didn't. Jackson showed them things they'd never seen before. He did pirouettes, slides and somersaults. He even did a grand jeté – a huge, gazelle-like leap – that his ballet teacher had taught him. The crowd went wild. He'd never had such an incredible reaction. They clapped, they stamped, they cheered. The Italian never had a chance.

The next week, the Italian came back with an even more athletic performance and he won by just a whisker. Jackson thought the judgement had been unfair but, even so, throughout the next week he spent every free moment working on new techniques: moves that the Italian wouldn't be able to compete with.

And so it went on throughout the year: August, September, October, November. Every week, dozens of people would enter the competition and every week either Jackson or The Italian would win. By the end of November they were neck and neck. That's when the owners of the Blocks Club came up with an idea. They'd have a "grudge match" – that's how it was billed on the posters. A Champion-against-Champion contest. Just like a wrestling bout but without the body-slams. Unlike the ordinary weekly dance-offs, there would be only two competitors. Best of all, in Jackson's opinion, they would be able to choose their own music which meant that, at long last, he'd be able to do proper, fully choreographed routines.

Throughout December, Jackson trained for the big event. When the weather was fine, he practised in the garden. When it was raining, he practised in his dad's garage. Twice a week he booked the local church hall which gave him space to try out the more spectacular moves.

And now, finally, the big night had arrived.

Half an hour had been set aside for the contest, starting at one o'clock. Each contestant would be required to dance three complete routines. After each routine, the panel of judges would hold up a score out of 10. On this special night, there was a panel of 'star' judges: a footballer who had once appeared in 'Celebrity Come Dancing', an elderly man who used to be a member of a TV dance troupe, a local fitness instructor and a woman called Doreen who had, apparently, starred in a James Bond film though nobody could remember which one.

By ten to one there was still no sign of The Italian.

"He's pissing me about," Jackson complained.

"What?" Eddie hadn't heard what Jackson had said. All he could hear was the relentless pounding of the music.

"It's nearly time," Jackson shouted, "Maybe he's not coming."

Eddie shrugged. "The snow."

"What?"

"Maybe he can't get through the snow…"

But then they saw him. Wearing a white suit, black shirt, white tie, he was dazzling. The crowd parted as he made his way towards the dancefloor. The disco lights picked him out, making him seem to glow in the darkness.

"What the Hell…" Jackson couldn't believe what he was seeing. This was not The Italian's style at all. The Italian was flashy. He wore multi-coloured shirts, Gucci jeans. Sometimes he even wore glow-bracelets that shone neon-like in the darkness. The Italian was showy. The Italian was vulgar. And yet here he was, in a black shirt and white, three-piece suit. Just like Jackson's hero. Just like Travolta.

"You all right?" Eddie said.

"What? Me? Yeah, I'm fine. Why shouldn't I be?"

The Italian was looking at Jackson. He was smiling. No, not just smiling. He was smirking. The bastard was smirking at him. Jackson smiled back. The smile was practically a sneer. He'd soon show The Italian a thing or two. Jackson would dance tonight as he'd never danced before. He planned to wipe The Italian's smile off his face once and for all.

"Ladies and Gentlemen…." – the DJ's voice cut over the track he'd been playing. A drum roll blared through the speakers. The brass section of an orchestra played a fanfare – "Ladies and Gentlemen, the time has come. The moment you've all been waiting for. The Grudge Match of the Century…." – another fanfare – "Can the two contestants come forward please!"

The Italian was already near to the DJ's desk. A spotlight shone on him. The DJ said, "In the red corner," (there was no red corner but he said it anyhow), "a big hand please for Mr Salvatore Grandini, The Italian Stallion!" (people applauded apathetically but the sound was drowned out by pre-recorded applause played through the loudspeakers). "And in the blue corner," (there wasn't a blue corner either), "show your appreciation for 'Flying Feet' Jackson." (more pre-recorded applause).

"Flying Feet?" Jackson winced. This was a serious competition. He'd slogged his guts out preparing for this and the damn' DJ was treating him like a circus act. Oh well, that's just the way people were in this godawful town. As soon as Jackson got his chance, he'd get away. He'd go to some place where talent was appreciated.

The DJ called Jackson and The Italian over to his desk and they drew straws to decide who would dance first. The Italian drew the longer straw and decided he would go second. At one o'clock sharp, the DJ announced the start of the competition, the floor was cleared and Jackson's first chosen record was played. He'd decided to kick off with a classic from the 1980s – 'London Nights' by The London Boys – a stomping tune with a massive bass beat. The London Boys had been terrific dancers and Jackson's routine recreated many of their best moves. Jackson was sensational. By the time he'd finished, the crowd was on its feet applauding. Sweat was pouring off Jackson as he took his bow. Then he had to wait to see the scores awarded by the four judges. Here they came: 10, 9, 8, 10. Better than he could have hoped for. Two perfect 10s. The 8 came from the fitness instructor who seemed a bit of a miserable git as far as Jackson could tell.

Then it was The Italian's turn. His music was 'Requiem' which was another of the London Boys' hits. Jackson couldn't believe it. The Italian never danced to retro music if he could possibly avoid it. The chances of him picking a song by the same group that Jackson had picked were so remote as to be almost impossible.

"Someone's been informing on me," Jackson thought. But who knew that he had been rehearsing a London Boys routine? The club DJ? That was a possibility. But Jackson had only told him the week before. He doubted if that would have given The Italian enough time to choreograph his whole routine. Who else then? Eddie? Yes, he'd mentioned it to Eddie. Shirley? Had he mentioned it to Shirley? He didn't think so. Maybe someone had been spying on him when he'd been practising in the church hall?

The Italian's routine had been closely based on the London Boys' original routine just as Jackson's had. Angry as he was, Jackson had to admit that The Italian was good. He even did a perfect roll-out and back-flip. Now here came his scores: 9, 10, 9, 9. The only perfect 10 had come from the fitness instructor who'd given Jackson a miserable 8. So after that round, they were level-pegging. They had both scored 37.

For the next round, Jackson stayed with the '80s and danced to Sylvester's classic electro dance hit, 'Menergy'. For his routine, The Italian danced to 'You Make Me Feel (Mighty Real)' – also by

Sylvester. For God's sake! That was no coincidence. He'd must have been spying on Jackson. That was cheating. That surely wasn't allowed.

Jackson scored 9, 8, 7, 8. A total of 32. Not as good as he'd hoped for. The Italian scored: 7, 10, 6, 7. The fitness instructor was the one who gave the perfect score, which was ridiculous. The Italian had screwed up two important moves. There was something fishy about that fitness instructor. Still, The Italian's total was only 30, which meant that this round was a clear win for Jackson. Everything now depended on the final round.

Jackson had saved all his best moves for this one. His music was the Evelyn Thomas classic, 'High Energy'. Jackson did cartwheels, leaps through the air, twirls, even some breakdance moves. He pulled out every stop. And in spite of slipping after one particularly athletic jump (some idiot had slopped their drink onto the slippery floor) Jackson was convinced that The Italian couldn't possibly surpass his performance.

Jackson practically held his breath waiting for the scores. Here they came: 9, 6, 8, 8. Jesus, no! Only 31. He'd been hoping for better than that. The damn' fitness instructor had given him a mere 6. That man was deliberately under-scoring him!

When The Italian took to the floor, Jackson half expected him to have chosen another Evelyn Thomas hit. But he hadn't. As soon as he heard the opening notes, Jackson knew what it was: The Bee Gees' 'You Should be Dancing' – which was, in Jackson's view, one of the definitive greats of disco music, from Jackson's favourite film ever – 'Saturday Night Fever'.

Jackson stared wide-eyed. He couldn't believe what he was seeing. The Italian was doing the exact same routine that Travolta had done in the film: the hip swivels, the pelvic thrusts, the arm-snaking movements. Everything. He *was* Travolta. He looked like Travolta. He moved like Travolta. It was almost like being taken back in time to 1977 to see Travolta himself, in his godlike prime. And the funny thing was, this wasn't how The Italian danced. Not usually. The Italian always went for spectacular moves whether or not they fitted with the music. He was a clever dancer, not a subtle one. But not tonight. Tonight, he seemed to dissolve into the music. He was magnificent. Jackson almost cried to see him.

Jackson knew in that moment that he had lost. Nobody could have competed with The Italian's final dance. It was flawless. Perfect. Jackson hardly even bothered to look at the scores when the judges held up their cards. The footballer held up his: 10. Then came the fitness instructor: 9. Odd, he'd given The Italian 10s before. Then there was the man who'd been a TV dancer once: 10. And finally the woman named Doreen who claimed to have been in a James Bond film: 10. The Italian had scored a total of 39. Almost the maximum possible score. But Jackson couldn't complain. Because the guy deserved it.

And then the DJ announces that The Italian was the winner and the crowd is cheering. The Italian walks over to Jackson and holds out his hand and he commiserates with Jackson, and Jackson congratulates The Italian. And already the DJ is playing some more music. Some modern shite. And the dancefloor is filling up. And Jackson desperately wants a drink.

Now Eddie is there, with his arm around Jackson's shoulder, telling him how good he'd been, that he should have won and Jackson is saying, "No, I shouldn't. I need a drink." Now they are sitting at a table, at the back of the club, under the columns, away from the dancefloor and Jackson doesn't really want a drink any more but he sips the Blue Moon that Eddie bought him. The cocktail doesn't really taste of much. Just alcohol and sugar. So Jackson watches the people dancing and they look like oil paint on the surface of water, swirling together, making patterns in time with the music. And Jackson thinks, "I must be drunk," but he doesn't feel drunk. He's only had one cocktail and he hasn't even drunk it all yet. But he feels like he's floating in air. "…want to dance?" "What?" Who said that? Oh, it's Shirley! Where did she appear from? "Nah, not now. I'm all danced out." "Yeah," says Shirley, "I saw you. I thought you was a lot better than the other guy, honest to God." "Nah, Shirley, nah, I wasn't…"

But he goes and dances with Shirley anyway. God knows what the music is. Some modern shite. Superfast electro-beat but no melody, no funk, no soul. At the edge of the dancefloor he sees The Italian. Over by the DJ's desk. The Italian is talking to that creepy bloke. Piers. The one Bear had warned Jackson about. Maybe it was Piers who'd been spying on Jackson? If The Italian hadn't damn' well copied Jackson's first two dance routines, there was no way the guy could have won. He cheated. That's what he did. The bloody Italian bloody well cheated!

"What the Hell you on about?"

How did Jackson end up here? By the DJ's desk. One minute he was dancing with Shirley, the next he was screaming blue murder at the Italian – "You copied everything I did. You must have been spying on me!"

"It was you who copied me, sunshine. If anyone's a spy, it's you!"

"And anyway, I won a round, you won a round, we drew on the first one. That should be a draw. So how come you end up winning?"

"I scored more than you did."

"Oh yeah, and why is that?"

"Because I'm better than you are."

"You bloody liar. You bloody rotten cheat!"

The Italian pushed Jackson away with one hand, as if he was swatting a fly. "Go away, little man. If you can't be a good loser you shouldn't have entered, should you?"

"You're a cheat, that's what you are!"

The Italian turned away from Jackson. Jackson caught hold of The Italian's sleeve. The left-hand sleeve of his immaculate white jacket. That was too much provocation for The Italian. He turned back towards Jackson, put his hand over Jackson's mouth and nose and pushed his head back so hard that Jackson fell onto the floor.

Now here was Eddie again, helping Jackson to his feet. "Not worth it, man," he was saying.

Jackson wanted to punch The Italian. He wanted to kick him, bite him, do anything he could to hurt him. The Italian had cheated. He hadn't won fair and square. Jackson wanted to make him pay for what he'd done!

But Eddie was restraining him. "There'll be another time," Eddie was saying, "No point making a scene here. You'll only get yourself barred."

Eddie was right, of course. There was no point getting into a brawl in the club. Besides which, The Italian was bigger than Jackson. Taller and stronger. There was no way Jackson could win in a fight. But the time would come. Oh yes, the time would come when Jackson would be revenged.

"...time to go."

"What?"

"I said," Eddie repeated, "it's late. Time to go, I reckon."

"What's the time?"

"Ten to two."

"Another ten minutes then."

It was while Jackson was on his way to the cloakroom to get his coat that he noticed the sleazy guy, Piers. He was right at the back of the club, in the darkness under the balcony. He was talking to Bear. That struck Jackson as weird. It had been Bear who'd warned him against Piers in the first place. They were up to something. Bear was handing something to Piers. They were both smiling. Laughing. Why were they laughing? They were laughing at Jackson. That was the only explanation. The Italian had made a fool of him and now everyone was laughing at him.

"What's up, man?"

It was Eddie again. It seemed like Eddie was following him around. Why was he doing that?

"That guy, Piers," Jackson said, "He's doing a deal with Bear."

Eddie looked around. "Where?"

"Over there..." But, when he looked, there was nobody there. They'd snuck off. In secret. Jackson knew that Bear had double-crossed him. Bear had told Jackson that he'd cut him in on a deal, get him in on the dealership network. All Jackson had to do was invest five hundred pounds. But what was it that had Bear said? He'd said that if Jackson couldn't stump up the funds then he'd find someone else who could. Piers! The dirty, rotten bastard! Bear had warned Jackson that Piers was dodgy, said he couldn't be trusted. And all the while, Bear and Piers were hatching up a plan between them. A plan to cut Jackson out of the deal!

"...not gonna let them make a bloody fool of me!"

"What?"

"Where's Annie?"

Jackson didn't recognise the woman in the cloakroom.

"Annie. Where's Annie?"

"You know what time it is?" the woman said as she handed him his coat, "Annie knocked of ages ago."

It was still snowing. Heavier than ever. The snow on the ground came up well over Jackson's ankles. It trickled down inside his shoes as he walked through it. He didn't care. The snow made him feel happy. He stood there, just watching it falling. Big, feathery white flakes. Transforming the grimy streets of the miserable town into a great big undulating wave of pure whiteness. And then he blacked out.

Stayin' Alive

He was in the underpass. He was bent over, with his hands on his knees. His breath was rasping hard and fast as though he had been undertaking some kind of strenuous activity. What was he doing in the underpass? He didn't remember going there. He'd got his coat from the cloakroom and he'd walked out of the club. He remembered feeling dizzy. And the next thing he knew, here he was, in the underpass. He straightened up. His back ached. As though he'd been punched in the kidneys. He gritted his teeth against the pain.

Here, in the darkness of the underpass he could see nothing. Some distance away, to the right and to the left he could see snow falling by the light of streetlamps beyond the underpass openings. The opening on his left led towards the club. The opening on his right led back into town. He'd have to get a taxi to take him home. He hoped taxis were still running so late and in such bad weather. Otherwise it would be a long, cold trudge. He began to walk towards the opening on the right. He nearly tripped over. His foot had struck something lying on the ground. It was too dark to make out what it was. Carefully, he took little steps, feeling where the obstruction lay with the toes of his shoes. It was something quite big. All at once he realised that it was a body. Whose body? A down-and-out? Maybe. He knew they slept down there sometimes. Or maybe someone had been hurt? Mugged? There wasn't enough light to see. And Jackson didn't have a torch with him.

He had his phone though. He felt inside his jacket pocket. His fingers were numb with cold. He took out the phone and pressed a fingertip against the ID sensor to activate it. The screen produced just enough light to make out the contours of his hand. He knelt and held the screen close to the body on the ground. He had to hold the screen just a few inches away in order for the pale light to show him what was there. It was a body all right. A man's body. Very still. The coat was open showing a light-coloured suit beneath. The face was…

Jackson recoiled. He must be mistaken. His heart was pounding. He wanted to run. He had to take one more look. He leant closer again. The dim blue/red light from the screen of his phone showed the pale contours of the man's face. There was no doubt about it. It was The Italian. But, my God, what had happened to him? His head was bent back, as though his neck had been broken. The front of his white suit was stained dark with great splashes of – in the darkness it looked like tar or black ink but Jackson knew that it must be the sticky, oozing crimson of arterial blood because blood was still flowing from the ragged gap, like the bite of a savage animal, where The Italian's throat had once been.

Jackson stood. He thought he was going to be sick. He put his hand to his mouth. His hand was sticky. It smelled. There was a sickly taste in his mouth. A strangely metallic taste like…

"Like blood," Jackson thought.

He was panicking. Terrible thoughts and images filled his mind. He must have passed out. That would explain why he couldn't remember how he had got from the club to the underpass. Someone must have attacked him. Maybe the same person who'd killed The Italian. That was the only explanation. Jackson had to go for help.

No.

How would someone else see the situation? Jackson had been arguing with The Italian. Lots of people must have seen that. And now here he was, alone in the underpass, with The Italian lying dead at his feet. That looked bad. People might jump to conclusions.

He had to get away. Before someone found him there. He ran to the left, back towards the opening through which he must have entered the underpass after leaving the club. He saw the shadows before he reached the opening. Long shadows that moved in waves over the soft ripples of the settled snow. Two people. Coming down the incline towards the underpass. Jackson turned around and ran towards the other end of the underpass taking care not to trip over The Italian's body as he went.

"What the…?"

"Don't move, son!"

He ran headlong into them. One grabbed him and pulled his arms behind his back.

"You got him, Wilson?"

"I think so, sarge."

One of the men grabbed his arm, bent his wrist, twisted and Jackson yelled in pain. Then the other man was telling him he was under arrest.

"What the Hell? I haven't done anything!"

"You are under arrest for assaulting a police officer."

"I never…."

"You don't have to say anything but it may harm your defence if…."

"For God's sake, man. Someone's been hurt!" He didn't dare say 'killed'.

"Anything you do say may be…."

"In the tunnel! Someone's been…"

They were handcuffing him. He felt the cuff go on. Heard it snap shut. They were pulling his arms further behind his back. Warning him not to resist, not to make any sudden movements.

"I haven't done anything! Why are you arresting me? I haven't…."

They dragged him to the top of the underpass, up to the road. There was a police car there. Lights flashing. They bundled him into the back seat. He kept asking what was going on, why were they arresting him? He kept telling them about the body in the underpass. They didn't seem interested. The car moved off, its wheels spinning, slipping in the snow.

REQUIEM

The cell was a bleak, sterile white box. No bars, no windows. Just four walls and a grey metal door. There wasn't any furniture. Just a bench that was built into the back wall. You could sit on the bench or you could lie on it. There was a toilet with a bowl but no lid. The ceiling was about ten feet above the floor. Strip lights were built into the edges and there was a camera pointing downwards from one corner. There were noises coming through the walls from every direction: banging, clanking, shouting, screaming. People in other cells.

The noise continued through the night. Jackson didn't sleep at all. At eight o'clock in the morning, he washed at a small sink that was built into the wall next to the toilet. He drank some water from his hand. It tasted of chemicals so he spat it out again. He still had his watch so he could tell the time but the bastards had taken his mobile phone so he couldn't phone anyone to tell them what had happened. Then he sat on the bed and waited. Surely somebody would be along soon. Then it was nine o'clock. Jackson banged on the door – "Any chance of breakfast?" There was the ceaseless wailing and banging from the other cells. At half past ten the door opened and someone threw a bag containing a bread roll into his cell before banging the door shut again. Jackson opened the bag and ate the roll. It was just bread. No butter. No jam.

At twelve o'clock he banged on the door again and shouted – "What's going on? You can't keep me in here all day!"

From another cell a voice answered, "Shout all you like, son! They won't hear you."

By one o'clock, Jackson was starting to panic. He was also starting to hallucinate. Lack of sleep, probably. And dehydration. He lay on the bed staring up at the camera in the corner of the room. He was convinced it contained an eyeball. A huge, human-looking eyeball that swivelled in a socket to follow Jackson whenever he moved.

At six o'clock, people in other cells were shouting. One panicky voice screamed out, "They're all over me! For God's sake, get them off me!"

When Jackson stared at the walls, it looked as though they were rhythmically bulging in and out, like a breathing animal. After a while, Jackson started to lose track of time. The hours went by but nothing in the cell changed. He looked at his watch: half-past three. He had no idea whether it was half-past three in the morning or half-past three in the afternoon. The stark white lights were on by day and by night. He didn't know how long he'd been in the cell. Was it one day? Two days? Longer than that?

"Let me out! Let me out!" he was banging on the door. Why did nobody answer?

"There's nobody there," someone shouted from another cell.

"Jackson, is that you?" Was that Eddie's voice?

"Eddie! Eddie! Can you hear me?" But nobody answered.

Jackson lay back on the bench, closed his eyes, tried to sleep. He dozed fitfully. But the bright white light and the constant background hubbub of people talking, crying, shouting and screaming kept him awake.

Then the lights went off.

The darkness was complete. At first, he panicked. He had grown used to the light. He could no longer see the eyeball camera. He wondered if it could see him. He lay in the darkness listening to the noises from the other cells. The noises were joined by the beat of his own heart. In the absolute darkness, his heartbeat reverberated through his head. And finally he fell asleep.

There was a face – "Wake up!"

Someone was with him in the cell. A man, his face, pale and gaunt. Jackson sat up with a start. It was a policeman. In uniform. The cell door was open. Pale grey light filtered in.

"What's happening?"

"You can clear off out of here is what's happening," said the policeman.

"I'm not being charged?"

"What with?"

"I don't know. I got arrested. I thought someone would…"

"There isn't anyone."

"What d'you mean?" said Jackson.

"What I said. There's no one here. Not in this station. Only me. I decided to take pity on you."

"You're letting me go?" said Jackson.

The policeman nodded.

Jackson couldn't make any sense of this. "You're serious. I'm free to go?"

"Don't get excited," the policeman said, "There's nowhere to go to."

"What?"

"Everything's changed."

"What? What d'you mean?"

"What I said. Everything's changed."

Jackson opened the door to his cell and walked down the passageway that led to the outside world. Nothing could have prepared him for what he saw. He stared in horror. But then a thought came into his head. He remembered somebody telling him that opportunities don't come along very often. When an opportunity does come along, you should seize it.

Jackson smiled.

Saturday Night in the City of the Dead – Underpass

When he opened his eyes, Jackson found that he was sitting out on the balcony with Eddie.

"I had a weird dream," he said, "It was like… oh, never mind."

Eddie was smoking sparkle-powder and drinking Chivas Regal from the bottle. Twenty floors below, the motorway shimmered, silvery white in the heat of the midday sun. They watched a pack of dogs chasing a girl along the overpass until some kid with a gun shot at them but missed. The dogs ran off, yowling with rage, and the girl – they couldn't see what happened to her and they didn't care.

"We should get some guns," said Eddie.

"You should have thought of that before," Jackson said, "Where'd you get a gun these days?"

"You can get anything for the right price."

"The right price? What have we got that anyone else would want?"

Eddie had no answer for that. They didn't have anything. Only the tower block. They had that. And all the stuff they'd scrounged from the apartments. Like the sparkle-dust and the Chivas Regal.

Eddie sat naked on a striped canvas deckchair out on the veranda. Jackson watched a drop of sweat running down his body, over his chest, and into his bellybutton.

"We should get us a business," Jackson said.

"What kind of business?"

"I don't know. A nightclub maybe?"

"You'd need electricity for a nightclub. You'd need a generator."

"We can find a generator."

"You'd need fuel. You'd need petrol or oil or something."

"We can nick that too."

Eddie swigged back some whisky. "What'd they pay us with?"

"Who?"

"The people that come to our nightclub. They'd have to pay us with something. Like food or booze or something."

Jackson thought about that. In the Time Before, someone could waggle a plastic card at a machine and it would buy stuff. Or they could give you bits of coloured paper from a wallet and everyone pretended it was worth something. Now, all that plastic and paper was as worthless as it looked. No wonder the wheels of commerce had ground to a halt.

"We could sell drugs," Jackson said.

"We haven't got enough to sell. Once my stash runs out, that's it."

"We could make drugs then. Set up a lab."

"You know how to do that, do you?"

"No. But… maybe we could find someone who does."

"Even if we did, we'd have the same problem. What'd they pay us with?"

"Their houses?" Jackson suggested, "They could give us their houses."

Eddie yawned. "We got this whole bleedin' tower block, this whole soddin' high-rise shithouse all to ourselves. What'd we do with more houses?"

Jackson thought about that for a while. He said, "Let's be famous."

Eddie didn't catch on right away. He was not a quick thinker. Jackson had to explain it to him. Even in the Time Before, it wasn't just money that people wanted. It was success. Fame. Being successful, being famous, was the ultimate reward. That's why poor people wanted to be rich and why rich people kept on working even though they didn't need more money.

"You reckon?" said Eddie. He stood up and urinated over the balcony.

"Don't do that," said Jackson.

"Why not?"

"It attracts attention. A soldier might see you."

"Ain't no soldiers for miles."

"A crusty might see you. A red-eye, one of the East Side gangs."

"Does it matter?"

Jackson was losing patience with Eddie. "'Course it matters! Anyone who sees us here might coming looking for us."

"You want to be famous, don't you?"

Jackson thought of explaining that fame didn't come from pissing over balconies.

"Anyway," Eddie went on, "I don't see the point of being famous. I mean, in the Time Before, you had to be famous to get money so you could get food and booze and somewhere to live. But now, we got this whole damn' building to live in. There's plenty of food and booze to be scavenged. So the way I see it, our best course of action is to lie back and enjoy it."

Jackson shook his head. "You don't understand. It can't go on like that. Stuff will run out."

"We can get more."

"What's the point? Every day's the goddamn' same. You got to have ambition…"

Jackson hated the anonymity of his life. He hated it with a passion that he couldn't begin to explain to Eddie. Jackson had always wanted to 'make it' whatever that meant. He had never been content to be a part of the mindless herd of humanity. Maybe that's why he hated the red-eyes so much. They were the logical evolution of the human species – mindless beasts that only lived for the sake of living.

Eddie was strolling off the balcony into the room behind. "I'm going down to floor 7," he said, "There's a chick on floor 7. I'll prob'ly…" But he never finished the sentence. There was a gigantic flash of flame in the far distance, shooting skyward. Then came the sound of a deafening explosion. The building shook. The bottle of Chivas Regal fell from the table and smashed. There was a long, low rumble that you could feel as much as hear. Way out on the east of the city a great plume of grey-white smoke roiled upwards.

"Shit, man!" Jackson said, "What a waste of Chivas Regal."

They waited until twilight before venturing out. Eddie thought the explosion might have been a pipe bomb, a fertilizer bomb, something like that. The gangs out east were always blowing things up. There was some sort of feud going on between the Red Skull

Gang and some other gang. The Red Skull Gang was the most vicious gang in the city. They didn't care who they killed – Infected or Normal, it was all the same to them. Their symbol was a red skull and crossbones.

If one of the gangs got control of a building, the other gang was likely to mount an assault to try to get them out. There had been fires before. But not an explosion.

"That's no pipe bomb," Jackson said.

"How d'you know?" said Eddie.

"It was too big."

"Could have been a big pipe," said Eddie.

The sun was low in the sky now. The windows of the tower blocks shone gold and red. They were making their way cautiously towards the southern suburbs. Looking for booze. It was no good looking in supermarkets or town-centre stores. They'd all been looted long ago. It was still possible to find a few bottles in some of the corner shops on the fringes of town but the houses made easier pickings. At first, Jackson had avoided houses. Partly because he'd felt guilty about scavenging from houses that looked just like his mum and dad's old house. And partly because so many houses contained decomposing bodies and the stench had made him feel sick. He had long ago got over those qualms. Scavenging was scavenging. If you didn't do it someone else would. Anyway, the bodies didn't stink so much any more. Or, if they did, Jackson didn't notice it.

They took all the narrow little back roads where there weren't any shops, so they'd be unlikely to meet any gangs of scavengers or hunters, and where there weren't any tower blocks, so people with guns wouldn't be able to take pot shots at them, and where the roads were too small for Challenger Tanks and Stormers to go through.

"My theory is it was a Stormer," said Jackson.

"What was?"

"That explosion this afternoon."

"What's a Stormer?"

In the Time Before, Eddie had lived out in the suburbs. He hadn't been in the city when the Army had moved in. First the armoured reconnaissance vehicles had come – the Scimitars and

Jackals. They'd dealt with the first stage of the clean-up: rounding up the living, shooting the Infected. Then the tanks had rumbled into town. Nothing could stand before them. They demolished the low-rise buildings and fired on anyone who refused to surrender. That's when the gangs started occupying the tower blocks. They thought the higher up they went, the safer they'd be. But then the Stormers arrived – tanks fitted with banks of high velocity missile launchers. They'd been designed to bring down helicopters but they worked just as well on tower blocks.

A young man with a straggly beard and long, greasy hair was shambling across the street. He paid no attention to Jackson and Eddie. Jackson took the hunting knife from the sheath strapped to his belt, went up to the man, grabbed his long hair, jerked back his head and deftly cut his throat. The man had been a red-eye. That was the only way to deal with the bastards.

"I think I knew that guy," Eddie said, "From the Time Before, I mean. Peter his name was. Art student, I think."

"Yeah?" said Jackson. He wasn't really interested.

They were walking through a residential area now. A nice looking place. Big houses, detached and semi-detached. Very select. Very posh. The sort of place that solicitors and accountants and the managers of small but profitable retail outlets would once have lived.

"What you looking for?" said Eddie, "More Chivas Regal?"

"I was thinking a couple of single malts might be nice this time," Jackson said, "Some of the peaty ones. Talisker maybe. Or Laphroaig. But I wouldn't turn my nose up at a Macallan."

"Didn't you used to drink cocktails? What was that one you liked? Blue Moon?"

"Yeah, but where would I get the ice?"

The Time Before. Eddie was always going on about it. Jackson wasn't interested. That was dead and gone. Back in those days, the labels on your clothes or the make of your aftershave had seemed somehow important. Not any longer. Now survival was important. But mere survival wasn't enough. Not for Jackson. He had ambition. He wanted to succeed. At any cost. He'd always wanted to be famous. He still did.

"Remember my name," he said.

"What?"

"It was a song. Irene Cara. I'm gonna live forever. You remember that song?"

"Oh yeah," Eddie wrinkled his brow, trying to dredge up old memories, "Yeah, I think so."

They'd both brought rucksacks to put any swag into. The rucksacks were empty at the moment, apart from a couple of tins of baked beans that they'd scrounged from the debris of a small shop. One of the houses had a lawn out front with a white wrought-iron bench in the middle. They sat on the bench and took the tins of beans out of their rucksacks.

Far out to the east, smoke was still billowing into the air. They opened the tins and ate the cold beans with a couple of spoons that they'd brought with them. It was the sort of junk food Jackson had hated. These days, though, you had to take what you could get.

"Could have been the crusties," Eddie said.

'Crusties' was their word for anyone older than about thirty, who'd survived the great plague.

"What, who blew up that building, you mean?"

"Might have been."

"Why'd they do a thing like that?"

"They want everything to go back the way it used to be."

"You think they're killing red-eyes?"

"I think they'd kill anyone who's not a crusty."

"Funny…" said Jackson.

"Yeah," Eddie chuckled to himself. After a while he stopped chuckling because he didn't know what he was chuckling about. "What's funny?" he said.

"This lawn."

Eddie looked at the lawn. It was the same as any other lawn. Just grass. "What's funny about it?"

"No weeds."

Eddie carried on scooping cold baked beans into his mouth. Jackson was always saying stuff that didn't make sense. Best to ignore him.

"This lawn's been here all summer with no one to look after it."

"Yeah."

"So where are the weeds?"

"Beats me."

"And why's the grass so short?"

That was when the man came out of the house and started shouting at them.

Later, sitting in the dismal, dusty front room, drinking Broken Orange Pekoe tea from bone china cups, the man told them about Eleanor. He showed them the photographs in their decorative frames on the mantel-piece. The smiling, dark-haired young woman leaning over the parapet of a bridge, waving at the photographer; now she was holding hands with a young man; then she was wearing a wedding dressing, kissing the same young man. The young man was the same man who was showing them the photographs. He looked older now.

"We were married last September," he said. He turned to Jackson, "Did you lose… anyone?"

"Not really."

Not really? Jackson thought. I only lost my mother and father. My little brother. All my friends, except for Eddie. But that was commonplace. Everyone had lost people. No good dwelling on it.

"You?" The man was talking to Eddie.

Eddie stood up, walked over to the windows, looked through the lace curtains at all the other houses in the street. "Nice area, this," he said, "Where'd be the best house to go scavenging?"

The man's name was Donald but Jackson decided to call him Donnie. Donnie didn't have any neighbours. Not living ones. There was nobody left alive in the entire street apart from Donnie. So they went scavenging in a big white house at the end of the street. The house had belonged to a man called Fescot who had been a doctor. It turned out that Dr Fescot's house was a good choice. They found full bottles of Talisker, Lagavulin and Ardbeg, a few nearly-full bottles of some other malt whiskies plus a couple of cognacs and a calvados. They found Dr Fescot in the kitchen, slumped over the kitchen table. There was a crystal tumbler in what was left of his hand and a half-full bottle of 12-year old Fettercairn close by.

"That's a nice drop of stuff," Jackson commented, but he left the bottle there anyhow out of respect for the dead.

Donnie took Jackson and Eddie to a couple of other houses after that but the booze wasn't of the same standard. At some point,

Jackson told Donnie about his plan to be famous and successful. "The way I see it," Jackson explained, "is that you either need to have something that people want or you have to have something that scares them half to death. Appeal to their greed or appeal to their fear."

It had been obvious to Jackson from the moment he'd met Donnie that here was an intelligent man, someone who, unlike Eddie, would be able to get to grips with Jackson's ideas.

"I see what you mean," said Donnie, "And I know exactly what you should do."

"You do?"

"I do."

"What?"

"Start your own army."

It was such an obvious idea that, once Donnie had explained it to him, Jackson was amazed that he hadn't thought of it himself. The army could give people what people wanted: safety. They could also instil fear: because if people didn't do what they were told to do, well, there would doubtless be repercussions. Jackson appointed Donnie to the position of Chief of the General Staff. Donnie moved into the tower-block and occupied the rooms on the twenty-first floor.

The next day, Jackson, Donnie and Eddie went around town armed with spray cans. They went to the multi-story carpark in the town centre. Jackson found a red-eye girl hiding behind a black BMW. He clubbed her to death with a walking stick that he was carrying for just that sort of occasion. That was the only way to deal with red-eyes. Then they got to work with their spray cans. On the concrete walls on each floor they sprayed the slogan: "Join The NuArmy – For A Better Tomorrow". They went into the main shopping mall. On the walls and the few remaining unbroken windows of the deserted shops they sprayed "Join The NuArmy – Enforce Freedom". They walked through the town centre and on every blank wall they sprayed "Join The NuArmy – Kill Red-Eyes!"

Under each slogan, they sprayed "Central Plaza, midday, tomorrow" so that anyone would know the place, and the time. They didn't put a date because nobody could remember what date it was any more. This was to be their first rally.

The next day, the sun shone. Only one person turned up at the rally – a girl called Dolores. She was dressed in a weird outfit made of sacking, chains and an antique leather flying helmet with goggles positioned just above her forehead.

"You come to join up?" said Jackson.

"Join up what?" Dolores said.

"The NuArmy," Eddie said.

"The New what?"

"Army."

"Army?"

"Didn't you see the adverts?" Jackson said.

She shook her head. "I saw you three hanging about here like idiots. I came to see what was going on?"

They explained about the NuArmy. Dolores said, "Oh, cool." She was recruited and given the rank of Sergeant.

"You a Goth?" Jackson asked.

Dolores practically spat at him – "Does it look like I'm a soddin' Goth?"

"Well, yeah, it does."

"Well, I ain't. I'm a clockwork punk."

"Yeah? What's that?"

"It's like a steampunk only clockwork"

"Oh. Cool."

"What are you?" Dolores said.

"What do you mean?"

"What are you? Punk? Post-punk? Metal-head? Scum-rocker? You look kind of scruffy. I was wondering what it was called."

Scruffy? Jackson took a look at himself. He was wearing crumpled chinos, walking boots that had seen better days and a grubby tennis shirt. He also hadn't washed in quite a while and his stubble was half way to being a beard.

"I'm undercover."

"What?"

"You know, like Al Pacino in Serpico."

"What?"

"You never seen Serpico?"

Dolores shook her head.

"See, Al Pacino is a cop. In New York. And the other cops are corrupt. You know, extorting money, and stuff. So he goes undercover. To expose what's going on."

"And you're an undercover cop?"

"Well, not exactly."

"Take my advice," said Dolores, "Do something about your appearance. Have a shave. Do something with your hair. Maybe get some underarm deodorant."

So Jackson went scavenging through the wreckage of a department store. He found some razors and shaving foam, some French soap, hair wax and aftershave – Givenchy Gentlemen, which had always been his favourite. He also scrounged some better clothes: Armani, Gucci, Balenciaga. He'd been letting his standards slip. That would all have to change.

Dolores came back to the tower block. She took a room on the twenty-second floor, right above Donnie.

"Did you hear that explosion?"

"Which explosion?" Dolores said.

"A big one. When was it, Eddie, a couple of weeks ago?"

"Two, three weeks," Eddie said.

The four of them – Jackson, Eddie, Donnie and Dolores – were sitting out on the balcony, watching a couple of tramps having a fight in the middle lane of the motorway. Jackson had washed and shaved. He was wearing an Armani shirt and Gucci jeans. The day was sunny and Eddie was naked again. "Trying to top up my suntan," he said.

Dolores was sitting on the concrete floor next to him, drawing with a pencil in an old notebook. She was a good artist. She'd been going to art college, she said, before the snow came. She never glanced at Eddie. He said she should draw him but she said she wasn't interested.

"The tower block?" Dolores said, "Yeah, I was squatting a few streets away. It blew out the windows. We moved into another house after that, a bit further away. One that still had windows."

"So who blew the place up?" Jackson said.

"The Red Skull Gang, I think."

"I knew it!" said Eddie, "This is some kind of gang war."

"Nah, not a gang war," said Dolores, "I mean, they didn't blow it up to get even with another gang or nothing."

"So who was in the building, then?" Jackson said, "The one they blew up?"

"Some old people is all. Some old crusties."

Jackson laughed. "You're having me on. The old crusties are harmless enough. Why'd the Red Skull Gang blow up a building full of old crusties?"

"Protection money," Dolores said, "The old folks refused to pay protection money."

That's when Jackson decided that, if they were going to bring back law and order, they had to take on the gangs. He called a special meeting of the entire NuArmy (they'd recruited a teenager called Kevin the day before so that made five of them). Jackson explained his plan. They would issue an ultimatum. Either the gangs obeyed the law or else… well, they'd have to face the consequences.

Kevin said, "There's one problem."

"What's that?" said Jackson.

"The Red Skull Gang's got guns."

That evening, as Jackson and Eddie were sitting on the balcony watching dimly flickering lights far off in the streets of the twilight city, Jackson said, "Do you remember Bear?"

"Yeah. Why?"

"What happened to him?"

"The same as happened to everyone else, I suppose."

"Except for us."

"Yeah," Eddie agreed, "Except for us."

Jackson took a long swig from a bottle. It was potent stuff. He nearly choked on it. He had to look at the label to see what he was drinking. Bunnahabhain. He didn't known how to pronounce it. But it tasted good.

"Why's that? Why didn't it affect us?" said Jackson.

"We must be immune."

"I was sick, wasn't I?" He remembered blacking out in an underpass. Being locked up in a cell. Then being let out. Wandering around town, the stink of decay everywhere. And then, for days, maybe weeks, throwing up, suffering from delirium, trying to find food and then not being able to eat it. It was a wonder he'd survived.

"How do you feel now?" Eddie said.

Jackson wasn't sure how he felt. He thought he was feeling a bit feverish, as a matter of fact. Though that might have been due to the whisky.

"How long have we been here?" Jackson said.

"Where? In the tower block, you mean? Ever since… you know. That night. When the snow came. That was January. It's July now, ain't it? Or August. Six or seven months then."

Six or seven wasted months, Jackson thought. He tried to remember how he'd arrived at the tower block. His memories were fuzzy. He couldn't piece together the details. He'd been sick. That much he remembered. Somehow Eddie had found him and looked after him. And then, when the Army had arrived, Eddie had hidden him. In an apartment in the tower block.

"How did Bear know Donnie?" Jackson said.

"Who?"

"Donnie."

"Donnie?"

"Bear had some business dealings with a guy called Donnie."

"That's my name," said Donnie.

"Oh yeah," said Jackson, "Well, it's a pretty common name, I guess."

"Is it?" said Donnie.

"I think so."

"Hmm. You're probably right."

Jackson wondered what had happened to the people who'd been rounded up after the Army had come. Stories had been going around that they were sent to camps. The official line was that it was for their protection. That's what the loud-hailers had said, when the Army had rolled into town: "The Government has established safe havens where you will be looked after and protected. Anyone who is hungry will be fed. Anyone who is ill will be treated." But that didn't stop the rumours. Nobody knew where the rumours had come from because nobody knew of anyone who'd come back after they'd been taken to a camp. People didn't know who to trust any more. So they trusted nobody.

One evening, towards the end of summer, Jackson, Eddie and Dolores went out east. Dolores had told them where the Red Skull Gang hung out. It was in an old building that used to be a nightclub. Jackson knew the place from the old days. The club had been called The Blocks.

Eddie said they should parley first. "Diplomacy first. Force later," is how he put it. A small delegation should go to the club, make friendly contact with the gang and see if they could persuade them to abide by the law. So Jackson, Eddie and Dolores went there. Donnie wasn't around for some reason. Jackson hadn't seen Donnie in ages. Maybe he'd moved out of the tower block?

They took the narrow side streets that night so as to avoid confrontations with roaming bands of red-eyes. Jackson didn't mind red-eyes. He enjoyed killing them. But Dolores said that Jackson should try not to be too violent. Jackson thought that was a stupid idea but he went along with it anyway because he liked Dolores.

It was a clear, sultry night and the full moon was bright enough for them to see where they were going. They eventually arrived at a part of town that Jackson knew well from the Time Before. There was the old wine bar, Swizzy's. He'd thought it was a pretty snazzy place back in the day. Now it was a wreck, like most of the other bars and shops and pubs. The plate glass window had been smashed and the tables and chairs lay in pieces. The old bar was blackened as though someone had lit a fire there.

Jackson tried to recall the last time he'd been here. Everything had been covered in snow. The grimy old streets had looked clean and white. Now they were filthier than they'd ever been. There were wrecked cars on the side of the road, their windscreens reduced to glassy fragments glittering on the road surface. Up ahead, he saw the underpass. His heart skipped a beat. What was it about the underpass that scared him? Something had happened there. Something terrible but he couldn't remember what.

There it was: the Blocks Club. It looked no different from the way it had looked all those months ago, before the world had changed. The neon light above the door was still working, surprisingly, with the faulty "o" flickering on and off, just as Jackson remembered it.

"Evening, gents." Hell's bells! There was Big Billy, standing, as he always had, under the little archway over the door to the club, "You members, are you?"

Jackson couldn't help but laugh. "It's me, Billy. Jackson. You can't have forgotten."

Big Billy smiled broadly, "Oh yes, sonny, and how old are you exactly? There's a strict entry policy here, you know. Billy was going through the old routine again. He'd always teased Jackson about his age.

"I'm older than I look," Jackson said.

"Let me be the judge of that," Big Billy replied, "I will require a formal statement of your age, kid, before I can let you in."

Jackson tried to remember how old he was. Eighteen? No, surely he was older than that. It seemed like years since he'd been to The Blocks. It was hard to believe it had only been a few months.

"I'll vouch for him," said Eddie.

Billy grunted. He didn't smile. He didn't make a joke of it as he had done in the old days. The inside of the club hadn't changed. Jackson said hello to Annie, the cloakroom attendant. He didn't have a coat to check in because the night was too warm for one. Then he went into the main body of the club. The lights were flashing, the glitter-ball was twirling, the old seductive *boom-boom-boom* of the bass speakers was resonating through his chest. Jackson wondered where they'd managed to get electricity.

"They must have a generator," he said.

"What?" said Eddie.

Jackson drew closer to Eddie and shouted into his ear in an attempt to compete with the relentless *boom-boom-boom* of the music: "Generator. They must have a..."

"Hey guys! Where've you been?"

Who was the man who was talking to him? Jackson tried to remember. Oh yeah, it was Piers. The bloke that Bear had warned him about.

"I been around, man, how 'bout you?"

"Here and there. Here and there."

"Come on, we need to get away." That was Eddie. He was leaning towards Jackson, shouting into his ear.

"Get away? Why? We only just..."

"Let's go."

"What about the Red Skull Gang? We haven't even…"

"Something's not right."

"What?"

"This place. Something about it isn't right."

Piers was on the dancefloor now. Dancing with Shirley. Jackson waved but Shirley didn't notice.

"As far as I can see, *everything* is right here," Jackson said, "It's the rest of the world that's wrong."

"That's what I mean," Eddie said.

"You go if you want," said Jackson, "Dolores and I will…"

"Who?"

"Dolores."

"Who?"

Jackson looked around. He couldn't see Dolores. In fact, he didn't remember her coming into the club with them. But she'd been with them earlier. So she must be there somewhere.

Jackson searched for any other familiar faces. No sign of Shirley. No sign of Bear. He couldn't see Piers any more either. He must have left. *Boom-boom-boom* the bass speakers went. No wonder everyone was leaving. It was the music. It was terrible. No melody. Nothing you could dance to. Just *boom-boom-boom*…

He was throwing up. He was sitting on a step outside the front door of the club. He must have drunk too much. He hadn't drunk anything in the club, had he? But earlier on. He seemed to remember sitting on the balcony drinking whisky.

He looked around for Eddie. He saw someone standing, barely visible in the darkness, on the other side of the street.

"Eddie?"

"Yes."

"What happened?"

"You were sick. You'll feel all right again soon."

Jackson stood up. He felt shaky on his feet. He glanced back at the Blocks Club. The neon sign had been turned off. The doors were shut.

"How long have I been here?"

"Don't you remember?"

"Not really."

"Come on, you'll be all right again soon."

Eddie had his arm around Jackson's shoulders now. Jackson felt woozy. Eddie supported him as they walked together towards the end of the street. They turned the corner. There was the underpass.

Jackson stopped. Even when there had been streetlamps here, the underpass had always been dark. Now the only illumination was the thin, silvery light of the moon. Barely enough to see by. In the underpass it would be pitch black. Who could tell what might be lurking down there?

"Something bad happened down there," Jackson said.

"That was a long time ago," Eddie said.

They were walking down towards the underpass. Eddie was holding Jackson tightly. Jackson wanted to pull away but Eddie's grasp was too strong. Jackson stared, wide-eyed, into the opening of the underpass. It looked like a gigantic mouth that was about to swallow him. The closer they got, the greater Jackson's terror became. Now they were entering the underpass. Everything was dark. He could see nothing. Not even the walls. Not even the ground. Then someone leapt from the darkness, seized Jackson by the throat and…

"Got another one, here, sarge."

"Put him in the truck."

What was happening?

He was by the roadside, lying on the grass verge. He could see a tower block rising high above him. There were helicopters with spotlights shining onto balconies, shining into windows. Lights everywhere. Someone was shining a light into his eyes. There were soldiers, all over the place. There were armoured vehicles. A soldier roughly pulled him to his feet. They were lining people up. The soldiers were bundling people into a truck. Jackson's hands were cuffed behind his back. What was going on? *Yow!* Someone stuck a needle into his arm. Then everything faded to blackness…

"Where am I?"

Jackson tried to get up. He was shivering uncontrollably. He felt feverish. He wanted to run away. But he couldn't move. His heart was pounding, *boom-boom-boom*. "Don't worry, old man, you'll feel a lot better after this."

He opened his eyes. A grey-haired man was smiling down at him. There was a dark-haired woman there too. She was wiping Jackson's mouth with a cloth. There was the smell of vomit. The man and the woman were wearing white coats. Jackson looked around. He was in a small, white-painted room. He was lying in a bed. No, not just lying there. He was strapped to the bed so that he couldn't even move his arms and his legs.

The man was wearing a name tag on his white coat. It said: "Dr. A. G. Fescot". The woman had a name tag too. It said: "Dolores Diaz, Staff Nurse". She stepped away from Jackson and tossed the soiled cloth into a waste bin.

"What am I doing here?" Jackson said, "Let me go! Please! Let me out of here."

"Do you think he knows we are here?" Nurse Diaz said.

She'd been looking at the patient for several minutes, trying to ascertain whether or not he gave any indication of awareness. He was struggling against the straps and making strange gargling noises in his throat but there was no sign that he was lucid or capable of reasoned thought.

"Oh, no," said Dr Fescot, "The last glimmer of intelligence was long ago extinguished. When they are at this stage, they still look human. But intellectually, they have more in common with a rat or a stoat than with you or me."

Nurse Diaz leant over Jackson and pulled back the top lid of his right eye. "Still very red," she said.

"This one is far gone," said the doctor, "He's one of the violent ones. He seemed quite a decent lad when they brought him in. But there was always that unfortunate tendency to violence. We tried our best. But it's been a steady decline, sadly."

Nurse Diaz was holding an empty syringe now. She dabbed something wet onto Jackson's upper arm, stuck the hypodermic needle in and withdrew some blood.

"Careful with that sample, Nurse," the doctor said, "For all we know, it could hold the breakthrough we are looking for. If it does, he could end up famous. Do you want to be famous, old fellow?"

Jackson stared at the doctor. What was he talking about? "No!" he shouted, "I don't want to be bloody famous. I want to be bloody free!"

"Blabber-blabber-blabber, that's all he ever says." The doctor chuckled. He enjoyed his work.

Doctor Fescot opened the door of the room. The door opened inwards. Jackson briefly glimpsed an antiseptic-looking corridor beyond. He was in a hospital. There was two symbols on the outside of the door. One was a biohazard symbol: three rings overlapping a circle. The other was a red skull and crossbones.

There were pillows propping Jackson up. There was a window directly in front of him. The sky was clear blue. The sun was shining. It looked like summer. There were seagulls. The hospital overlooked a small town. The sun gleamed on the rooftops. In the distance the sea glittered. Between the town and the sea there was – what was it? It looked familiar. It was a fenced-off area. Inside the fence there were buildings, rows of chalets, a fairground with a carousel and a big wheel. Jackson vaguely remembered going there once. It was a holiday camp.

As the door closed behind the doctor, the nurse approached Jackson with another syringe. He tried to tell her that there was nothing wrong with him, that it was all a terrible mistake, that he shouldn't really be here. Then the syringe went into his arm and the white room faded into the distance.

When he opened his eyes, Jackson found that he was sitting out on the balcony with Eddie.

"I had a weird dream," he said, "It was like… oh, never mind."

Eddie was smoking sparkle-powder and drinking Chivas Regal from the bottle. Twenty floors below, the motorway shimmered, silvery white in the heat of the midday sun. They watched a pack of dogs chasing a girl along the overpass until some kid with a gun shot at them but missed. The dogs ran off, yowling with rage, and the girl – they couldn't see what happened to her and they didn't care.

Winter Cruise

Mrs Chivers wrapped her thick woollen scarf tightly around her neck and strolled along the deck. The night was cold and blustery. To think that, in just a few days from now she would be in the Azores – and less than a week after that, Antigua! It promised to be the experience of a lifetime. Even though it had cost her more than she could really afford, she felt sure it would be worth every penny.

Since her husband Frank had died, seven years earlier, she had lived a solitary existence which, frankly, had become increasingly tedious. Life in a sleepy Suffolk village offered few opportunities for unbridled excitement. Coffee mornings and bingo nights in the local village hall had become the highlights of her social calendar. She craved adventure!

Quite suddenly, in late October, as she watched the leaves swirling down from the trees under the impact of an autumn storm, she decided that she could not face the unrelenting dark, wet misery of a British winter. And the snow! She particularly hated the snow. This winter she would escape from it all. The romance of the sea was calling to her. She had always dreamt of going on a luxury cruise. Frank had promise to take her "one day" but that day had never arrived and Frank was now long gone.

She didn't quite know what a cruise entailed. She had read about cruises in detective stories – but they always involved a murder. And she had seen ocean-going liners in films – but they always ended up with the ship turning upside down or striking an iceberg. She didn't think that sort of disaster was very likely to happen in reality. Not these days. Even so, her view of life aboard a cruise ship had undoubtedly been formed by reading those books and watching those films. In her mind, a cruise ship embodied the height of luxury. It would have a sumptuous oak-panelled restaurant and a huge ballroom with crystal chandeliers. Her fellow passengers would comprise a mix of cultured, interesting and occasionally somewhat exotic people. The captain, of course, would be dashing and handsome and he would no doubt invite Mrs Chivers to dine at his table.

That her idea of a cruise ship was outdated became immediately apparent the moment she first set eyes on the ship in Southampton dock. The sight of it made Mrs Chivers feel dizzy. It was vast. Immense. Far bigger than it had looked in the photograph in the holiday brochure. The decks seemed to rise up forever. It resembled nothing so much as a massive housing estate perched precariously on the hull of an oil tanker. Mrs Chivers had imagined that the ship would be a sort of floating five-star hotel. This was more like the suburbs of a small town suffering from delusions of seaworthiness.

Boarding the ship had gone smoothly, though she had felt butterflies in her stomach when she had walked through the passageway that led from the departure lounge to the deck. It was so high above the ground! However, once she was on board, the crew members had all been so polite and helpful that she really couldn't complain.

Her room was on Deck 5. She would never have found it without the assistance of the pleasant young woman who showed her to the lift and then took her all the way to her room. It was quite a nice room, furnished with a settee, a small table and two chairs, a wardrobe, a TV set – everything she could possibly want. The only thing it lacked was a view. The fact of the matter was that her room was not one of the better ones. It was called an 'obstructed ocean view' cabin, which meant that it had one small round window the view from which was partially obscured by some exterior pipes of unknown purpose.

When the ship set sail from Southampton on the 12th of December, Mrs Chivers was both excited and a little frightened. She was looking forward to visiting all those exotic places – Antigua, Jamaica, Trinidad, St. Lucia and the rest – but she was also frightened that she would be lonely.

"Don't be so silly!" she chided herself that evening, as she smoothed out the creases in her dove-grey evening gown and titivated her hair before going to dinner, "There are literally thousands of passengers on this ship. All I have to do is find the cultured, interesting and exotic people. Like in the books and films."

The first people she found were the Dobson family from Bournemouth. They were sitting at the next table to Mrs Chivers. Mr and Mrs Dobson made a determined effort to strike up a conversation with Mrs Chivers while their teenage son Alfie conveyed greasy morsels of food to his mouth with the aid of his fingers while simultaneously watching something of engrossing interest on his mobile phone.

"We been on loads of cruises," Mrs Dobson shouted across at Mrs Chivers, "New York, Spain, Finland, you name it we been there. How about you?"

Mrs Chivers replied casually that this was her first.

"Your first!" screeched Mrs Dobson; "It's her first cruise, Bill," she informed her husband.

"Your first, is it?" Bill yelled to Mrs Chivers. "She won't know the ropes then, will she, Margie?" Bill said to his wife. Then, in case she had missed this astute remark, he repeated it for the benefit of Mrs Chivers – "You won't know the ropes then, will you?"

Margie shouted, "Don't you worry, dear, we'll show you the ropes. We go on cruises all the time, don't we Bill?"

"We do," Bill confirmed, "All the time. If anyone can show you the ropes, we can!"

Mrs Chivers thanked them for their solicitude but assured them that she was quite capable of handling whatever ropes might chance to come her way.

The Dobson family weren't quite the sort of cultured, interesting and exotic people which the books and films had led Mrs Chivers to anticipate. Nor was the dining room the oak-panelled haven of refined elegance that she'd hoped for. Not that it was scruffy or self-service. Far from it. The tables were all covered in crisp white cloths, the silver and cutlery were properly arranged and the serving staff were smart and efficient. But there was undoubtedly a lack of intimacy. As with everything else on the ship, the dining room was vast. It was also crowded and noisy. As for the décor, the furnishings tended less towards oak and more towards stainless steel and smoked glass. What is more, as far as she could see, Mrs Chivers was the only person who had bothered to dress for dinner. Henceforth, she resolved to avoid the main dining room as much as possible. According to the guidebook that had been placed in her room, the ship boasted no less than eight "mouth-watering eateries catering to every taste". She would take some time to select a more intimate "eatery" at which to dine in future.

As she stepped into the lift to go back to her room, Mrs Chivers was horrified to see the three Dobsons suddenly leaping in with her just before the doors closed. Little Alfie Dobson was still engaged in some apparently fascinating activity on his mobile phone.

"Ooo, we meet again!" enthused Mrs Dobson.

"So it would appear," replied Mrs Chivers, coldly.

"What deck you on then?"

"Deck 5," said Mrs Chivers.

"'Ear that, Bill? She's on Deck 5!"

"You're on Deck 5, are you?" said Bill.

"I am," Mrs Chivers agreed.

"We're on Deck 5, aren't we, Bill?"

"We are!" Mr Dobson confirmed.

"How remarkable," observed Mrs Chivers.

"We'll be neighbours then, won't we!" – Mrs Dobson made this sound like one of the most thrilling discoveries of her life.

"Ah," said Mrs Chivers.

*

Mrs Chivers spent the next few days exploring the ship. She found that there was a nice coffee parlour on the seventh deck that served excellent cappuccinos. There was a tea room on the eighth deck that not only served tea made from proper tealeaves rather than teabags but also had some very nice scones. She had made an extensive tour of the restaurants and had quickly dismissed the Mogul Experience (too spicy), the Noodle Delight (too noodley) and the Bahama Buffet (self-service). She had spent some time consulting the menu of the Olde British Steak House but decided that she couldn't face steak ever single night for over a month. Eventually she found a restaurant called The Dandelion Diner on Deck 6. By the standards of the ship, The Dandelion Diner was remarkably small – it had just ten tables – and the food was very much to her taste. They served fish, pork and lamb chops, meat pies and fresh vegetables.

Mrs Chivers dined at the same small table next to a window every day. After dinner she would find a window table in one of the lounges and watch the sea. One evening there was a man whom she'd seen on the television telling amusing anecdotes in the Sunset Cocktail Lounge. She enjoyed that, though to be truthful his anecdotes weren't quite as amusing as he seemed to think they were. The next morning, she went to have her hair done. The day after that, she had her nails done. It was on the fourth day at sea that she met Mr Stickleton. Mrs Chivers arrived in the Dandelion Diner at seven o'clock, which was her usual time for dinner, and found that a man was sitting at her table.

"Good evening," she said, "I'm afraid there appears to have been some mistake."

The man stood up. He bowed slightly when he returned her greeting, "Good evening, dear lady. Some mistake, you say?"

"This table," she explained, "is taken."

"Taken?"

"Reserved."

"That is true," Mr Stickleton replied, smiling, "But if you wish to join me, I should have no objection." And he sat back down again.

The man had misunderstood her. He seemed a very nice man, however. Very polite. Cultured, one might say. And elegant. He had dressed for dinner. That at least was in his favour. Most of the male passengers came to the restaurants wearing jeans and open-neck shirts. Some even wore shorts and sandals. The gentleman sitting at her table, however, was most correctly dressed in a black dinner jacket and bow tie. The red cummerbund was, perhaps, something of an affectation but it was one that seemed, oddly, to suit him rather well.

"What I mean," said Mrs Chivers, "is that the table is reserved for me."

"Ah no," the man shook his head sorrowfully, "I fear, madam, it is you who are mistaken. I reserved this table this morning. It is the table I always take on this ship."

The gentleman was clearly mistaken. Having discovered the Dandelion Diner, Mrs Chivers had thought it circumspect to reserve this particular table for her sole use throughout the remainder of the voyage. However, she was disinclined to argue. Besides which, there was something about the man that she found interesting. Attractive even, though she blushed at the thought.

She smiled, "I blame the computers. Never mind. It's such a lovely view from this table that it would be nice to share it with someone, don't you think?"

The gentleman smiled, "I do indeed, madam."

"Rosemary," she said, "If we are to share dinner, I think we might use our first names…"

She waited a moment. The gentleman looked somewhat embarrassed. He glanced down and mumbled something.

"I beg your pardon?" Mrs Chivers said.

The gentleman looked up and said in a firmer voice, "Horatio. My name, madam, is Horatio Stickleton."

"Pleased to make your acquaintance, Horatio."

During the meal, Mrs Chivers discovered a good deal about Mr Horatio Stickleton. He had been named not after Admiral Nelson, as she had at first supposed, but after the fictional captain, Horatio Hornblower. Mr Stickleton did not care for the name. "My father, you see," explained Mr Stickleton, "was a great admirer of Mr C. S. Forester's seafaring novels. It is only a wonder to me that he did not legally change our family name to Hornblower and have done with it!"

Mrs Chivers laughed at that. In fact, she laughed at a good deal that Mr Stickleton said. There was something essentially witty about him. Witty and elegant. It was his habit to take a cruise each winter, he told her. He'd been to Norway, Iceland, Newfoundland, Sardinia, The Canary Islands. So many places! And he had so many tales to tell. In Norway he'd been mistaken for the film star David Niven and was treated to a free bottle of Champagne by a star-struck restauranteur – "Which would have been flattering, I suppose, but for the fact that Mr Niven died donkey's years ago. He'd be about 110 by now, so I'm not sure being mistaken for him is a very great compliment." In Iceland he'd been swimming in a thermal hot pool when a passing Great Dane happened to fall in – "The damn' dog couldn't swim. Would've drowned if I hadn't rescued it. Mind you, giving the kiss of life to a slavering brute like that is an experience I don't wish to repeat!" And in Tenerife he'd been thrown into prison on suspicion of smuggling drugs – "It was a large bag of Mint Imperials. Take them wherever I go. The British consul had to fly over from Las Palmas and vouch for my innocence. The consul and I sucked our way through about two dozen mints before the local police would believe that they weren't cocaine!"

Mrs Chivers strongly suspected that Mr Stickleton's anecdotes were fictitious but she didn't mind. They were a good deal more amusing than the anecdotes that the man from the television had told in the cocktail bar.

From then on, they shared the same table at dinner every day. They found they enjoyed one another's company. When the ship stopped at its first port of call at Ponta del Garda in the Azores, they went ashore together. They wandered through the palm-lined streets and stopped at a harbourside café for an espresso and a local delicacy called a queijadas which reminded Mrs Chivers of a small treacle tart only spicier.

The next five days were spent at sea as the massive ship made its way towards Antigua. Had it not been for Mr Stickleton's company, those days would have seemed interminable. Not that there was a shortage of things to do on board. Indeed, there were so many leisure activities that it was hard to keep track of what was happening from one moment to the next. There were two swimming pools, one outside and one indoors, there was a fully-equipped gym, a sauna, innumerable bars and lounges, a shopping arcade, a cinema, a theatre, there were yoga and pilates classes, you could learn to paint and you could learn to dance. There were discos in the evening and bhangra dancing in the afternoon. But Mrs Chivers couldn't muster enthusiasm for any of those activities. The very idea of a woman of her age going to a gym or dancing in a disco was preposterous. She had no interest in yoga or swimming, she didn't even know what bhangra was and the shopping arcade contained no shops that sold anything she wanted to buy.

*

If Mr Stickleton hadn't been there, Mrs Chivers might have ended up whiling away the entire voyage knitting scarves for her nephews and nieces. She had brought half a dozen balls of wool and, if she ran out, she assumed that more might be available to buy in Antigua. But since meeting Mr Stickleton, her balls of wool and knitting needles lay unused. There was so much else to do. Even just walking around the ship and talking took up a surprising amount of time.

They met for breakfast in the main dining room on Deck 6 every morning at eight thirty. Initially they had taken breakfast at nine but since this was also the time favoured by the Dobson family, Mrs Chivers had suggested that eight-thirty might be more convenient.

"I could meet you at your room," Mr Stickleton had suggested but Mrs Chivers had demurred. For one thing, a gentleman caller might excite the wrong sort of speculation about her morals. For another thing, Mr Stickleton had told her about his balcony room on Deck 14 which was clearly of a much higher calibre of luxury than her modest 'ocean view' room. She had not wanted him to see her inferior accommodation and conclude that she was totally impecunious.

In Antigua Mrs Chivers and Mr Stickleton visited St. John's Cathedral with its startling white facade and towers, then they spent a lazy afternoon wandering the length of the quay where their ship, along with a couple of smaller cruise ships, was docked.

In Santo Domingo they hired a local guide to take them on a tour of the ancient buildings: the imposing 16th Century Cathedral of Santa María la Menor; the castle of Alcázar de Colón where (the guide informed them) Christopher Columbus's son had lived; and the mediaeval fortress of Fortaleza Ozama set upon a spectacular promontory overlooking the glittering, azure waters of the Rio Ozama. Eventually they grew tired, gave their guide a generous tip, and found a small café in a quiet side street where they sat drinking orange juice while enjoying the simple pleasure of each other's company.

*

On New Year's Eve, the ship was at sea, en route from Kingston, Jamaica to Willemstad, Curaçao. The day had been sunny and cloudless. The night was warm and calm. Mr Stickleton and Mrs

Chivers spent the early part of the evening walking around on the deck, gazing at the stars glittering in the velvet blackness of the sky. Then they went to the smallest and most intimate bar on the ship and drank Margaritas because those were Mrs Chivers's favourite cocktails. As the midnight hour drew closer they went to the main Atrium, a vast four-storey-high area at the centre of the ship. It was crowded. The ground floor was packed with people dancing to loud pop music. The balconies overlooking the dancefloor on each of the three storeys above were equally crowded. People were drinking and shouting, wearing paper hats and throwing coloured streamers. Seeing that Mrs Chivers and Mr Stickleton were hatless, a steward handed them two hats – a cardboard top hat for Mr Stickleton and a bowler hat decorated with a green feather for Mrs Chivers. At any other time, they would have felt silly – undignified – to be seen wearing such silly headwear in public. But the mood that night was so extravagant, so buoyant, that it seemed the most natural thing in the world.

Mrs Chivers looked at the big screen dominating one end of the Atrium. It showed a huge digital time display which was counting down, second by second. At that moment, they were just two minutes and ten seconds away from the new year. On an impulse, Mrs Chivers leant across to Mr Stickleton and said, "Let's go and dance!"

"What?" his expression showed his surprise.

"Dance," she said, "Down there. Quick!"

They placed their glasses of Champagne onto a nearby table and scurried down the stairs from the first storey, where they had been standing, to the heaving mass of people on the ground floor. The bodies were squashed together so tightly here that they had to push with some force to make their way onto the dance floor. Mr Stickleton grasped one of Mrs Chivers's hands and put his free arm around her waist. There was no time for dancing, however, because an amplified voice was now shouting through the loudspeakers: "Here it comes, folks… 10, 9, 8, 7, 6, 5, 4" – everyone was counting along with him now – "3, 2, 1 – Happy New Year!!!"

The speakers blared out Auld Lang Syne. Through the windows, they could see fireworks, which presumably had been set off from the top deck of the ship, exploding in the blackness. And then everyone was joining hands and singing: "Should old acquaintance be forgot and never brought to mind? Should old acquaintance be forgot for the sake of auld lang syne? For auld lang syne, my dear, for auld lang syne, we'll take a cup of kindness yet, for the sake of auld lang syne."

After that, the loudspeakers blasted out some sort of South American music and the more energetic or inebriated passengers did an elaborate conga around the dancefloor. Mrs Chivers and Mr Stickleton didn't feel up to doing the conga so they left the Atrium and found a passageway leading to an outside deck. It was a warm Caribbean night. Mr Stickleton held Mrs Chivers tightly to him. They stared into one another's eyes for a few moments. Then they kissed. They kissed long and repeatedly and passionately.

*

The following day, Mrs Chivers skipped breakfast. This was not because she lacked an appetite. Nor did she have a hangover. While she may, on the previous evening, have imbibed rather more than was her custom, she certainly had not been drunk. The reason she skipped breakfast was that she was embarrassed. She hadn't kissed a man since her husband Frank had died seven years earlier. And she hadn't kissed any man *but* Frank since before their marriage which had been almost fifty years ago.

She sat looking mournfully into the mirror on the wall of her room. "What on earth were you thinking of?" she said to herself, "Acting like some silly teenager. It's undignified. Improper. For Heaven's sake, woman, he'll think you are nothing but a tart!"

In truth, she couldn't be entirely sure whether *she* had kissed Mr Stickleton or whether *he* had kissed her. It had happened all at once, impetuously, without thinking, as though it had been inevitable. Fated. As though it had been completely and utterly *right*.

By lunchtime, she came to the conclusion that she was being foolish to stay in her room. There were still more than two weeks left of the cruise. She couldn't avoid him all that time. And she most certainly couldn't stay cooped up in her room.

So she brushed her hair, put on a sensible beige skirt and jacket and made her way to lunch. The Dandelion Diner didn't serve breakfast or lunch so Mrs Chivers had continued to eat those meals in the main dining room and Mr Stickleton had usually joined her. When she arrived, Mr Stickleton was already sitting at their regular table. She walked across. He glanced up at her then turned away to look out of the window.

"Oh, God!" Mrs Chivers thought, "He can't even bear to look at me."

"Shall I sit down?" she asked timidly.

He glanced at her, "Of course," then he immediately glanced away again.

"Mr Stickleton," she said.

"Yes?"

"I missed having breakfast with you."

"I'm so sorry," he said, turning to her again, "I couldn't face breakfast."

"You? You mean to say you didn't come to breakfast?"

"No. Well, isn't that what you just said?"

"No," she couldn't help but laugh, "What I meant was that *I* didn't come to breakfast. So you are saying that didn't come either?"

"No."

"Why ever not?"

"I thought you might not want to see me. After last night. I was such an idiot. I should never have… forced myself upon you."

She really laughed now. A full throated howl of a laugh. She laughed so much that she ended up choking and had to take several long sips of water to get herself under control again.

"I thought *I'd* forced myself upon *you*!" she said, and she began laughing all over again.

"You?" Mr Stickleton seemed to be seeing the funny side of it now and he too began laughing, "No, of course not. It was all my fault really. Because, you see, I…"

"What?"

"You see, I…"

"What?"

"Well, I…"

"For God's sake, man. Get to the end of the sentence, can't you? I'll be dead of old age if you don't hurry up."

"Well, you see, my dear Mrs Chivers. I do believe I love you."

She stared at him. Her mouth dropped open. She closed it. It was no good – it dropped open all over again. Mr Stickleton turned away, blushing slightly, to look out of the window.

Mrs Chivers took another long drink of water.

"Well, Mr Stickleton," she said at last, "The truth of the matter is, I think I reciprocate."

"I beg your pardon?"

"What I mean to say is that I do believe I may, er, you know, as it were, well, love you too."

Seconds later, Mr Stickleton snapped his fingers at a passing waiter and ordered a bottle of Champagne.

"Then I think," he said gently, holding Mrs Chivers's hands, "that it may be time that we started to use one another's first names on a, as it were, more regular basis. Don't you think so, Rosemary?"

"I certainly do think so, Horatio."

"Vincent," he said.

"I beg your pardon, I thought you said your name was…"

"What?"

"…that you were named after Horatio Hornblower."

"Ah yes. But my middle name is Vincent. To be frank with you, that is the name by which I prefer to be known."

Suddenly there was a raucous screech from just behind Mrs Chivers's left ear: "Ooo, lovely bubbly! Must be a celebration!" It was the awful Mrs Dobson. That was the principal peril of eating in the main dining room. The Dobsons had a tendency to occupy an adjoining table and shriek at Mrs Chivers throughout the meal.

"Champers, 'ey? Let me guess," said Mr Dobson, "Wedding anniversary!"

Good Lord! Mrs Chivers thought, *They think we're married!*

"Nothing quite so celebratory, I fear," replied Mr Stickleton, gloomily, "We are commemorating the death of Johann Bernoulli."

Mr Dobson smiled uncertainly.

"The singer!" Mrs Dobson explained, for the benefit of her husband, "You know, the one that sang that song for the World Cup."

"The mathematician," Mr Stickleton corrected, "You are perhaps familiar with his work on the calculus of infinitesimals?"

"Oh, dead is, he?" said Mr Dobson, "Shame."

"'Ere, Alfie, where the hell did you get that carving knife?" Mrs Dobson had suddenly turned her attention to her loathsome child, "Put it down this instant you brat or I swear I'll swing for you!"

Mrs Chivers smiled. Even the dreadful Dobsons didn't seem quite so bad when she was with Mr Stickleton – or, rather, Vincent. The name suited him better than Horatio. Yes, she decided, Vincent suited him very well indeed.

*

From that moment on, the cruise had been perfect. Mrs Chivers – Rosemary – had never for one moment thought there could be another man in her life after Frank had died. Mr Stickleton – Vincent – told her that he had felt the same: after his beloved Elsa had passed on, eleven years earlier, he had assumed that his would, from that time on, be a solitary existence. And now, here they were, behaving like two teenagers who'd never known love before.

In the days that followed, they spent time getting to know one another better. Vincent told Rosemary about his eventful life. He had worked for the Foreign Office, living for some years in west Africa, then in the Philippines and Indonesia. It all sounded terribly exotic. He had one child, a son, and a granddaughter. Rosemary, by contrast, had barely done anything worth mentioning. She'd lived in a quiet little village and taught in a quiet little school. Since retiring, she'd tended to her garden, read lots of books and done lots of knitting. Her experience of the world was sorely limited. She had rarely been out of her native Suffolk until embarking upon this "once-in-a-lifetime" cruise. Vincent laughed at that – "Once in a lifetime, be damned!" he said, "If something's worth doing, it's worth doing repeatedly."

So they started planning for their future. Even at their mature years, there really could be a future to look forward too. A future together. Vincent had a small cottage in Dorset, he said, quite near to the sea – "I say small but it's got five bedrooms and sits in forty acres of land." Rosemary gasped. "Too big for an old fellow like me, really. But perhaps with a woman's touch…?"

Yes, Rosemary concluded, there really was a future for her after all. A wonderful, happy, carefree future.

Little did she know what was coming. The world was about to change. There would be no carefree future for Rosemary. Or for anyone else.

*

"Attention. Attention, please. This is the captain speaking."

That was odd, Rosemary thought. The captain never said "Attention" in his announcements. In fact, as a general rule, he didn't say very much at all. Every so often he'd tell you something about latitudes and longitudes and the names of islands that you were passing, but he never said "Attention." He just said, "Hello" or "A very good afternoon, ladies and gentlemen."

This was obviously something special. She put down the magazine she had been reading while lying on the bed in her room. For a panicky second, she recalled the films she'd seen which had been set on cruise ships. There was invariably a murder or a collision or some other kind of disaster.

"We have received a weather report," the captain said, "indicating heavy falls of snow in Britain and the Continent. If this continues, it is possible that when we arrive at Southampton, passengers may experience delays in travelling to their final destinations. If you require assistance in booking hotels in Southampton or if you need to make other travel arrangements upon arrival, my crew will be happy to provide you with all possible assistance. The situation in Southampton at present indicates heavy snowfall but this may, of course, change by the time of our arrival. I shall update you further when I have more news."

She breathed a sigh of relief. Snow! Is that all? Well, she didn't care much for snow but really she didn't think it was worth a special announcement.

Rosemary looked at the date on her bedside clock: January 13th. They weren't due to dock at Southampton for another three days. Maybe the snow would have melted by then. At least, the authorities would surely have cleared the roads. And the trains would be running, wouldn't they?

"Did you hear the announcement?" she asked Vincent later on, as they sat on one of the observation decks watching the choppy grey sea.

"Yes. He's not the chattiest of captains as a rule. Odd that a damn' weather report merits his personal consideration, don't you think?"

Rosemary was knitting a scarf for her brother's daughter, Claire, but she couldn't concentrate. "Yes, it does seem odd. Oh, I can hardly face getting back to all that cold, can you? I don't like winter at the best of times. But after all the sunshine we had in the Caribbean, I'm afraid I may freeze to death."

Vincent patted her hand – "Don't worry about that, my dear. I'm sure I shall find some way to keep you warm."

*

Rosemary went back to her cabin and turned on the TV. She'd barely watched television at all since boarding the ship. She was curious to find out more about the weather in Britain.

The news was full of depressing world events: wars in Africa, bombs going off in the Middle East, riots in France. She smiled. The news these days seemed to be much the same every day of the year. When they showed some videos of the riots in Paris, the thing Rosemary noticed most was the snow. It looked more like Alaska than France. "Why would people want to go rioting in that weather?" she wondered. Not that she understood why people would want to go rioting in any weather. But if they were absolutely determined to have a riot, at least you'd think they'd have the sense to do it when the sun was shining!

She glanced through the porthole of her cabin. Other than the pipes outside the window, there was nothing much to see. Just darkness. But wait a minute, there *was* something. Illuminated by the light from her room, a few small, sleety snowflakes were falling. Rosemary's heart sank. They were drawing near to the end of the cruise. The reality of a bleak British winter filled her with dread.

*

When she woke up next morning, Rosemary looked out of the window and saw – nothing. Not the sea, not the sky, not even the pipes that usually obscured her view. The glass of her window was nothing but a circle of pure white. At first, she couldn't figure out where everything had gone. It was only when she looked more closely that she realised that the circle of whiteness covering the window was made of tiny crystals – snow!

"Just our luck!" she told Vincent over breakfast, "One day away from home and it's snowing."

"I shouldn't worry," he replied, "You know what snow's like. In Britain anyway. Here today, gone tomorrow. Quite a different matter in Iceland, of course. Did I ever tell you about the time I was in Reykjavik when a walrus appeared, waddling down the road? Well, they say the Icelandic Walrus is extinct but here was one coming right towards me and it didn't look happy…."

Once Vincent started off on his anecdotes, there was no stopping him. Rosemary nibbled at her toast and marmalade and struggled not to spit crumbs over the table-top whenever she laughed, as she invariably did, at his increasingly absurd yarns. Even though the snow was now whipping past the windows, she was no longer concerned. She had embarked upon this cruise alone and lonely. She was returning with a companion, someone whom she might even love, and (she sighed when she thought of it!) with whom she might live for the rest of her life. What did a little bit of bad weather matter?

On the way of out the dining room, they bumped into the Dobsons who were on their way in. Mr Dobson was wearing a multi-coloured Hawaiian shirt. Mrs Dobson had a straw sombrero on her head. Their son Alfie was wearing shorts and sandals. Rosemary was on the verge of asking if they had been expecting better weather but she didn't have a chance to get the question out because Mrs Dobson was already babbling away like a fool – "You seen the state of the snow? We been watching it on the telly. The whole of Britain's practically ground to a halt. Surrey's had the worst of it, I heard. And Scotland's totally cut off."

"No loss!" said Mr Dobson and guffawed, then had second thoughts and added, "You two ain't Scottish, are you?"

Rosemary and Vincent assured him they were not but by that time Mrs Dobson was already chattering away again – "I heard they've sent the Army into London. There's loads of power cuts, apparently. Mind you, it's the old age pensioners I feel sorry for. They'll be dropping like flies, I expect."

"'Ere!" said Alfie, looking Rosemary hard in the eye, "How old is you two?"

"Old enough," Vincent replied, "not to care if we accidentally push small, malodorous children overboard."

*

Vincent tried to persuade Rosemary to go outside with him onto the Oceanview Boardwalk in order to get a better look at the snow. She laughed at the suggestion. She could see the snow well enough from indoors where it was dry and warm. Why would she want to go outside to see it?

"Because it may be the only chance you'll ever have," Vincent replied, "to see snow on a cruise ship."

For a man of his mature years and dignified bearing, there was something rather childlike about Vincent. "You just want to play snowballs, don't you?" she teased him.

He raised an eyebrow. "Well, now that you've suggested it, I have to say the possibility does have some appeal."

Rosemary insisted on getting changed into more suitable clothing before venturing out of doors. She went to her cabin and put on an overcoat, a scarf, a woolly hat and some sensible, sheepskin-lined boots. This was what she called her "England outfit". It's what she had worn on the journey to Southampton at the start of the cruise and it's what she planned to wear once she stepped foot again on British soil.

She had arranged to meet Vincent in the Pool Bar on the top deck. He was dressed magnificently in tweed jacket and corduroy trousers beneath a heavy greatcoat that had a short cape attached. He called it his Inverness. Rosemary thought it made him look like a character from Sherlock Holmes.

The Pool Bar was enclosed in a large, glass-topped enclosure, rather like one of the smaller hot houses in Kew Gardens. There was a swimming pool and a drinks bar and, one level above those, there was a balcony. It was on the balcony that Rosemary and Vincent were standing. They walked towards the glass-paned doors which slid open as they approached. Immediately, a gust of freezing air blew into the warm humidity of the Pool Bar. Rosemary drew her coat more tightly about her and, with a degree of reluctance, stepped out onto the Boardwalk, the doors sliding silently shut behind them.

It was a surreal sight. Not only was the deck covered in snow but so too were the sun loungers. Two parallel lines of the reclining loungers faced one another, frostily deserted in the cold morning air. They were already covered by a good two inches of snow. It was hard to believe that only a few days earlier passengers had been sunbathing on them. There were numerous footprints in the snow, showing that Rosemary and Vincent hadn't been the first people bold or foolish enough to venture beyond the warm interior of the ship. Indeed, at the other end of the Boardwalk they could see a group of youngsters throwing snowballs at one another.

Rosemary thought she saw a glint in Vincent's eye. "No!" she said, "Don't you dare even think about it!" Her breath plumed in the air when she spoke. The snow was still falling and the wind was lashing it into her face. She shivered. She'd loved the snow when she was a child. She was no longer so fond of it. "Come on," she said, "Let's get back inside."

They had only been outside for a few seconds. Later, after it was all over, Rosemary wondered if that was what had saved them.

*

There was a bit of excitement during lunch that day. An elderly gentleman sitting two tables distant from Vincent and Rosemary, suddenly had a terrible nosebleed. A waiter came to help him but the man had managed to staunch the blood with a handkerchief and so the waiter went away. Then, ten minutes or so later, the man suddenly had a coughing fit.

At the next table, the Dobson family was thoroughly enjoying it all. Little Alfie Dobson was so fascinated that he even put aside his mobile phone in order to concentrate better on the spectacle. It was

Alfie who first noticed the blood spray. "Look, dad!" he screeched, "That man's coughing blood all over the place!"

Rosemary and Vincent turned to see what was wrong. Alfie was quite correct. The man was coughing violently and when he did so a fine mist of blood droplets issued from his mouth. The white cloth on his table was already stained pink as a consequence. Vincent leapt to his feet and went over to the man. He spoke quietly to him and the man mumbled something in reply. Then Vincent snapped his fingers and summoned a waiter. Then another waiter came over. Soon an officer in a white uniform appeared and took charge of the situation. Between them, the officer and the waiters helped the man out of the dining room while other members of staff quickly removed the soiled tablecloth and disinfected the table top.

"Bet he's gonna die," Alfie shouted happily. He had been using his phone to take a video of the sick man.

"So are we all going to die," Vincent said, "Some sooner than others unless they learn good manners."

By mid-afternoon, rumours had started circulating that some sort of sickness was spreading through the ship. Vincent and Rosemary spent the afternoon wandering around, gazing out at the densely falling snow. Many of the younger people thought it was enormous fun. They were out on the decks larking about, building snowmen, throwing snowballs. Rosemary's brief venture onto the Boardwalk had more than sated any small interest she might have had in the snow and she was resolved to stay in the warm interior of the ship henceforth.

"Terrible stomach ache…" – she was vaguely aware of a man and a woman walking down the corridor behind her.

"It's probably something you've eaten," the woman was saying.

"There's a rumour there's a bug going around," the man replied, "The doctor had to be called for the woman in the stateroom next to mine."

Later on, as Rosemary and Vincent were taking afternoon tea in the Bahama Buffet, she overheard a woman at another table saying, "…just dropped to the ground she did. Blood everywhere."

"Oh my God!" another woman replied, "I've heard there's a disease doing the rounds. One of those tropical ones, I suppose. Someone probably picked it up in Trinidad or Barbados."

"Then we'll all get it, I suppose."

"Why do you say that?"

"Stands to reason, doesn't it – one gets it, we all get it. Air conditioning, you see."

*

That evening, Vincent took Rosemary to the theatre. She hadn't been to the theatre in more than twenty years. Rosemary had assumed that the theatre would be a small one. She was wrong. As with everything on the ship, it was gigantic – a huge amphitheatre containing row upon row of red-plush upholstered seats; and, above those, two more tiers of balcony seats.

The show itself was breath-taking. There were dancers and singers and an orchestra. The costumes were marvellous, the lighting was spectacular. She doubted if you'd see anything better in the West End of London. She didn't much care for the music which was mainly songs from popular musicals, but even so she had a wonderful time, made all the better by Vincent's company. When the show ended, they went to 'Le Fizz' Cocktail Lounge on Deck 7 and drank Champagne which made Rosemary get quite giggly.

After leaving the Cocktail Lounge, she and Vincent went their own ways. Vincent offered to accompany Rosemary to her cabin on Deck 5 but she declined his offer. The truth is, she was afraid that he might want to come into her cabin for a small nightcap; and that really wouldn't have done at all. Someone might have seen him enter and Rosemary did not want to get what she thought of as "a reputation."

As she exited the lift on Deck 5, she was nearly knocked over by someone running past. Then she saw some more people running along the corridor. They were yelling and laughing like maniacs. Literally screaming at the top of their voices. Rosemary pressed herself against a wall in order to avoid them. They gave every appearance of being oblivious of her presence. They were totally out of control. Some of them were holding bottles of beer or wine. One young woman was almost completely naked.

"Teenagers," Rosemary muttered to herself, "No respect for other people these days."

It was odd though. She'd been on the ship for over a month now and she'd never seen such rowdy behaviour before. She knew there were discos in the evenings and no doubt some of the youngsters had a bit too much to drink sometimes. But Deck 5 had always been a haven of tranquillity. Rosemary couldn't work out what had got into them!

Once back in her cabin, Rosemary switched on the television with the sound turned down low while she sat on the edge of the bed and took off her shoes. The TV was showing yet another news report about riots. In France, she supposed. On the screen she saw gangs of people fighting and looting and generally behaving abominably. Everywhere there was deep snow, much of it churned to slush due to all the people cavorting about in it.

She tutted to herself, "That's the French for you!"

She took off her earrings and put them into the jewellery box on her dressing table. She was about to take a shower when something on the television caught her eye. The camera was panning over a huge, surging crowd when it happened to show a familiar landmark in the background. Nelson's Column. Which meant that the rioting she'd been watching wasn't in France at all. It was in London.

Why were people rioting in London? She turned up the volume of the TV. The newsreader in the studio was talking: "…there has also been rioting in Birmingham, Leeds, Manchester and several other towns. As we came on air, Downing Street announced that the Prime Minister will chair a meeting of the emergency COBRA committee this evening and he is expected to make a statement at around ten o'clock tonight.

"And now back to our main story. The health crisis afflicting Britain's elderly population has taken a turn for the worse tonight as it's been revealed that…"

Rosemary pressed the Off button on the remote control. After such a wonderful cruise, the last thing she wanted to hear was bad news from back home. She'd find out about that soon enough. For the time being, she wanted her final couple of days on board to be cocooned from all the troubles of the world beyond.

*

Rosemary was awakened by a loud thumping noise. Blearily, she opened her eyes and gazed around her cabin. There was not much to see apart from the digital readout of her bedside clock. It said: 05:32. Far too early to get up. She closed her eyes, turned over, snuggled up to her pillow and wriggled down under the blankets.

Thump! Thump! Thump! There it was again. She squirmed above the blankets and listened. Someone was whispering her name. She turned on the bedside lamp. Then she checked the clock again: 05:33.

Thump! Thump! Thump! The thumps were quieter this time. Not much more than light taps, really. She got out of bed and put on her slippers. She went over to her cabin door and put her ear against it. "Rosemary," – there was that whisper again, "Let me in." It was Vincent.

Let him into her cabin at half past five in the morning! What on earth was he thinking of?

"Vincent," she whispered back, "Do you know what time it is?"

"Please, Rosemary," he whispered, "let me in. It's important."

She hesitated a moment, her hand hovering uncertainly over the door handle.

"Rosemary, please."

She opened the door and peeked through the gap. Vincent was wearing his Inverness cape and a big black hat. At any other time, Rosemary might have complimented him on his elegance. At that moment, she thought he was behaving very oddly and was about to give him a piece of her mind.

"Really," she said, "I can't think what on earth…"

She didn't have a chance to finish the sentence. Vincent pushed her door open, strode into her cabin and locked the door behind him.

"It's like a battlefield out there!" he said.

Rosemary smiled. She was still annoyed with Vincent for waking her so early and she wasn't too pleased about having him barge into her room either. But his absurd sense of the dramatic never failed to amuse her.

"Have you been drinking?" she asked, suspiciously.

"Drinking?" he replied, as though the concept was new to him, "Certainly not! I've been too busy trying to escape."

"Oh, really, Vincent! Is this another of your anecdotes? Like the Walrus and the Great Dane?"

"Rosemary, you must listen to me. This is not a game, you know. This is a matter of life and death!"

It suddenly occurred to her that she was wearing her nightdress which was a totally inappropriate garment when locked in a bedroom with a man. "Go into the shower room," she said.

"What?"

"The shower room." She remembered that Vincent occupied a more luxurious room which, no doubt, had a proper bathroom. "I prefer a shower to a bath," she added by way of explanation, "when I'm on holiday. It's through the door on your left."

"Why do you want me in the shower room?"

"I need to put some clothes on."

"Oh. Ah. Yes, quite."

"Whatever you want to say to me can be said while you are in there."

Vincent went into the little shower room and spoke through the gap in the door. He told Rosemary that he'd been woken by sounds of a scuffle outside his room. When he'd gone to see what was happening he'd found half a dozen people fighting in the corridor.

"Drunken passengers?" Rosemary asked.

"Maybe some of them were," Vincent said, "But two of them were employees of the ship. Stewards, I think."

"You should report them."

"That would do no good, I fear. I waited until everything was quiet. Then I got dressed and went outside."

"They'd gone somewhere else by that time?"

"All but one of the stewards. He was lying on the ground."

"Hurt?"

"Dead."

Rosemary laughed.

"What's funny about that?"

"You're pulling my leg, aren't you? This is one of your stories."

"No!"

"All right. You can come out now."

"You don't seem concerned that someone was killed outside my room."

"Pah! If I believed every tale you told me…"

Rosemary was interrupted by three penetrating electronic beeping sounds. She put her hands over her ears.

"What on earth was…?"

Then a familiar voice came through the speakers – "Ladies and gentleman, this is the captain. We have had a few problems on decks 9, 10, 13 and 15 involving fighting among some guests. Security staff are present on all decks and are taking appropriate action. Please do not leave your cabins and staterooms. I repeat, please do not leave your cabins and staterooms until this problem has been fully resolved. I thank you for your understanding. I shall update you on the situation shortly."

Rosemary stared blankly at Vincent. "Someone was really…?"

"Killed, yes," he confirmed.

"Outside your room?"

"Right outside."

Rosemary felt unsteady on her feet. She sank back onto the edge of the bed and sat there staring. After a few moments, she said, "There's a half bottle of whisky in the minibar. Would you care for a small glass?"

"I would care for one very much indeed," said Vincent.

*

Ten minutes later, the captain made another announcement: "I would like to update you on the situation which I mentioned in my last announcement. I can assure guests that the disruption on decks 9, 10, 13 and 15 is being actively and effectively dealt with. The ship remains safe and secure. I would, however, ask guests to please remain in your rooms. Until further notice, we shall be operating room service for all meals. Menu cards for breakfast, lunch and dinner are provided to allow you to choose your meals. If you wish to order breakfast, please place your completed card outside your stateroom by seven o'clock this morning. If you only wish to order lunch or dinner, please have your card ready by ten o'clock at the latest. Thank you for your patience and cooperation. As the situation evolves, I shall, of course provide you with more information."

Rosemary was stunned. "They want us to stay in our rooms all day?"

"Until further notice, at any rate. That's what he said."

"I can't stay here all day!" Rosemary protested, "There's nothing to do. There's nothing to see."

"You have a porthole," Vincent pointed out.

"There's a pipe outside it. They gave me a small discount because of it."

"At least, we are together."

"Well, I certainly can't stay all day here with you. People will talk."

"They won't know. They'll all be locked inside their own cabins."

"The ship's staff will talk. The people who bring us our food will talk. My room steward will talk. Before you know it, the entire ship will be saying that I've been entertaining you in my room."

Vincent smiled indulgently, "I rather doubt if our celebrity is sufficient to cause much gossip."

But Rosemary was adamant. "No, no, it really won't do. You'll have to go back to your own cabin."

"I can't! It could be dangerous out there."

"The captain didn't mention any fighting on Deck 14."

"What?"

"Your room is on Deck 14, isn't it? That's what you told me."

"Yes. Yes, of course."

"Well, the captain only mentioned decks 9, 10, 13 and 15. You could get the lift to Deck 14."

"But that's right between decks 13 and 15!"

Rosemary was silent for a moment. Then she said, "Odd that he didn't mention Deck 14, since the fight was outside your room. Especially if, as you say, a member of staff was…"

"Probably didn't want to cause panic."

"Does that seem probable?"

"Oh, yes. There are all sorts of protocols, you know, that they are obliged to follow in these circumstances."

"No," Rosemary was quite resolved, "I don't believe that. If the captain said there is no fighting on Deck 14 then there is no fighting on Deck 14. For goodness sake, Vincent, the captain wouldn't lie to us. You really must return to your room."

"Oh, but it's so stuffy there. I'll have nothing to do but stare at the walls."

"Nonsense. You have a balcony stateroom. You could sit outside if you wanted to."

"In this snow!"

"In your Inverness overcoat, you could."

"It's called a cape. An Inverness cape."

"Indeed, since your cabin is so much more commodious than mine, it may be altogether for the best if I were to come there with you."

"You can't do that!"

"Why ever not?"

"It would case a scandal."

"Poppycock! Since you've visited my cabin, I think it's only right that I visit yours. Come on, we may as well go now before the security people try to stop us."

"I wouldn't advise is. We don't know what the situation is out there."

"Oh, don't be such a sissy! I'm prepared to risk it if you are."

"Ah, well, there is one more slight problem."

"Yes?"

"Well, you see, my room. How can I put this? I may have given you a slightly inaccurate impression. Regarding, that is, the, er, balcony."

"What's wrong with the balcony?"

"There isn't one. In fact, to be perfectly honest, there isn't even a window."

"What manner of tall tale are you concocting now? Don't tell me you are living in a broom cupboard!"

"I may as well be. I have an inside room on Deck 9 rather than, as I may inadvertently have given you to believe…"

"A balcony room on Deck 14!"

"Quite."

Rosemary stared at him wide-eyed. Then her body began to tremble. Then it began to shake.

"Oh dear," said Vincent, "I do hope you are not angry."

She shook her head and her body increased its frequency of oscillation.

"You're not going to cry, are you?"

It was then that Rosemary could hold it in no longer. With a great snorting whoop, she let out a braying laugh. Having begun to laugh, she continued laughing. Her laughter took all of four minutes to subside, by which time she had formulated a plan.

*

"You know, I really don't think we should be doing this," Vincent whispered.

"Why ever not?"

"It's probably illegal."

Rosemary dismissed Vincent with a wave of a hand – "We're paying customers. And, as the saying goes, the customer is always right."

They were walking down the port-side corridor of Deck 5 towards the rear of the ship. Apart from themselves, there was nobody in sight. There were locked cabin doors to their left and locked cabin doors to their right. They had a clear view ahead for only about thirty feet. At that point the passage made a sharp turn to the right. They walked slowly, making as little noise as possible, which wasn't difficult thanks to the plush carpeting.

Rosemary had always hated being told what to do. Being told to stay in her room had immediately made her determined to leave it. There was something very suspicious about all the fighting on the various decks. Fights didn't suddenly break out in multiple random places. That made no sense. And why decks 9 and 10, 13 and 15 but not decks 5, 6, 7, 8, 11, 12, 14 and all the rest?

"You appear to be acting like an amateur sleuth," Vincent whispered.

Rosemary took this as a compliment. "Perhaps that is better than acting as an amateur prisoner which is what the captain was suggesting."

They arrived at the dogleg bend in the corridor. They stopped. Rosemary moved towards the corner and peered around it cautiously.

"Anyone there?" Vincent whispered.

"Nobody who will trouble us."

They went around the corner. A body lay on the floor. Blood was still flowing from the place where the head had once been; the plush carpet all around was sticky with it.

"I think," said Rosemary, "that our dear captain may have understated the severity of our problems."

Vincent grimaced. Two dead bodies in one morning was more than enough for his sensitive stomach. He had a prescient feeling that this might not be the last dead body he'd encounter before the morning was through.

"Who is it?" Vincent asked, "Anyone we know?"

"Could be the American lady from cabin 5073. But in the absence of the head, it's hard to know for sure."

"I wonder where the head is?" Vincent said.

"More to the point," said Rosemary, "I wonder where the ship's security are? I seem to recall the captain assuring us that his security team were present on all decks, taking control of the situation."

"Cooee!"

"What?" – Rosemary turned around sharply. The voice that had Cooeed had definitely not been Vincent's.

"Oh, my God! What are *you* doing here?"

"We heard voices," – it was Mrs Dobson. Probably the last person that Rosemary wanted anywhere near her at a time of crisis, "In the corridor. Whispering. So we came to see who it was and, who should it be but you!"

"But Mrs Dobson…"

"Call me Margie."

"Margie. You should stay in your cabin. Didn't you hear the captain's announcement?"

Margie giggled – "Oh yeah, we heard it. So did *you*, I expect!"

Margie's husband, Bill, was there too, sheltering, it appeared, behind his wife. He was holding a baseball bat.

"What's that?" Vincent asked.

"A baseball bat," Bill Dobson replied.

As this didn't seem an adequate explanation, Vincent added a supplementary question, "Why are you holding it?"

"It's Alfie's," Margie said. This didn't seem like an adequate explanation either but before Vincent had the opportunity to pursue the matter further, he was interrupted by Rosemary – "Well, you can't come with us."

"Why not?" Margie said.

"Because where we are going is…well, it's dangerous."

"Where are you going?"

"Well, we are going to… well, the fact of the matter is, I can't divulge our destination."

"Why not?"

"You'd follow us."

"We'll follow you anyway," said Margie.

The logic of this argument was inescapable.

"Ugh! What's that?" Margie added, having only then noticed the headless body on the floor.

"It is a headless body," Vincent said, since stating the obvious seemed reasonable in the circumstances.

Margie winced as though headless bodies in cruise ship corridors were, to her, as distasteful as cockroaches in takeaway curries. "What's it doing there?"

"Currently," said Vincent, "not a great deal."

Bill Dobson was staring, wide-eyed, at the decapitated corpse. His face was pale with a slight green tinge. If they didn't get away from there pretty damn' quickly, Rosemary feared that Bill might faint. "Come along!" she snapped, "No time to be dawdling!"

Skirting the headless body, they continued to move along the corridor. A few yards away stood a lift. By the lift there was a sort of crossroads of corridors formed by a passageway that connected the port and starboard sides. Rosemary glanced down this passageway to make sure there was nobody hiding there. Then she sprinted past the lift, continuing down the port corridor in the sternward direction. There was another dogleg in the corridor up ahead. They moved cautiously past this with Rosemary still taking the lead.

"Shouldn't we report it to someone?" Margie Dobson asked.

"Report what?" said Rosemary.

"The body. The one without a head."

"If you can find someone to report it to, by all means do so. But as far as I can see, members of the ship's crew are noticeable by their absence."

Just then someone appeared in the corridor ahead of them. It was a member of the crew. He was wearing a white uniform with epaulettes decorated with a reassuring quantity of gold embroidery which meant that he was an officer of some sort. Rosemary had never worked out which officer was which and what their responsibilities were. All she knew for sure was that a white uniform with gold-embroidered epaulettes meant that this was somebody in charge of something.

The officer was now standing with his back flat against the left-hand wall. He was peering around the corner into the hidden stretch of corridor from which he had just emerged. He gave the impression that he had seen something that he didn't much like. In the next moment he was running flat out towards Rosemary, Vincent and the Dobsons. As he sped past, he called out, "Good morning, ladies and gentlemen..." Then he disappeared down another corridor and that was the last they saw of him.

"Extraordinary behaviour," Vincent commented.

"I wonder what he was running away from?" Margie said.

This mystery was soon solved. There were noises coming from the stretch of corridor just beyond the dogleg corner where they had first seen the officer. In that direction lay the Atrium. There was a loud bang, like an explosion. Then a scream. Then there was the sound of – well, it was hard to be sure, but it sounded very like a pack of wolves growling.

In the next moment they found out what the officer had been running away from. A group of shambling, dishevelled youths emerged around the dogleg. The way they were walking seemed somehow inhuman, almost as though they were having to work out how to take each step rather than doing so automatically.

One of them caught sight of Rosemary and her companions and shouted: "Oy! You! We're coming for you!"

"Quick," said Rosemary, "The lift!"

She, Vincent and the Dobsons ran to the nearby lift. Bill Dobson arrived there first and punched the button on the door. By luck, the lift was already waiting there so they immediately bundled themselves in. But where to go next? Where would be safe?

The sound of stumblingly running feet and bestial growling grew in volume as the band of youths drew ever closer. Rosemary punched the button marked 'Deck 8' and the lift doors started to close. Never before had she realised quite how long it takes for the doors of a lift to close. They did so with alarming slowness. Eventually the two doors were within inches of meeting in the middle when suddenly a hand poked itself through the gap. The lift doors stopped moving. They clearly contained some kind of safety mechanism that was activated in just this sort of circumstance. The doors began to open again.

Standing before the lift doors was a young man with long straggly hair, strangely red eyes and a maniacal grin on his face.

"Oh, bother!" said Rosemary with feeling.

"Take that!" said Bill Dobson with even more feeling. As he said it, he swung his baseball bat and struck the long-haired youth squarely upon the centre of the cranium. There was a sickening crunch. Blood trickled down the young man's face. But still he stood there, staring and grinning as though the realisation that he had just been struck by a baseball bat had yet to work its way through to his brain. The lift door was quicker to realise that events had moved on, however: it was closing once again. Just before the two doors finally drew together, the young man slumped to the ground. Then the lift was moving upwards to Deck 8.

"Good shot," Vincent remarked.

"It's left a dent in the bat, unfortunately," Bill Dobson replied, "Our Alfie won't be pleased."

"Ah yes, Alfie," returned Vincent, "Where is the dear child?"

"That's the funny thing," said Margie, "He must have scarpered in the night. Gone wandering around the ship, I suppose. Leastways, he wasn't in his bed when we woke up."

"That's why we came out," Bill added, "We was going to look for him."

The lift doors opened. Facing them was a blank wall in the austere, antiseptic colour-scheme favoured by the interior designers of the ship – which is to say, shiny, black and trimmed with chrome. Deck 8 was one of the 'leisure decks'. There were no cabins here at all. Towards the front of the ship, the facilities on Deck 8 were aimed at fitness fanatics. It had a gym, a spa, a sunroom, a sauna and a yoga studio. The rear part of Deck 8 was reserved for drinkers and eaters. There was a bistro, two bars, a coffee shop and an Asian restaurant.

Rosemary had chosen Deck 8 as their destination for two reasons: first, it was one of the decks that had not, according to the captain, been a scene of violence; and secondly, because they would (she hoped) be less likely to encounter other passengers than on the occupied decks. They turned right, towards the front of the ship. First they passed through an airy circular area containing a shop that sold fine whiskies and brandies. Soothing winter-themed music was playing from wall-speakers. Dean Martin crooned, "Let it snow, let it snow, let it snow…"

They walked past the pedicure salon and into the gym. Everywhere was eerily deserted. Then they heard a metallic clanking, rhythmic and regular: *clank… clank… clank…*

"What the heck is…?" Margie whispered.

Rosemary put a forefinger to her lips and signalled that they should walk onwards. This they did, quietly, ever alert, listing, watching. The gym was huge. There were exercise bikes in ranks, there were free weights, there were rowing machines. The entire left wall was formed by plate glass windows. In the cold winter light they saw a blizzard raging outside. And still there was that *clank… clank… clank…*

"Look, over there." Margie pointed to a weight machine at the far end of the gym. A stack of oblong cast-iron weights were contained within a vertical metal framework. The weights were attached to a woven metal cord which ran up through the framework and over a pulley. At the other end, the cord was attached to a horizontal bar. A man was sitting on a bench beneath the pulley, regularly pulling the bar down with a grunt of effort. As he did so, the cord pulled the stack of weights upwards two feet or so inside the metal framework. Then the man on the bench relaxed his arms and the weights settled back down again. It was the noise of the weights dropping with each repetition of the exercise that was creating that rhythmic *clank… clank… clank…*

Rosemary walked over to the man. He was engrossed in the effort of his exercise, head down, eyes clenched, breathing hard, pulling the weights, releasing them, pulling them, releasing them, *clank, clank, clank…*

"Excuse me," Rosemary said, "I hope you don't mind my disturbing you…"

Margie walked over and interrupted, "I'm looking for my son. He's about this high," (she held her hand to her forehead), "Fifteen, dark hair, I wondered if you might have… Oh!"

The "Oh!" was an instinctive reaction. So was the way she put her hands over her mouth and took a big step backwards. The man had stopped hefting the weights. He looked up. He was breathing hard from the exertion of training. He looked first at Margie, then at Rosemary. He was a man of about twenty, with short blond hair and a powerful physique. He was the sort of man that Margie would have found attractive. But for the eyes. His eyes were filled with blood, they were swollen and ugly and diseased-looking.

"Go away!" the man said.

Margie was all too happy to do as he said. She retreated back to where Vincent and her husband were standing. Rosemary stayed where she was. "What happened?" she asked.

"I don't know," the man said, "All I know is that if you don't go, I will hurt you."

"Hurt us? Why?"

He shook his head. "I don't know. I don't bloody know! I know that I want to hurt people. Just go. Please. Just go!"

He returned to his exercises. It was as though he was trying to channel a violent compulsion into the effort of moving the weights. As though he was trying not to make himself stronger, by building muscle, but weaker through mental and physical exhaustion.

The captain's announcements hadn't been entirely truthful. He had made it sound as though a few random acts of violence had broken out on board. As though this was nothing out of the ordinary. Just a result of high spirits or drunkenness. But there was more to it than that. Death was loose on the ship. Nobody was safe.

Margie was shaking her head in frustration. "How the heck am I going to find my son?" she said.

Rosemary thought to herself: the question is not "how" you'll find your son but "if".

There was a "Bing-bong!" tone from the speakers. An unknown voice said, "Code Bravo. Atrium. Deck 5. Code Bravo. Atrium. Deck 5. Code Bravo. Atrium. Deck 5."

"What does that mean?" Margie asked.

"Oh, it's, er, one of their codes, you know," said Vincent, "They have codes for medical emergencies and fires and passengers overboard and terrorist attacks and collisions with other vessels. They even have a code to summon a cleaner to a vomit incident…"

"So which one is Code Bravo?" Rosemary asked.

"Yes, er, now, that's quite a good question, I think. Trouble is, I can't seem to recall. I think it may be a medical emergency. Or possibly a terrorist incident, or…"

"Yes, well never mind. No doubt we'll find out soon enough."

They backtracked away from the gym, heading towards the rear of the ship. They went past the whisky shop once more (through the speakers Frank Sinatra was singing "Winter Wonderland") and into a lounge with windows offering a clear view of the mayhem on the outside deck, three storeys below. The deck was filled with people sliding in the slushy snow, pushing and shoving one another, throwing snowballs. At one end of the deck, the snow was bright red. Rosemary stared with horror at a pile of bodies lying there, disfigured and mutilated. "Oh my God," muttered Margie. She was starting to panic – "Where's Alfie? For God's sake, we have to find Alfie."

There was the sound of gunfire. It was coming from the deck directly above them on level 9, which was an accommodation deck.

"Surely they don't allow guns on board," Bill Dobson said.

"Does the crew have guns?" asked Rosemary.

There was another gunshot.

"We can only hope so," said Vincent.

The penetrating beeps preceding an emergency announcement blared from the speakers: "Ladies and gentlemen, the signal you have just heard was the general emergency signal. This is your captain speaking. May I have you attention, please. For all crew, please report to your emergency positions. For all guests, please report to your muster stations at this time. Do not use the lifts or elevators. I repeat: report to your muster stations at this time Thank you for your cooperation."

Rosemary looked at Vincent. Vincent looked at Bill. Bill looked at Margie. Margie looked at Rosemary. None of them knew how to get to a muster station.

"Where did they send you in the safety drill?" Margie asked.

They had gone through the safety drill on their first afternoon aboard ship. All the passengers had.

"They sent me to the theatre on Deck 7," Vincent said, "which is where the theatre balconies are. But I think they said that in a real emergency we should go to Deck 6 which is where the theatre stalls are. The stalls were being cleaned when we did the drill which is why we couldn't go there. What about you?"

"They sent us to the main dining room," Margie said, "But they said that in a real emergency we should go to the lounge on Deck 7. We couldn't use Deck 7 for the drill because it was in use…"

"By our lot," Vincent interjected, "Queuing up to get into the theatre. And we were only there because Deck 6 was being used by the cleaners."

Vincent looked at Rosemary.

"They sent me to the Atrium on Deck 5," she said.

"But did they tell you where you should go in a real emergency?"

Rosemary nodded, "The Atrium on Deck 5."

"Well, then," said Vincent, "I suggest that's where we go. Let me see, the Atrium is four decks high, which mean that the upper level is here on Deck 8. Which means we'll be able to take the stairs down to Deck 5."

Rosemary didn't seem overjoyed by the suggestion. "Wasn't that where the announcement said there was a Code Bravo incident?"

"Oh yes," said Vincent, smiling, "So it did. Well, it seems we may be about to discover what Code Bravo means after all."

They could smell the smoke long before they got to the Atrium. Looking down from the balcony, they saw the fire burning on the floor of Deck 5, four levels below them. What exactly it was that was being burned they couldn't make out. The smoke smelled of wood and chemicals and fat. There was a group of youths down there smashing just about everything they could lay their hands on and throwing the wreckage into the flames. Two staff members appeared, holding fire extinguishers. One second the staff members were shouting, telling people to get out of the way. The next second they were engulfed by a mass of people swarming over them like a colony of army ants.

"Oh, my God!" Margie cried. Her voice attracted the attention of one of the youths on Deck 5. He glanced up, saw the four people staring down from the balcony on Deck 8, and shouted to his companions, "Follow me, guys!" Within moments, half a dozen youths were running up the staircase towards them.

"What can we do?" Margie shrieked. Deck 8 had no accommodation so there were no rooms to hide in. They couldn't take the stairs to the lower decks or they'd run straight into the youths on their way up. They'd have to go up to a higher deck and hope that the fire didn't take hold and trap them there.

Just a few yards away there was a stairway leading to Deck 9. Vincent led the way. "Quick. I know a place we can go."

People were milling about in confusion. "We're looking for the muster stations," one voice said. "Follow me," said another. "Why, do you know where the muster station is?" asked a third. "No," said the previous voice, "but I'm following someone who does."

Vincent barged through a small gaggle of passengers and ran up the stairway on the outer port side of the ship. Rosemary, Bill and Margie followed. Half way up the staircase, there was a small platform at the mid-point of a zig-zag that allowed the stairs to fit into the narrow stairwell. It was here that they ran into a two people running down. A large, middle-aged woman was struggling with a suitcase while a smaller, middle-aged man was carrying two big holdalls. Encumbered as they were, the man and the woman completely blocked the stairway. The woman gave the impression that this was entirely Vincent's fault: "You shouldn't be here!" she bellowed; "…shouldn't be here," the small man echoed.

"Didn't you hear the captain?" the woman bellowed, "You should be in the muster stations."

"…muster stations," the little man repeated.

Vincent was having none of it. He seized the woman's case, ignoring her bellowed protestations, then seized the little man's holdalls, ignoring his muttered repetitions of the woman's protestations, and he bundled the luggage into a heap on the stairway platform.

"Now, if you would be so good," Vincent said, pushing past the man and the woman. The others pushed past too. Then Vincent turned to the obstructive man and woman and warned them – "I would advise you to return to your room and lock the door. Whatever you do, don't go down those stairs."

The woman ignored him. She picked up her case and she continued on down the stairs. The man picked up his holdalls and followed. Rosemary and her companions were halfway along the port corridor of Deck 9 when the screaming began. It was muffled by distance but there was no mistaking the bellowing tone of one scream and the little echo of a scream that followed it.

"Well," said Vincent, "they can't say I didn't warm them!"

Vincent slipped his key-card into the slot on door 9097 just as they heard the footsteps arriving on the deck from the direction of the stairwell. Fortunately there was a sharp turn in the corridor just between the lift and the cabin area which blocked them from their pursuers' view and gave them just enough time to get inside Vincent's cabin before being seen.

The cabin was small and, with four people crammed inside, a bit claustrophobic. It was dominated by the unmade bed. The cabin layout was similar to Rosemary's cabin apart from the fact that, being on the inside of the ship, there was no window. Vincent looked at the others and put a finger to his lips. They didn't need any encouragement to stay quiet; as long as they did so, their pursuers wouldn't know which room they were in – or so they hoped.

Bang! There was the sound of something being struck against a wall. The sound came from the far end of the corridor, near the stairwell. *Bang!* It sounded as though it was something hard, maybe metal, striking against the walls and the doors of cabins; then a man's voice, calling – "Come out, come out wherever you are!"

"Put the lights off," Rosemary whispered.

Vincent did as he was told. He wasn't sure if the cabin lights would show through the narrow gaps around the edges of the door but it wasn't worth taking the risk. In the darkness they felt even more trapped than before. Margie started making little whimpering noises. *Bang! Bang! Bang!* The sound was coming ever closer to their cabin.

"They'll find us," Margie whispered.

"What's wrong with them?" Bill added.

"There's madness in the air," said Vincent, "You've seen the television news, haven't you? Rioting in France, Germany, London. Whatever's causing it, it would appear that the sea is no barrier."

"Shhhhh…" said Rosemary.

In the confining darkness, they huddled together, hardly daring to breathe, listening to the sounds from the corridor outside.

Bang! Bang! Bang!

"There's one in here! I can smell him." That was a man's voice. It was impossible to tell how many people were out in the corridor. Two at least. Maybe more.

"Which one?"

"9121"

"That's Mr Williams's cabin," Vincent murmured, "He's a retired garage-owner. Elderly. Late eighties. From Chelmsford. Nice man."

Then there was an almighty racket: banging, crashing, smashing. The sound of a door being stoved in. "What do you want?" That was Mr Williams's voice, "My money? Take it. Here, take my wallet."

The sound of laughter. High, raucous laughter. Two people laughing. So there were just two of them out there. The other youths who'd originally been with them must have gone off in search of different victims.

"We don't want your money, chummy. We want you!"

"Why? What do you want with me?"

"Never mind the damn' questions. Just get up and…"

Smack!

"What was that?" said Margie, "Did someone hit the old man?"

Vincent flung open the cabin door.

Margie gasped – "What are you doing? They'll see us."

But there was no stopping him. Vincent wrenched the baseball bat from Bill's grasp and strode down the corridor, towards the two thugs. The door closed behind him and Bill immediately put his back against it in case either of the two women had any notions about following the foolish old gent who'd taken his baseball bat.

The next few moments were full of sound and fury. "Get him!" "Watch out!" "Aaaahhhh…." And various other noises indicative of hard objects making forceful contact with less hard objects which, with a bit of imagination, might well have been various parts of human bodies. Then there was silence.

"He's dead," whispered Margie dramatically, "Poor Mr Vincent gave his life for us!"

In the next moment, the door opened a crack. An eyeball peered in at them. It was not an eyeball that they recognised. It was an eyeball with a grey iris overhung by an equally grey, bushy eyebrow.

Bill Dobson jumped back.

"It's all right," said the voice belonging to the eyeball, "I'm quite harmless."

"I can vouch for that," Vincent's voice added, "This is Mr Williams."

Bill opened the door wider.

"You can call me Peter," added the elderly man, "You can call me other things too if you like. Most people do. But Peter is my name."

"What happened?" Rosemary asked.

Vincent shrugged. "An unfortunate disagreement. But it's all over now."

"There was a thump. Just before Vincent left," Rosemary said, "We thought they'd killed you."

"Me?" said Mr Williams in obvious astonishment, "Not bloody likely. I bashed one of them with a bottle of Bombay Sapphire Gin which I happened to have close at hand. That must have been the thump you heard. It was lucky for me that the bottle didn't break."

"I thumped the other one," Vincent added, twirling the baseball bat proudly, "Quite a few times, as a matter of fact."

They all trailed out of the room into the corridor. Five doors down from Vincent's room, there was a scene of devastation. The door to Peter Williams's cabin had been smashed to smithereens. Lying among the wreckage were the bodies of two young men.

"You killed them?" said Margie.

"It had to be done," Vincent replied calmly, "Kill or be killed. That's what they always taught us."

"You were in the Army?" Bill asked.

Vincent shook his head. "The school cricket team. Winchester. We were a bloodthirsty lot. Played to win. I always thought playing cricket was a worthless talent to have. But it taught me how to swing a bat," he threw the baseball bat into the air where it turned through a perfect circle before he caught it again, "Which is a handy skill to have in a tight corner."

Just then one of the bloodied bodies lying on the floor moved. It pushed itself into a sitting position and stared around blearily. Then the other one began to move too.

"Of course," Vincent muttered, "I was always much better as a fielder. I never was a very good batsman. I could have another crack at them, I suppose."

But Bill had already grabbed the baseball bat. "I think you've only made them angry. I'd say the faster we get away from here the better."

Vincent bent down and grabbed two short iron bars that were lying nearby. They appeared to be barbell bars which had been pilfered from the gym. Those were the objects with which the two youths had been banging the walls and doors. "I shall arm myself with this. Here's one for you, Peter."

"Thank you, Vincent. Most considerate."

"I suppose," said Rosemary, "you don't trust us mere women with weapons."

Vincent struggled to find a diplomatic response. He settled for an undiplomatic one: "No."

By now they were all running along the corridor towards the lift.

"The captain said don't take the lift," Margie reminded them. Rosemary ignored her; she pressed a button to summon the lift and they all piled in.

"Up or down?" said Rosemary.

"Down," said Vincent, "We can go to your cabin."

Rosemary pressed the button for Deck 18. "They'll be expecting us to go down. So we'll go up!"

"I am not confident that your reasoning is sound," said Vincent, "However, it appears I have no choice in the matter."

Just as they stepped out onto Deck 18, the emergency signal screeched from the loudspeakers once again, "Ladies and gentlemen, this is the captain. Would you all please return to your staterooms. The Bravo incident which I reported earlier is now under control. There was a small fire in the Atrium which has been extinguished. I repeat, the Bravo incident is now under control."

The captain gave a hesitant little cough before continuing – "However, I'm afraid we have one or two other problems..."

*

They weren't the only passengers who'd migrated to the upper decks. A few dozen people had congregated in the Ocean Splendour restaurant at the front of Deck 18. When Rosemary, Vincent and the Dobsons arrived, all heads turned in unison. A tall, elderly man with a Buffalo Bill moustache was standing next to the door of the restaurant; he was holding a small revolver which, according to the ship's regulations, he should not have brought aboard but which, in the current situation, nobody thought was a particularly egregious infraction. He gave the four new-arrivals a quick inspection and passed them as fit for admission – "Come on in, folks," he said, "Not much to do but the view's fine."

From his drawling accent, it was obvious that the man was American. "Texas?" Bill asked.

"Missouri," drawled the man.

"Near enough," said Bill.

The man with the revolver scowled. His fingers seemed to be twitching slightly. Vincent put his arm around Bill's shoulders and rapidly hustled him away towards the plate glass windows at the front of the restaurant.

They found a table for four and settled themselves in the vacant chairs around it. Margie had barely been sitting for a few seconds before she got up again. She whispered to Bill and tugged at his sleeve. Reluctantly, Bill got up too. The two of them went wandering among the other tables asking the same question at each – "Have you seen a boy, fifteen, about this tall, dark hair?"

Nobody had.

"So," said Rosemary, "is there anything else I should know?"

"In what respect?" Vincent replied.

"About you."

"Me?"

"Like, for example, how much of what you've told me is true?"

Vincent harrumphed, "I would never speak a word of a lie, dear lady."

"Apart from your luxury balcony stateroom on Deck 14, you mean. The one you told me all about with the personal veranda and the en suite Jacuzzi. When, in fact, you have a poky little inside cabin on Deck 9."

"Well, well, I…"

"It turns out your cabin is even cheaper than mine!"

"It was all that was available. Otherwise I should certainly have, um, you know, booked a, er, balcony…"

"I'm guessing the cottage in Dorset with five bedrooms and forty acres may be an exaggeration too?"

Vincent was starting to blush. "Perhaps not quite five bedrooms. No, not quite five. And the acreage, yes, the acreage may have been somewhat overstated. But I do live in Dorset."

"In what? A semi-detached? An end of terrace?"

"A one-bedroom flat."

"My God!" Rosemary exclaimed, "You are incorrigible. I suppose the job with the Foreign Office never existed."

"I worked in an employment exchange."

"And the round-the-world travel?"

"The Isle of Man was the most exotic place I'd been to before this cruise."

"Your deceased wife."

"I never married."

"In fact, there is not a single thing you've told me that bears any resemblance to the truth."

"There is one thing."

"Oh yes? And what may that be?"

Vincent's blush went a shade deeper – "I love you, Rosemary."

"Ha! Pull the other one!"

"But it's true."

"And how do I know that you are not a gigolo? A philanderer? A serial seducer of lonely widows on cruise ships? In short, how do I know that you aren't a conman!"

"You surely can't believe such a thing!"

"To be perfectly frank, Vincent, I no longer know what to believe. Why would you tell me all those tall stories unless you planned to, well, unless you planned to trick me into… into…"

"Into what?"

"Well, I don't know. Whatever it is that conmen trick lonely old widows into doing."

Vincent sighed deeply. "I spent a large part of my admittedly meagre life savings to come on this cruise," he said, "I wasn't sure if it was a waste of money because, after all, I might just as well have stayed at home in my little flat and been lonely as locked myself inside a cruise ship cabin and been lonely. And then I met you! And everything changed. I was smitten."

"Smitten?"

"Completely. I'd go so far as to say it was a case of smitten at first sight. But I realised that a lady such as you could find nothing of interest in a man such as I. I am, to be blunt, rather a boring old codger."

"That," said Rosemary, "you certainly aren't!"

"So I – how can I put it? – I embroidered upon the truth slightly."

"Which is your way of saying that you told me a pack of lies."

"But I say again that the only important thing I told you was, and *is*, absolutely true. I am madly in love with you, my dear."

Vincent took Rosemary's hands in his and gazed deeply into her eyes. Rosemary thought about withdrawing her hands. But she did not. In the next moment, they found themselves drawing closer, ever closer to one another. Rosemary closed her eyes. Vincent puckered his lips…

"Here you go! Two custard slices and a Danish Pastry."

The romantic moment was lost. Margie Dobson was standing there with a plate containing an assortment of brightly coloured and inedible-looking cakes.

"I thought you'd gone searching for your son," Rosemary said tersely.

"Alfie? Oh, he'll turn up, don't you worry. There's a whole load of cakes and stuff over on that counter over there. All going free. Pity to waste them."

That was when the helicopters arrived.

*

There were three of them. At first they looked like grey, ghostly birds vaguely discernible through the swirling snow. As they drew nearer, their shapes became more fully defined – like great, steely robotic dragonflies with powerful swirling blades that whooshed loudly overhead. The ship had a helipad on the nineteenth deck right above the restaurant on Deck 18 and when the first copter came down, the noise was deafening.

From the restaurant it was impossible to see exactly what was happening on the deck above but they presumed that some sort of rescue mission was in progress. The nature of that mission became clearer minutes later when two armed men burst into the restaurant and shouted at them to put their hands on their heads. One of the armed men pointed an assault rifle at the man from Missouri who, quick to get the message, threw his revolver onto the ground. The other armed man picked it up. Then, deciding that the people in the restaurant were not the targets of their mission, they ran towards the stairwells and made for the lower decks.

One by one, two other helicopters arrived, and more armed men passed through the nineteenth deck on their way to the lower levels. They swarmed down the stairways and filtered into the labyrinthine network of corridors and hallways that ran through the body of the ship.

Every so often there was the sound of machinegun fire, clattering harshly in the distance. For the next hour the battle raged. Through the windows of the restaurant they were able to look down upon the boardwalk on the fifth level. It was a scene of total carnage. By the end of hostilities the white of the snow had been stained a deep, repulsive red.

It was over an hour after the arrival of the helicopters that the shrill emergency tones once again sounded through the loudspeakers. Then: "Ladies and gentlemen, this is your captain speaking. I am pleased to tell you that the emergency situation has now been brought under control. I repeat, the emergency situation has now been brought under control. Please stay in your staterooms if you are already there. If not, please return to your staterooms. I thank you for your kind cooperation."

Later, weeks later, after Rosemary had understood the full scale of the catastrophe, she wondered who had sent the helicopters to their ship. And why? Maybe at the start of the great plague, the Government had thought they might be able to contain it. Maybe they thought that, by dealing with isolated outbreaks, it could all be brought under control. Nobody thinks that any longer, of course. But right at the start, people still clung to their sense of optimism.

"Well," said Vincent, "that's it then. The excitement is all over. Quite fun, what!"

Rosemary glared at him.

"What about Alfie?" wailed Margie, "What's happened to my son? They could have shot him!"

Vincent, who didn't appear to be particularly disturbed by this possibility, said, "I am sure the little scamp will be quite all right, my dear. You know what children are. He's probably in the games room or playing on the adventure slide on the top deck."

Margie's face froze in horror – "The top deck! Where the helicopters landed!"

Rosemary gave Vincent a surreptitious but painful dig in the ribs with an elbow.

"Or possibly," Vincent said, "on some other deck."

They made their way back to the staircase then. There were only a few dead bodies lying on the stairs and they were soon back on Deck 5. Rosemary and Vincent accompanied Bill and Margie Dobson to their cabin. Bill held his wife tightly while she snivelled persistently into a soggy Kleenex. He slid his key card into the slot and opened the door. As he did so, Margie let out a squeak of surprise. "Alfie! Oh, Alfie, love!"

There, sitting on the floor of the Dobsons' cabin, was their son. Alfie was staring at something in his hands.

"There," said Rosemary, smiling, "You've found your Alfie. All's well that ends well."

But there was something wrong with Alfie. He was making a low, keening noise, almost like an angry dog. He looked up at his mother and there was no recognition in his eyes.

"What's wrong, love?" – Margie took a step towards her son. She gasped and stepped back again. There was something wrong with Alfie's eyes. They were bright red. His hands were red too. They were covered in blood. The little boy stood and began shufflingly to walk towards his mother. There was something, wild, feral, dangerous in his expression. He dropped the thing that he had been holding. It landed on the floor with a sickening squelch. It was some kind of offal.

"Where did you get that?" Margie said, "Did you get it in the kitchen, Alfie?" But she didn't think he'd got it there. The offal looked too fresh. Suddenly the boy leapt at his mother. In that split second, Margie Dobson slammed the door in her son's face. They could heard the boy scratching and snarling on the other side.

From the far end of the corridor, they saw a soldier approaching, holding an assault rifle as though ready to fire. As the soldier got close to them, he said, "Everything all right here, folks?"

Margie answered almost too quickly – "Yes, fine. Everything's fine here. Really. Couldn't be better."

"You should get into your cabins," the soldier said, "Lock yourselves in. Is there anything in there?" He nodded toward the Dobsons' cabin from which the sound of scratching and growling was clearly audible.

"A marmoset," Bill said.

"A what?"

"It's a furry thing. A pet. With eyes. And a tail. We bought it in Antigua."

The soldier gave him an odd look – "It'll have to be quarantined." And he moved away to the far end of the corridor.

"What are you going to do?" said Rosemary, "About your son, I mean?"

"What do you mean?"

"He appears to be suffering from some kind of, er, mania," Vincent explained, "Perhaps the ship's doctor might be able to…?"

"He's fine!" snapped Margie, "And don't you dare say otherwise."

So Rosemary went back to her cabin and Vincent went with her. In the middle of the night there was another emergency siren. The captain announced: "Mr Mob to forward Oceanview deck." But there were no further announcements after that.

The following day, Rosemary and Vincent met for breakfast in the dining hall. It was still snowing outside. She mentioned the strange emergency announcement in the night and Vincent told her that "Mr Mob" was code for "man overboard" but Rosemary didn't know if Vincent was making that up. She still was unsure how much of what Vincent said was true and how much was pure fabrication.

As usual, Bill and Margie Dobson came to sit at the next table. They didn't seem as chatty as normal. Their son Alfie wasn't with them, Rosemary noticed, but she didn't think it polite to comment on his absence.

"Well," said Rosemary, "this has certainly been an eventful cruise. It will be odd to get back to ordinary, everyday life again."

"Oh, I rather think that our life from now on will far from ordinary," said Vincent.

He was right, of course. Rosemary had no idea quite how extraordinary their lives would be from that day forward. If she had, she might not have looked so happy.

An Awfully Big Adventure

"Enemy sighted!" Tommy whispered, "Up ahead. Just past the Pirate's Oak Tree."

Rosie and Simon were crouching down behind a big clump of yellow-flowered gorse. Tommy was their trail-finder so he had gone ahead and was hiding behind a willow tree close to the edge of the lake.

"Is it safe to come out yet?" Rosie asked.

"No talking in the ranks!" snapped Tommy, "I shall give the All Clear when the enemy, um, goes away."

"Retreats," said Simon.

"What?"

"That's what enemies do. They retreat. When the enemy retreats you must sound the All Clear."

"Well I can't see any enemy," Rosie said, "unless you count that tatty old duck over there."

Rosie stood up, stretched her aching limbs and walked boldly towards Tommy.

"That tatty old duck," said Tommy, "might be a bomb or... or a listening device or something. Besides which, look at all those reeds on the other side of the lake. There might be enemy combatants hidden in them. They hide underwater and breathe through hollowed-out reed stalks."

"Well, we'll just have to take our chances then," Rosie insisted, "because it's time for lunch and I don't intend to let any rotten old enemy contestants..."

"Combatants," Tommy corrected.

"...I don't intend to let them put me off my smoked salmon sandwiches and lemonade."

"You haven't got any smoked salmon sandwiches and lemonade," said Tommy.

"The enemy contestants don't know that though, do they!"

There was no arguing with Rosie. As long as Tommy had known her, she'd been pig-headed. He had first met Rosie at Christmas when mum had come to spend the holidays with Uncle Ernest and Aunty May who were Rosie and Simon's parents. From the very first day, Rosie had bossed Tommy around, telling him where to sit at dinner, what to wear when they went walking, which games they should play and which books he should read. Tommy found it irritating to be bossed around by a girl – especially by a nine-year old girl who was, after all, just a child whereas Tommy was eleven so practically a teenager. Rosie's younger brother Simon was quite different. He was much quieter than Rosie. He was also much brighter. In fact, Simon was also a good deal brighter than Tommy. And that too was irritating since Simon was only eight. Tommy assumed that Simon must be some sort of child prodigy; he seemed to know everything about everything.

"You could have her court martialled," Simon suggested.

"What?"

"Rosie. As the senior officer, you could have her court martialled for insubordination."

Rosie sighed. "The trouble with my little brother," she said, "is that he reads too many books and takes everything far too seriously."

"And that old oak tree," Simon went is, "isn't the Pirate's Oak. It's the Prelate's Oak."

"It is not!" Rosie said, "Everyone calls it the Pirate's Oak."

"Then everyone is wrong. It was called the Prelate's Oak after a prelate was hanged there in the seventeenth century."

Both Rosie and Tommy were desperate to ask Simon what a prelate was but they said nothing because they didn't want to give him the satisfaction of being able to tell them the answer. Simon's big fault was that he gloated. He especially gloated when he knew things that other people didn't. Since he knew thousands of things that other people didn't, he gloated quite a lot.

Rosie had brought a wicker picnic basket with her. She opened the lid and took out a tablecloth which she spread on a grassy bank by the edge of the lake. The three of them sat on the cloth while Rosie took out the food she had brought. There was a tin of sardines, some digestive biscuits, a tin of peaches and a bottle of water. As she took out a tin-opener and set to work opening the sardines, Simon said, "A prelate is a bishop."

"We know that!" Rosie and Tommy chanted in unison.

"Or sometimes an abbot," Simon added.

"I bet there are pirates in them there waters," Tommy said, after they'd had their lunch and were passing around the water bottle.

"On Hollybush Lake?" said Rosie, "Do you think it's deep enough for a pirate ship?"

"It's deep enough for a small pirate ship," Tommy said.

"You would only need a small ship, well, actually a boat, to bury treasure," Simon added.

"What's the difference between a ship and a boat?" Tommy asked and he immediately wished that he hadn't because Simon then proceeded to enumerate all the differences at long and tedious length while they packed the tablecloth, can-opener, cutlery and empty tins back into the picnic basket. It was probably because they were concentrating so much on the packing and also listening to Simon's boring lecture on ships and boats that they failed to notice the man watching them from the other side of the lake.

*

That evening, when they returned home, they lit a fire. They didn't light the fire to keep warm; the weather was mild. They lit it to cook their dinner. The fire was made from logs piled up in an old-fashioned open grate. Over this, a simple spit had been constructed. The spit had been Simon's idea. It was made of two columns of bricks, one on each side of the grate; an iron bar that had been taken from the garden railings was placed across the columns of bricks so that the middle of the bar was directly over the flames of the fire. Onto the spit was threaded a hefty leg of lamb. As the meat cooked, great gobbets of hot fat dripped onto the logs below, making the fire sputter and spark. From time to time, Tommy turned the spit to make sure that the meat was cooked evenly. The delicious smell of roast lamb permeated the house.

Rosie and Simon stood at the old ceramic sink washing small potatoes, which they'd dug up from the garden, in water that they'd brought back from the lake. When the potatoes were reasonably clean, they put them into a small saucepan containing some more water. When the meat was almost cooked, they put the saucepan onto the glowing wood in the grate and waited until the potatoes were done.

It was well into the evening by the time the food was ready. The table was laid with a green-checked tablecloth on which were three table-mats with knives and forks at the sides.

"For that which we are about to receive, maybe the Lord is truly thankful," Rosie intoned. Then the three of them set to and demolished the meal in just a few minutes.

"Is there a pudding?" Simon asked.

"You know there isn't," said Rosie, "We had the last tin of peaches for lunch. In a month or two there'll be apples on the trees and blackberries on the bushes. We'll have lots of puddings then."

There was a growling and a whimpering noise coming from the cellar directly beneath the kitchen.

"Harvey wants his food," Rosie said. She cut four big slices of lamb from the leg they'd been eating and put them onto a battered metal plate.

"I'll take it down to him," said Tommy.

"And you," Rosie said to Simon, "can help me with the washing up."

*

It was grey and misty the next morning so Simon and Tommy stayed inside, reading books, while Rosie tended to the garden. If only the old rhubarb patch hadn't been so choked with weeds, maybe they'd have been able to have stewed rhubarb for pudding. With the help of a spade and a trowel from the potting shed, Rosie spent half an hour pulling up clumps of grass and docks to give the rhubarb a bit more growing space. When she'd finished, she went to the end of the garden, just past the old compost heap near the orchard, and stood looking at the two mounds, each just over six feet long. There was a third mound too, a few yards away but Rosie didn't bother with that one. Each mound had a little wooden cross projecting from the earth at one end. Rosie put her hands, together, closed her eyes and said "The other night dear, when I was sleeping, I dreamt I held you in my arms. When I awoke dear, I was mistaken so I hung my head and I cried. Amen." It wasn't a proper prayer but she didn't know a proper prayer that was suitable so it would have to do. When Rosie opened her eyes, there were tears in them which may explain why she did not at first notice the man standing in the shade of the apple trees. When she did notice him, she gasped and jumped back a step, then glanced to see if Tommy and Simon were nearby which, of course, they weren't as they were indoors reading books.

"I hope I didn't scare you," said the man.

He had a nice voice, a deep, creamy sort a voice, a bit like her dad's voice had been. Rosie stared at him. He was younger than her dad. Thinner too. He was wearing jeans and brown boots and a white shirt that was only slightly dirty. He had a short black beard and there was a sort of twinkle in his eye that made him look nice and friendly.

"You did startle me a bit," Rosie said.

"Someone important?" The stranger looked towards the two mounds.

Rosie didn't want to talk about that. It was private. Not the sort of thing she wanted to discuss with a complete stranger. She nodded quickly and said, "I've been working in the garden. The rhubarb patch. It hasn't been very good this year."

"Horse muck is what you need," said the main.

Rosie raised her eyebrows – "Poo, you mean?"

The man laughed. He had a warm, cosy, chuckling sort of laugh. "Good fertilizer. That's what rhubarb thrives on. There's plenty of wild ponies roaming the hills. No shortage of rhubarb fertilizer."

"I suppose so," said Rosie, "Well, it was nice talking to you but I have chores to do, so, if you'll excuse me, I'll just…"

"Who's Harvey?" said the man.

Rosie gawped at him. "Harvey?"

"I heard you talking about him."

Rosie gawped again. "About Harvey? When did you…?"

"Last night. I…"

"You were watching us?"

"I happened to be passing. I heard you mention Harvey. I wondered who he might be."

"Not that it's any of your business," snapped Rosie, "but Harvey is, well, he's our dog."

"Ah yes, of course," the stranger smiled, "Funny, though, that I've never seen him outside the house. Do you keep him indoors all the time?"

"Of course not! He goes out at night."

"Ah yes, I see. That was a good joint of lamb you were eating last night. I could smell it in the smoke from your chimney. Where did you get it?"

"Get what?"

"Where did you get a joint of lamb? There are no butchers here. No supermarkets. I doubt if you have a freezer that works. So where did you get the lamb?"

"That's a silly question," said Rosie, "There may be plenty of wild ponies roaming the hills but there are even more wild sheep."

And she turned and walked towards the house without once glancing back to look at the stranger.

*

By nightfall the clouds had vanished from the sky, and the moon, being nearly at the full, illuminated the hills and woodlands that lay around the cottage. At some time close to midnight, the cottage door opened. Had a person happened, at that moment, to be sitting on top of a nearby hillside, that person would have seen a dark silhouette, outlined by moonlight, shambling out of the cottage door. The silhouetted figure would have turned its head this way and that as though scenting odours on the warm night air. And then, having decided on a direction, it would have been observed to go loping away at great speed before being swallowed up into the darkness of the wooded slopes.

*

"I saw Harvey."

Rosie had gone down to the lake with Tommy and Simon. It had been Simon's idea to collect aquatic life. There was an old galvanised metal bath in the garden and Simon was planning to make a pond of it so that he could study and draw its inhabitants. They had each brought jam jars and nets. Simon and Tommy had gone to the northern end of the lake where Simon hoped to find sticklebacks in a small stream. Rosie had stayed in the bay nearest the cottage. She was looking for caddisfly larvae under stones and roots. When she heard the man speaking to her, she didn't even bother to look up. She just carried on poking around in the mud where she thought she'd seen a larva of some sort.

"Last night," the man said, "About midnight. I saw him leaving the cottage."

"Oh."

"He didn't look much like a dog to me."

"Can you move out of the sunlight?" Rosie said, "If they see your shadow they'll dig deeper into the mud before I can get at them."

"Who is he, Rosie?"

Rosie looked up at him. "You know my name then? I suppose you should tell me yours."

"I suppose I should," said the man, "It's Michael."

"Well, Michael," said Rosie, standing upright and trying to look as dignified as she could with her feet stuck into muddy water, "you seem to be taking a lot of interest in us. I don't know why. Nobody's asked you to."

"I thought it would be friendly."

"It seems quite rude, as a matter of fact."

"I could show you how to make bread."

The sudden change of subject took Rosie by surprise. She had been about to say something but now she forgot what it was. What she did say was: "Bread?"

"In the oven," said Michael.

"There's no electricity."

"The oven doesn't need electricity."

"What are you talking about?"

"The fire. Where you roasted the lamb."

"What about it?"

"To the right of the fire, there's a big hole, a deep hole that goes way back into the wall."

"It's where the cat used to live," said Rosie, "Before the cat died."

"It's an oven," Michael said, "An old-fashioned one. You can heat it up with wood. If you know how. And then you can bake bread and meat pies and baked apples and cakes and…"

"The apples are not in season yet," Rosie said, "But I wouldn't mind some bread. We could have toast and marmalade for breakfast."

"Yes, we could," agreed Michael.

"Are you sure the cat's hole in the wall is an oven?"

The man nodded, "I used to have one just like it. You could make pizzas."

Rosie's eyes went wide, "Are you kidding me?"

"Not at all. With an oven like that you can cook anything you want to."

So that afternoon, Michael came to the cottage. He brought a big rucksack with him which Rosie hadn't seen before. Tommy and Simon weren't very pleased to see him. In fact, when Tommy caught sight of the tall, bearded man walking up the back garden path, he leapt out of the chair in which he'd been reading a James Herbert novel, which his mother had always said was quite unsuitable for him, and shouted through the window – "Go away! You can't come in here!"

Simon looked upon the new arrival with more calmness but equal suspicion. He sauntered out to meet the man, put out his hand to be shaken and introduced himself. Then he wanted to know who the man was, where he had come from and what manner of business he might have in this locality.

"My name," said the man, "is Michael Frobisher, I come from Thornton which is a little village near Bradford and my business here is no business at all. The towns these days are dangerous and insanitary so I have taken to exploring the countryside."

Thus, in a matter of seconds, Simon had discovered more about the man than Rosie had in her lengthy conversations with him.

"You must have walked a long way," said Simon.

"I've had a long time in which to do so," returned Michael Frobisher.

"He can make bread," Rosie added.

This assertion from Rosie was sufficient to quell Simon's suspicion and Tommy's anger. It had been a very long time since they had eaten bread and the prospect of doing so again was enough to allay any piffling concerns they might have about the character of the bearded stranger.

So Michael Frobisher came into the cottage and explained to them the workings of the bread oven set into the wall. They would need to gather twigs and small branches, he said, to set alight in the wall cavity. When a sufficient heat was generated, the smouldering twigs would be brushed out and the bread would be put in.

"The only thing we need then," he said, "is a door for the oven. We'll have to find some big flat stones or slates. We can seal them over the wall cavity with some sort of putty or a bread-and-water paste. Oh, and we'll need flour and yeast, of course."

"We have flour," Tommy said, "I've seen it in the cupboard."

"Ideally it should be strong flour. That's a special sort of flour that's used for bread. But if you haven't got any of that, we'll see what we can do with the flour you have."

"I don't think we have any yeast," Simon said.

"Then we shall catch some," said Michael Frobisher.

Rosie laughed. "You're being silly. You can't catch yeast."

"Oh yes, you can!" Michael Frobisher insisted, "You make up a paste of flour and water and leave it in an open bowl and quite soon the yeast will find it. It's called sourdough and it's the way all bread used to be made once upon a time."

Rosie and Tommy looked at Simon. If Michael Frobisher was telling lies, Simon would surely know.

"He's quite right," said Simon, "There are wild yeasts in the air. All over the place. I don't know for sure how you go about catching them but a bowl of flour and water sounds like as good a way as any."

So that afternoon, Michael Frobisher showed them how to prepare a flour paste for wild yeast and then the three of them went foraging for plants. Michael showed them the ones that were tasty and safe to eat and the ones to avoid because they would make you sick. They collected some plants called chickweed and wild garlic which Michael said would be good for salads and another plant called fat hen which he said they could boil.

Simon asked Michael Frobisher how he had come to know so many obscure and useful things. "Oh," Michael said, "I used to be a teacher."

That impressed Tommy and Rosie. A teacher was a person who was accustomed to taking control in difficult circumstances. They hadn't really had anyone in control since their parents had died. Simon was less impressed, mainly because he thought that Michael Frobisher was lying. When Simon asked him which subjects he'd taught, Michael Frobisher said, "Oh, you know, the usual things," which didn't seem like a good answer at all. Besides which, Simon couldn't think of any good reason why a teacher would know all about surviving in tough conditions. That, Simon thought, is the sort of thing a soldier would know about.

When they'd finished foraging they took what they'd gathered back to the cottage. Along the way, Michael Frobisher pointed out some whinberry bushes that would provide fruit for pies and some cup-shaped yellow mushrooms that he said would be nice when fried. They would come back another day to collect those.

Simon thought to himself that it looked as though the man was planning to stay some time with them. His sister Rosie was under Michael Frobisher's spell, it seemed. Every time he explained what some bush or weed was, Rosie beamed and said how interesting it was. Tommy wasn't much better. His initial antagonism had given way to a grudging acceptance of the man. Tommy was the oldest of the three children – eleven, almost twelve – and now he spoke to Michael Frobisher as an equal, man to man.

They ate the rest of the leg of lamb that evening and Michael Frobisher made a salad with some oil and vinegar and the leaves they had collected. He complimented them on the succulence of the meat and said it was the best meal he'd had in a very long time. The children tried eating the salad but they didn't much care for the taste of wild garlic and they liked the chickweed even less.

Afterwards, when the sun was beginning to sink low in the sky, Michael Frobisher said he'd better be going and Tommy asked where he lived and he said he was squatting in an old sheep pen up in the hills and Rosie gasped and said that was awful, especially since they had a spare room in the cottage. And so it was agreed that Michael Frobisher would stay with them that night. But neither Tommy nor Rosie had given any thought to the problem of Harvey.

It was as they were doing the washing up in the kitchen, with Tommy doing the washing, Simon and Michael doing the drying and Rosie putting the clean dishes in their proper places in the cupboards, that the problem of Harvey asserted itself in a manner that could not be ignored.

First there was the sound of banging, like fists pounding on a door. The sound came from beneath the kitchen, down in the cellar. Then there was a low moaning and finally there was a hoarse wail, like a cry of terrible anguish or pain.

"Great God!" said Michael Frobisher, "What is that?"

Rosie and Tommy weren't sure what to say. They looked at Simon. "It's my brother," Simon said, "Harvey. He's unwell."

The wailing from the cellar continued all the while. Sometimes it was like a howl, sometimes like a snarl. At one moment it receded to a mere whimpering. At another moment it was just a voice – a man's voice, crying in unbearable pain.

"What's wrong with him?" Michael Frobisher asked, "Is he sick? Is he…?"

"No, he's not sick!" Simon snapped.

"But you said…"

"I said he's unwell. That's not the same as sick. Not the way you mean. He's just not well."

Michael nodded. He waited a moment and then he said, very softly, "Then why do you keep him locked up in the cellar?"

*

There was a stone staircase leading down a narrow passageway to the cellar. Once upon a time, long before the children had been born, the cellar had been used for storing coal but the cottage hadn't used coal in a very long time. Rosie and Simon's parents had used the cellar for keeping tins of food and bottles of wine. At the bottom of the staircase there was a solid oak door. It was from beyond the door that the howling and screaming could be heard.

All four of them went down the steps. Rosie went first, lighting the way with a candle in an old metal candle-holder. The door at the bottom was locked. Rosie shouted through – "Harvey, what's the matter?"

The screaming stopped. Then there was an indistinct, breathy voice. It had the timbre of a man's voice but the whining tone of petulant child, "Someone there. Heard… a man. Who's there, Rosie?"

Rosie told Harvey about Michael Frobisher. She said he was helping them. She said there was nothing to worry about.

Then Michael spoke. "Hello, Harvey. Simon says you are unwell. Maybe I can help you."

There was a bitter cry from the other side of the door. "Let me out. They keep me in here. All the time."

Rosie looked at Michael Frobisher. By the dim light of the candle, he saw that there were tears in the girl's eyes. She shook her head and whispered, "We can't let him out. Not yet. It's not safe."

"What's she saying?" the voice behind the door screeched, "Don't listen to her. They keep me chained up. In the cold. In the dark. They beat me. I want to get out! I want to…"

"Harvey," Simon shouted, "you know that's not true. We don't keep you chained up. You can leave whenever you want."

Then Tommy took Michael Frobisher's hand and pulled him back up the stairs, "We're upsetting Harvey. He thinks we're up to something. If we leave him, he'll calm down after a bit."

So they went back up to the little living room next to the kitchen and after a while the sounds of screaming from the cellar stopped. The children told Michael Frobisher about Harvey. After Christmas and the New Year, there had been some snow so Tommy and his mum had decided to stay on for another week. Then the really bad snow came and that made things even worse. Soon after that, Simon and Rosie's parents had died. After Tommy's mum had died too there was just Rosie, Simon, Harvey and Tommy. Harvey was the eldest in the family. Almost eighteen. But there was something wrong with him. He was pale and sickly-looking. His eyes were bloodshot and sometimes blood leaked from under his eyelids. At first they thought he was going to die, just as their parents had. But he didn't. He recovered. Only he was never the same as he had been. He had wild mood swings. One second he would be screaming with laughter, the next moment he'd be in a mood of black despair. But mostly he was just hateful. He would shout at Rosie and Simon. One day he punched Tommy so hard on the side of the head that he knocked him out. Tommy had headaches for a week after that.

"When Simon and I were little," Rosie said, "Harvey looked after us. Now we look after him."

Later that night, they let Harvey out. They kept the keys to the cellar in a drawer in the kitchen. Tommy went down the stairs holding the keys in one hand and a candle in the other. He unlocked the cellar door and pushed it open slightly. Then he quickly ran back up the stairs. At the top of the stairs, Rosie and Simon were standing next to Michael Frobisher. Rosie was holding a long-handled sweeping brush. Simon had a big garden fork. By the flickering light of the candles, it was impossible to see far down into the stairway that led to the cellar. Presently, they heard the creaking of the cellar door, then shuffling footsteps coming hesitantly up the stairs towards them. The top of the cellar passageway opened into the main hallway of the cottage. Simon backed away and opened the front door.

The ragged wreck of humanity that shambled up the stairways was less a thing of terror than of pity. Its haunted eyes stared in fear from beneath a matted thatch of hair which, along with the straggly beard, formed a frame around the gaunt and haggard face. This creature was a pathetic travesty of a young man, little more than a monstrous impersonation of a human being.

As it stumbled into the hallway, the creature drew back from the four people watching it. Rosie prodded it with the long-handled brush she held while Simon kept the prongs of the garden folk inches away from it. Within seconds, it was all over. The creature launched itself at the open door and ran out into the darkness beyond.

"Will he return?" Michael Frobisher asked, as Simon shut but did not lock the front door.

"He always does," Rosie said.

"He never tries to escape?"

"Escape?" said Rosie, "What do you mean? He's our brother. This is his home."

*

The following morning, on leaving the cottage to go foraging, Michael Frobisher found the mutilated carcase of a sheep lying on the grass a few yards away from the front door. Now he understood how the children managed to obtain fresh meat.

*

Michael Frobisher showed the children how to make fishing rods with a bamboo cane and some string he'd found in the potting shed. The hook he made from a safety pin. He tied a wine cork onto the string a few feet away from the hook, to act as float. They went to the lake and Michael baited the hook with bits of cooked lamb. Then he cast out the line and waited for fish to bite. When a fish took the bait the cork bobbed. On the first two occasions when the cork bobbed, Michael pulled in the line but the fish had already got away. He twisted the safety pin a bit to make a better hook and tried again. On the third attempt, he pulled in a fine-looking trout which he killed by hitting its head with a stone. In the next hour, he caught another trout and a grey fish that nobody could identify. If he could just catch one more, they'd have a fish each for their dinner.

"Have you seen any other people?" Michael asked.

Rosie was lying on her back in the shade of the Pirate's Oak. She was staring at an iridescent blue damselfly that was darting about in the air above her. "Since mum and dad died, you mean? We saw some helicopters go over once. That's all."

"You haven't seen anyone like Harvey?"

"What do you mean?"

"You haven't seen anyone who's sick like him?"

Rosie sat up. On the other side of the bay she saw Simon and Tommy with their own fishing rod. As far as she could tell, they hadn't caught anything.

"Harvey's not sick. Not really. Mum and dad and Aunty Marie, that's Tommy's mum, they were sick. But they didn't get better. Harvey got better."

"You think so?"

Rosie frowned. "Of course!"

"There are other people like Harvey," Michael said, "People who got sick. And then… got better, sort of. I mean, they didn't die. But they never were the same as they used to be."

"I've never seen anyone like that."

Michael turned to look at the cork in case there was any sign of a fish biting. There was nothing. The lake was so still that it perfectly mirrored the clear blue sky and the yellow-and–black-striped dragonflies flitting over the water surface.

"There are dangerous people around," Michael said, "Not people like you and me. People who would hurt you if they had the chance."

Rosie thought about that. "Harvey wouldn't hurt us. I mean, he might by accident. We used to have a cat when I was little and sometimes he would scratch or bite. But that was only by accident. It's sort of the same thing, I think."

"But think what it would be like if Harvey wasn't your brother? If people *like* Harvey found you alone in the cottage?"

Rosie gave a shudder. "I've never seen anyone like that," she said again.

"But there *are* people like that. In the towns and the villages. So if you ever see any of them around here, you should hide. Stay inside the cottage. Lock the doors. Never let anyone in."

"We let you in!" Rosie was smiling, teasing him.

"I'm not like Harvey, though, am I?"

Rosie didn't much care for the way the conversation was going. She liked Michael Frobisher. She trusted him. He was a grown-up and he knew how to do things that the children did not. But Harvey was her brother. Michael kept talking about people "like Harvey" who were bad people. Harvey wasn't bad. He just wasn't very well.

"I won't be here always," Michael said, "I have to move on."

That thought hadn't occurred to Rosie. She was already starting to think of Michael as a permanent addition to their little family. Like some long-lost uncle who had come to take care of them.

"You're not going yet, are you?" Rosie said in panic.

"I don't know when I'll go. But don't worry. You won't be on your own much longer. One day soon some people will come to look after you."

"What people?" Rosie didn't like the sound of that. She felt safe with Michael. But she didn't want other people coming to the cottage. She'd heard stories about children being taken away from their homes and made to live with families they'd never met before. She remembered the misery Harry Potter had gone through when he'd lived with Mr and Mrs Dursley.

"They'll be people like me," Michael said in his calm, warm, comforting voice, "They'll keep you safe."

"They'll take us away, you mean?"

"They'll do whatever is in your best interests."

"Yup, they'll take us away."

"That all depends."

"On what?"

"On what they decide is the best thing to do when they arrive."

"How will we know who they are? How will we know they won't hurt us?"

"They will be wearing uniforms."

"Like in Star Trek?"

Michael smiled. "That sort of thing."

Across on the other side of the bay, Simon and Tommy were packing away their fishing rod and line. Tommy waved to Rosie and Rosie waved back. "Did you catch anything?" she shouted.

Tommy held up a fish. It was a tiny, miserable-looking thing. More of a sprat than a trout. Rosie laughed – "I've seen fatter goldfish than that!"

*

In the middle of the night, there was a sharp, loud bang. Rosie wakened in an instant. She sat up in bed and listened but she could hear nothing other than the distant hoot of an owl. She got out of bed and tiptoed along the passageway to the next bedroom where Tommy and Simon slept in bunks. She pushed open the door, expecting them to be awake too. But they were fast asleep. Simon was snoring quite loudly. Michael Frobisher slept in the small bedroom at the back of the house but Rosie would not think of waking him. It had probably been a dream, she told herself, and nothing more. So she went back to bed and slept until breakfast time.

*

"Did you hear anything in the night?" Rosie said as she ate a stale digestive biscuit.

"Simon was snoring," Tommy said.

"Nothing else?"

"No. Why?"

"Oh, nothing. I thought I heard… I don't know, thunder or something."

By the time they had finished breakfast, there was still no sign of Michael Frobisher. Tommy thought he was probably having a lie-in. Simon thought he might have left the house early to go fishing or foraging or something. None of them wanted to go and look in his room to see if Michael was still in bed because, as Rosie said, "He's a guest. And a grown-up. It would be very bad manners to go into his room. He might not be dressed!"

They decided to go and play Star Wars in the woods by the lake. Tommy wanted to be Darth Vader. Simon would be Luke Skywalker and Rosie would be Princess Leia. They would take some of the shorter bamboo sticks from the potting shed to be light-sabres.

The sun was shining so they went to the old quarry at the far end of the woods where they could jump up onto rocks which made the fighting more exciting. But after ten minutes of it, they were already bored.

"It's a shame Michael isn't with us," Rosie said.

"Who would he be if he was here?" asked Tommy.

Rosie tutted at him. "Don't be silly. Obi-Wan Kenobi, of course!"

So they went back to the cottage to see if Michael was awake yet. There was no sign of him. Finally they decided they would have to look in his bedroom. After all, he might be sick. All three of them tiptoed up the staircase and when they were outside the bedroom door, Simon and Tommy pushed Rosie forward.

"Why me?" she whispered.

"He's your friend," said Simon, "You invited him here."

So Rosie tapped delicately on the door and waited. There was no reply. She tapped again and said, "It's me, Rosie. Are you all right?" Still no answer. Then, more loudly, she called, "I can make a cup of tea if you like."

Silence was the only reply she received. There was nothing for it but to go into the bedroom and hope that Michael Frobisher had at the very least put on his underpants. Rosie pushed open the door. The room was empty. No sign of Michael Frobisher. And not much else either apart from the bed itself. Not even his rucksack.

"He must have gone out," said Tommy.

"Obviously!" Rosie replied.

"What's that?" said Simon.

"What?"

"On the bed."

There was a folded piece of paper lying on top of the blanket. Rosie picked it up. On one side was written: "To Rosie, Simon and Tommy."

Rosie unfolded the paper. It was a letter. There were a few long words, she noticed, so she passed it to Simon as he was a better reader. Simon read the letter aloud:

Dear Rosie, Simon and Tommy,

By now, you probably know what has happened. I promise you that it is for the best, though you may not think so at this precise moment. I hope we shall meet again in happier times and, if so, I hope you can find it in your hearts to forgive me. My job is not pleasant but it is necessary. Soon some friends of mine will come to visit you. I hope they will be with you within the next few days but I cannot be sure if that will be possible. Please remember that you must lock your door and never go near anyone who looks ill as Harvey did. I promise you, I have your best interests at heart.

Your dearest friend,

Michael Frobisher

"What does that mean?" said Tommy, "'You probably know what has happened'. I don't know what has happened? Do you?"

Rosie shrugged. "I think Michael has left us. That's what he must mean."

"His job isn't pleasant, he says," persisted Tommy, "What job? I thought he said he was a teacher. And who are these friends who are coming to visit?"

"Oh, I know all about that," said Rosie, "He told me. They'll be wearing uniforms so I suppose they'll be nurses and they will want to take us away to an orphanage or make us stay with evil foster parents or something. I told him I wouldn't go."

Simon had been quiet all this time. When he spoke now, he spoke quietly and seriously. "Not nurses," he said, "Soldiers. And Michael Frobisher wasn't a teacher. He was a soldier too. Where is Harvey?"

Suddenly Simon rushed from the room, ran down the stairs and then down the other set of stairs that led to the cellar. When he arrived there, he threw open the cellar door. Then he shouted, "He's not here. Harvey isn't here!"

He ran back up to the living room. Tommy and Rosie were there already. "What do you mean, he's not here? Didn't he come back last night?"

Then she remembered the bang she'd heard in the night. It had sounded like a gunshot.

They eventually found Harvey at the far end of the orchard. He was on the ground, beneath a big old russet apple tree. His face was mostly missing. The ground behind his head was covered in a mess of blood and flesh. Flies were crawling all over him.

Rosie, Simon and Tommy cried for Harvey and they cursed Michael Frobisher who had come there to kill him. Later that day they dug another grave in the garden, next to the ones that were already there. Rosie said the best prayer she could think of. It went "Ashes to ashes, dust to dust, today is bad, tomorrow is worse. Amen."

As the evening was warm, they went out to the Pirate's Oak and played at being buccaneers. When the sun started sinking towards the horizon, they went back to the cottage and locked the door.

"We need to move on," said Simon, "Tomorrow. Before anyone comes to find us."

"Don't you think that Michael was telling the truth," said Rosie, "when he said that some people would be coming to help us?"

Simon look at her as though she were mad. "Michael Frobisher killed our brother," he said, "What do *you* think?"

NOTES FROM THE APOCALYPSE

(Don't worry – no spoilers)

What will the apocalypse be like? In the stories in this collection, I've tried to imagine how a globally catastrophic event might affect certain individuals or groups of people. Now let me give you a bit of the background to those stories and also provide a few thoughts on post-apocalyptic fiction and its enduring appeal to readers. If you are reading this before you read all the stories, don't worry, I won't give away the plots.

IMAGINING ARMAGEDDON

What is post-apocalyptic fiction? And why do we enjoy it…?

In recent times, we have all learnt to live with the problems associated with a worldwide pandemic. Coronavirus Disease 2019 (COVID-19) has been responsible for the biggest global upheaval that most of us have ever experienced.

Our parents and grandparents may have lived through world wars. Their parents and grandparents would have been familiar with the ever-present scourge of diseases such as cholera, dysentery, typhoid, polio, diphtheria, tuberculosis and smallpox. In mid-19th century Britain, for example, more than half of all deaths were caused by infectious diseases, almost a quarter of all babies died before their first birthday, and the average life expectancy was around 40 years.

In modern Britain, life expectancy is almost twice what it was in the mid-Victorian period. Advances in science and medicine mean that we no longer expect infectious disease to be an everyday cause of death, even among the young. So when a new disease emerges, as with COVID-19, the sense of shock – the sense of our own vulnerability – is far greater than it would have been to earlier generations. Suddenly we realise that, for all our scientific and medical knowledge, we are not as completely in control of our lives as we had thought.

Post-apocalyptic fiction takes us into a world that has gone out of control. This sort of fiction tries to imagine the worst-case scenario – and then it takes one step further into the abyss. What if a disease were so deadly and so infectious that it killed most of the earth's population? What if the crops failed? What would happen if cultivated but deadly plants went on the rampage just as almost everyone in the world became blind?

Speculative fiction has, at various times, imagined all these possibilities. George R. Stewart described a world depopulated by disease in 'Earth Abides' way back in 1949. A global crop failure formed the basis of John Christopher's 1956 novel, 'The Death Of Grass'. And the deadly plants in a blind world are, of course, central to John Wyndham's classic 1951 novel, 'The Day Of The Triffids'.

It might seem odd that so many of us would choose to read, for pleasure, stories about global catastrophes. And yet, horrific fiction has an almost universal appeal. Probably one of the pleasures of reading this sort of fiction derives from the fact that, just like a nightmare, we can emerge from it unscathed. We wake from the nightmare or put down the book and realise that the world in which we actually live isn't quite as bad as the imagined world we've left behind.

If vampires and werewolves were real we would probably not be at all pleased to find ourselves locked inside a castle with one of them. But in fiction, we can enjoy the pleasure of watching other people dealing with horrific situations while we are quite safe, sitting next to a warm fire with the cat on our lap and a glass of wine ready to hand.

Another feature of most post-apocalyptic fiction is that the stories concentrate not on the global catastrophe itself (which might depress the reader rather than entertain) but on the experiences of individuals trying to get on with daily life in exceptionally difficult circumstances.

The classic post-apocalyptic books I mentioned earlier – 'Earth Abides', 'The Death Of Grass' and 'The Day Of The Triffids' – were all written in the 1940s and 1950s. It is easy to imagine why the apocalypse might have been on people's minds at that time. After the Second World War, most readers would have had personal experience of a real-life global catastrophe. When that war ended, a number of others sprung up in Malaya, French Indochina (leading to the Vietnam War), Korea and elsewhere. Meanwhile, the Cold War was getting ever frostier as people wondered whether nuclear Armageddon might be about to be unleashed upon the world.

That may explain the attraction of this genre in the middle of the 20th Century. But why is post-apocalyptic fiction still popular now, in the 21st century?

The trivial answer would be something along the lines of – oh, but we have new fears now: global warming, ocean acidification, tensions between Korea or Russia and the UK or USA, pollution, genetic modification, fake news, cross-species diseases and so on…

But maybe there is more to it than that. One of our greatest fears is, I think, is our reliance on technology. On the one hand, we fear that technology may be used against us: our mobile phones can be used to track us, our Internet profiles make it easy for criminals to find out who we are, where we are, what jobs we do, the names of our pets, and even more intimate information if we aren't very careful! On the other hand, our lives are so dependent on technology – computers, phone networks, electricity, powered vehicles – that we would feel helpless without it. Without our phones, how would we contact people? Without the Internet, how would we find up-to-date information or download eBooks or place orders with online retailers? Without ready access to our doctors and hospitals, how we would stay healthy? Without biologically engineered vaccines, how would we combat emerging diseases?

The entire infrastructure of our world depends on technology. Sometimes it's scary when we have it. But it would be even scarier if it were all to disappear.

There are many possible things that might destroy our technologically-centred lives, and writers have used all of them – EMP (Electro Magnetic Pulses, either manmade or generated by a phenomenon such as a solar flare), catastrophic climate change, nuclear war, mega-earthquakes or meteor strikes, natural or laboratory-created pandemics. Overnight, society as we know it is destroyed. This is such a terrifying possibility that, in our everyday life, it is altogether simpler to avoid even thinking about it. But, just like all our darkest thoughts, sometimes it can be curiously pleasant to experience the nightmare – and then wake up from it.

Welcome to *The Exodus Plague*…

THE STORIES IN THIS BOOK

Here's a bit of background to the stories in this collection. There are no significant 'spoilers' here so it's safe to read this section even if you haven't yet read the stories…

Room 23a

You wake up and you have no idea where you are or why you are there. This is a classic scenario in paranoid fiction. It is what happens when Number 6 wakes in The Village in the 1960s TV series, 'The Prisoner'. It happens to Ethan Burke in the novel and TV series of 'Wayward Pines' and to "Rita" in David Lynch's film, 'Mulholland Drive'. It is, in fact, a theme that has been explored many times in paranoid fiction.

If you've read my novel, *Imprisoned*, you may recognise the central character in 'Room 23a'. In the novel he is no more than a very minor character in the first chapter. In that chapter, he behaves in a peculiar and seemingly nonsensical way. Maybe you wondered why that was. I know, I did! So, in this story, I try to find out.

Incidentally, the college of St Dunstan's doesn't really exist. So don't go to Cambridge looking for it. That said, it is very like one or two colleges that *do* exist. I was at one such college myself many years ago. The porter, the Master, the college rooms and quadrangles in this story bear some resemblance to their real-life equivalents. Though, to the best of my knowledge, no Cambridge colleges are currently participating in the Exodus Project. Then again, if they were, they probably wouldn't admit to it…

A Dirty Weekend in Blackpool

It's tempting to describe events on a global scale from the perspective of remarkable characters – exceptionally heroic people who fight against all odds with barely a quiver of their stiff upper lips. But the catastrophe would be just as devastating for ordinary, unremarkable people. Personally, when a catastrophe strikes, I am less interested in how the heroes (SAS operatives, CIA agents and so forth) would cope than how ordinary, everyday people would struggle through it. This story imagines what happens when two ordinary and unremarkable people happen to be engaged in an ordinary and unremarkable affair in an out-of-season seaside resort when they are plunged headlong into apocalyptic horror.

The Accordion Player and The Monkey

The main character in this story is a minor character in the early part of *Escape*, the third novel in *The Exodus Plague* series. You don't need to have read that novel before reading this story. If you have read it, however, you will be able to find out what became of someone who went to the same party as Justin Davenant (the main character in *Escape*) right at the start of the novel.

This story is set in London on the night of the Great Snow. London is a wonderful city in which to set a catastrophe. Think of the eerily empty London at the start of the film, '28 Days Later' or in John Wyndham's novel, 'The Day Of The Triffids'. The fate of London in the weeks and months that follow the events of this story is described in more detail in books 1 (*The Snow*) and 3 (*Escape*) of *The Exodus Plague* trilogy.

An Unexpected Guest

In *The Exodus Plague* novels, the main locations are the south-west of England, the university town of Cambridge, the seaside resort of Stony Cove and London. But, of course, the catastrophe would affect people in all kinds of different locations. In this story, I describe its effects on an old woman living on a remote hillside in Wales. I was born in South Wales and the setting here is similar to one of the more remote houses on the slopes of one of the old Welsh coal-mining valleys. The woman in this story lives alone in a little house with no close neighbours. So who is the stranger who has come to call? And why does the old woman let him inside? That is the question posed by this story. To find the answer, you have to know more about the woman herself. That's what this story is all about.

Saturday Night In The City Of The Dead

In 1977, British journalist, Nik Cohn, wrote an article for the New York Magazine about a young man named Vincent who was (according to Cohn), "the very best dancer in Bay Ridge." During the week, Vincent sold paint in a houseware store. But on Saturday night he took to the dancefloor at a New York disco and, for a few brief moments, became a star. Cohn's article was called "Tribal Rites of the New Saturday Night". It formed the basis of a film called "Saturday Night Fever" which starred a little known actor named John Travolta.

When the article was published, it seemed as though Cohn had unearthed an authentic disco subculture in New York. In fact, Cohn's article was pure fiction. "My story was a fraud," he later wrote, "I'd only recently arrived in New York. Far from being steeped in Brooklyn street life, I hardly knew the place. As for Vincent, my story's hero, he was largely inspired by a Shepherd's Bush mod whom I'd known in the Sixties, a one-time king of Goldhawk Road." And yet Vincent's story, and the film that it inspired, now seems to sum up the '70s disco era. Which just goes to show that sometimes it's hard to distinguish fact from fiction. You may want to bear that in mind when you read this story.

Underpass

In the 1970s, a British band called Ultravox recorded a song called 'Saturday Night In The City Of The Dead'. In the 1980s, John Foxx, the lead singer of Ultravox, left the band in order to create his own, more austere synth-based music. One of his songs was called 'Underpass'. I was a pop music journalist in the 1980s and, among numerous other stars, Foxx was one of the people I interviewed. I suspected that the imagery in his songs owed a debt to the science fiction writer, J G Ballard, whose stories are often set in bleak cityscapes full of high-rise blocks and motorways shimmering in the heat. Foxx admitted that there was indeed an influence.

So are the names of this story and the previous one purely coincidental? The name 'Underpass' popped into my head as soon as I began writing this story. It wasn't until I'd finished writing it, however, that I decided to call the preceding story 'Saturday Night In The City Of The Dead'. In my own mind, each story now has a backing track provided by the two John Foxx songs which give them their titles. If you aren't familiar with those songs, give them a listen on YouTube or an online music streaming service and see if you agree.

Winter Cruise

"Mrs Hamlyn lay on her long chair and lazily watched the passengers come along the gangway." – ah, the romance of an exotic cruise! The quotation above is not from my story but from a story called 'P&O' by William Somerset Maugham. I read that story when I was a young teenager. It made quite an impression on me. It tells the story of a woman of modest means taking a cut-price winter cruise. When I came to write the stories in this collection, Mrs Hamlyn suddenly popped into my head.

Maugham's story was written in 1926 when cruises would have seemed unthinkably exotic to most ordinary people. I deliberately did not re-read Maugham's story before writing 'Winter Cruise' because I didn't want mine to be an imitation of the Master. This was, perhaps, an unnecessary worry on my part because Maugham did not write post-apocalyptic fiction and I am fairly confident that his

Mrs Hamlyn did not have similar experiences to those of Mrs Chivers in my story!

What's more, the whole business of cruising has, of course, changed dramatically in the century since 'P&O' was written. Whereas Maugham's Mrs Hamlyn took a berth on a fairly small ocean liner, my Mrs Chivers boards a vast ship which seems to her like "a massive housing estate perched precariously on the hull of an oil tanker".

Big ships in fiction often come to a sticky end – or, if the ship itself doesn't, then some of the passengers do. In *The Poseidon Adventure*, the entire ship turns upside down. *Death On The Nile* involves a murder. And the Titanic, of course, in both the film version and in real-life, had a fatal encounter with an iceberg.

Mrs Chivers is well aware of these stories. However, "She didn't think that sort of disaster was very likely to happen in reality. Not these days."

And yet cruise ships are not immune from disaster. In 2012, the Costa Concordia cruise ship, with 3,229 passengers and 1,023 crew, struck a rock, rolled onto her starboard side and began to sink. Thirty-two people died. In February 2020, the Diamond Princess cruise ship was struck by one of the earliest major outbreaks of a newly identified disease, COVID-19. The 2,666 passengers and 1,045 crew were forced to remain isolated in the ship and 700 of them became infected with the disease eventually resulting in 14 fatalities.

A huge cruise ship can, in an instant, change from a luxury resort to a floating prison. This is yet another example of the technology (in this case the maritime technology needed to construct and run such vast ships) which can at one moment be for our benefit and, in the next moment, turns against us.

An Awfully Big Adventure

"Peter was not quite like other boys; but he was afraid at last. A tremor ran through him, like a shudder passing over the sea; but on the sea one shudder follows another till there are hundreds of them, and Peter felt just the one. Next moment he was standing erect on the rock again, with that smile on his face and a drum beating within him. It was saying, 'To die will be an awfully big adventure.'"

That is a passage from J M Barrie's 1911 novel, "Peter Pan; or, The Boy Who Wouldn't Grow Up." You will find that "To die will be an awfully big adventure" is frequently misquoted as "To live will be an awfully big adventure". There are some grounds for this due to the fact that, some time after Peter says the line in Barrie's stage version of "Peter Pan", a narrator adds: "If he could get the hang of the thing his cry might become 'To live would be an awfully big adventure!' but he can never quite get the hang of it…"

While my story takes the title from this quotation, there is nothing else of Peter Pan to be found in it. Or is there? It is, after all, about a group of children who, like Peter, Wendy and 'the lost boys' spend their time having adventures, free from adult supervision. In Barrie's Peter Pan, I've never been entirely sure whether adults are seen as comforting authority figures or whether, on the contrary, they are the villains. Peter certainly doesn't much care for them…

"…he was so full of wrath against grown-ups, who, as usual, were spoiling everything, that as soon as he got inside his tree he breathed intentionally quick short breaths at the rate of about five to a second. He did this because there is a saying in the Neverland that, every time you breathe, a grown-up dies; and Peter was killing them off vindictively as fast as possible."

In this story, the childhood idyll is shattered when a grown-up appears out of the blue. He seems to be a very nice, knowledgeable, helpful grown-up. Then again, he *is* a grown-up, so you never can tell…

This story is in a long tradition of British yarns about children having thrilling adventures – you will find something similar in everything from Enid Blyton's "Famous Five" novels to Arthur Ransome's "Swallows and Amazons". In the Blyton and Ransome books, no matter how hair-raising the adventures, everything turns out all right in the end. Not so in this story…

A MESSAGE FROM THE AUTHOR

Thank you for reading my book. I hope you enjoyed it.

Writing books takes a great deal of time and effort. I love writing them and it is one of the best things in my life to hear from readers who enjoy reading them. But the biggest problem I face is trying to let potential readers know that I even exist. There are millions of books for sale on Amazon and elsewhere and it is really hard for my books to compete against titles produced by big publishing companies with huge marketing budgets.

You can help me!

Reviews are incredibly important to me. They let potential readers know if they might enjoy reading one of my novels. I would therefore be really grateful if you could take a few moments to leave a short review on Amazon. You can do that by clicking one of the two links on the next page or (on other Amazon sites) by clicking the 'Write a Customer Review' button on the book page.

Thanks again for reading my book!

Huw Collingbourne

To download **free stories** now and to be the first to hear about new books, join Huw's mailing list at:
http://www.darkneon.com/newsletter

Leave a Review

Amazon (USA)

https://tinyurl.com/5aff36fx
or
https://www.amazon.com/review/create-review?asin=1913132153
or scan this QR code:

Amazon (UK)

https://tinyurl.com/77apjkfd
or
https://www.amazon.co.uk/review/create-review?asin=1913132153

Now Read On...

The stories in this book take place in the world of *The Exodus Plague*. If you would like to read much longer stories about the experiences of people caught up in the events which precipitated the world into the final catastrophe, you may like to read *The Exodus Plague* trilogy of books. Here's the first chapter of the first book – *The Snow*...

You can find the Exodus Plague series on Amazon by scanning the above bar code or via this URL:
https://tinyurl.com/7d2rukta

The Snow

(Chapter 1 of the first book in *The Exodus Plague* series)

1

There was blood in the snow. It was the first sign of life I'd seen for over a week.

I'd been snowed in for about ten days by that time. I don't remember much about the first couple of days. I was too sick to get out of bed. I had no idea where I was or what was happening. I lay staring into the darkness for hour after hour. The darkness was filled with shapes: luminous creatures whose heads were all eyes and whose bodies were like eels squirming across the ceiling and slithering down the walls. Fever raged in me. I couldn't tell what was real and what was delirium. When I woke on the third day, the bedsheets were soaking with sweat. That was the day the power went off for the last time.

I think there'd been a power cut the day before too. I'm not sure because I wasn't thinking straight at the time. And even if I had been, I wouldn't have paid much attention to it. In the depths of the countryside, you get used to power cuts. They happen all the time. The power flicks off for a few seconds, or sometimes for a few hours. Then it comes back on again. So when the power went off for the final time, it took me a while to notice. Night fell and the room was pitch black so I forced myself to get up and look for candles. That was when the cold really started to get to me. Power lines must be down, I told myself. After all the snow we'd been having, that was only to be expected.

The snow had started falling in early January. Small flurries at first. A light dusting over the hillsides. It was picturesque, people said. Like a Christmas card. In the second week of January it began to fall in earnest. There was something weird about it. On the first night anyway. The snowflakes seemed to shimmer in the darkness. It was at about that time that I started to feel a bit under the weather. I'd never seen such heavy snow before. Relentless. Day after day it kept on falling. Soon the fields and the roads were buried under deep mounds. Little wonder if some powerlines had come down, then. That was only to be expected. The power would be back on again soon, I thought. But, of course, it wasn't.

I stayed in bed. I piled blankets on top of me but I still couldn't get warm. The sheets were cold and clammy. When, after a few days, the fever started to abate, I couldn't bear to lie in damp sheets. The cold in my unheated bedroom was bitter and penetrating. The windows were covered in hoar frost. Ice had formed on the surface of the glass of water I kept on my bedside table. I had to do something or I would freeze to death.

I went downstairs, into the kitchen. There's an old cast-iron, wood-burning stove there. I made up a fire and I settled down on the settee. I wrapped myself in a duvet and I heaped up some blankets and an old overcoat on top. I sat there, in front of that fire for a few more days, adding logs to keep it going every once in a while. And then, one morning, the fever finally broke. And, although I was frail and tired, I felt almost human again. The headaches had gone, the retching coughs and the hallucinations had gone, I no longer felt the leaden weight of tiredness that had drained my energy to the point where I had barely been able even to think.

I was consumed with hunger. I hadn't eaten anything for days. I looked in the fridge to see what food there was. There was a bit of hard cheese, a few withered-looking vegetables and some sour milk. I had better luck when I searched the cupboards. There were plenty of tins: beans, soup, sardines, fruit. I reckoned I'd manage to keep going until the snow melted and then I would go into the village to buy some more food. You have to remember that I had no idea how bad things were. I still thought this was just a bit of cold weather we were having, that the snow had brought down some power lines and everything would get back to normal pretty soon.

Still the snow kept falling.

With no electricity, I was totally cut off. There was no TV, no Internet. The battery in my phone was dead and there was no way of recharging it. Which meant that I had no news of the outside world. I was isolated. Now that I was feeling better, I didn't mind that too much. At least it kept the stress at bay.

The fact of the matter is that I'd been going through a bad time. Before the snow, I mean. The usual stuff. Too much work, too little money. I worried about the work and I worried about money. Most of all, I worried about the way my life was going. I'd started to have panic attacks. My friend Marie warned me that if I didn't slow things down I was heading for a breakdown. Whatever happened to Marie, I wonder? The last time I saw her was on Christmas Eve down in the Farmer's Rest, which is a pub in the village. I don't suppose I'll ever see her again now.

Over the next couple of days, after the fever broke, there were times, while I was sitting by the fire reading a book or drinking a glass or two of wine, when it seemed to me that being cut off by the snow wasn't such a bad thing after all. Even the power cut had its good side. With no phone and no Internet, I couldn't take on any new students or upload any new lessons. My time was my own; I could spend it doing whatever I wanted.

I'd better explain about my students. I'm a guitar teacher. Well, I was, anyway. I'm not sure what I am now. Back then, I spent my time teaching students to play whatever type of guitar music took their fancy. Usually they came to my home. Occasionally (for an additional fee) I went to theirs. When I first started, I had been expecting all my students to be teenagers wanting to learn to play hard rock. In fact, most of my students were over thirty. A couple of them were pensioners who wanted to play like Buddy Holly and Hank Marvin. One enthusiastic woman in her forties had taken a fancy to playing classical guitar "just like Segovia". I taught her as best I could but I explained that playing like Segovia was an ambition that neither she nor I could ever expect to achieve. If I'd been honest, I would have added that she would have had a better chance if she'd started learning about thirty-five years earlier. But when your students are your livelihood, sometimes it doesn't pay to be too honest.

Just in case you think that teaching guitar is a fast route to easy money, let me put you right. The guitar lessons didn't earn me anything like enough money to live on. So I also taught online. I recorded a couple of video courses, I taught one-to-one lessons via Skype. I also published a few books.

It's not what I wanted to do. What I wanted to do was play Heavy Metal in a band. I'd tried it once or twice but it had never worked out. I won't give you all the sordid details. It was the old story of bad management, clashing egos and not enough work to go around. Not that it would have made any difference in the long run. Once the snow came, all that ended. Ambitions, careers, the things we'd always taken for granted – abruptly they all became things of the past.

But wait, there's more…

More Books…
To be one of the first to hear about new books, join the mailing list at: at: http://www.darkneon.com/newsletter

Books by Huw Collingbourne

The Exodus Plague

Book 1: The Snow
Book 2: Imprisoned
Book 3: Escape

The 1980s Murder Mysteries

Book 1: Killers In Mascara
Book 2: The Glam Assassin
Book 3: Death Wears Sequins

Thank you for reading.

Best wishes
Huw Collingbourne

Printed in Great Britain
by Amazon

10168724R00119